THE LIFE I LEAD

THE LIFE I LEAD

A NOVEL BY

KEITH BANNER

ALFRED A. KNOPF   NEW YORK   1999

Copyright © 1999 by Keith Banner
All rights reserved under International and Pan-American Copyright
Conventions. Published in the United States by Alfred A. Knopf,
Inc., New York, and simultaneously in Canada by Random House
of Canada Limited, Toronto. Distributed by Random House, Inc.,
New York.

www.randomhouse.com

Grateful acknowledgment is made to Warner Bros. Publications U.S. Inc.,
Miami, Florida 33014, for permission to reprint an excerpt from "The Flame,"
words and music by Bob Mitchell and Nick Graham, copyright © 1987, 1988
by Hit & Run Music (Publishing) Ltd. (PRS)/Red Bus Music (International)
Ltd. (PRS). All rights on behalf of Red Bus Music (International) Ltd. adminis-
tered by WB Music Corp. (ASCAP). All rights on behalf of Hit & Run Music
(Publishing) Ltd. for the U.S.A. and Canada administered by Hidden Pun
Music, Inc. (BMI). All rights reserved. Used by permission.

Knopf, Borzoi Books, and the colophon are
registered trademarks of Random House, Inc.

Library of Congress Cataloging-in-Publication Data
Banner, Keith.
The life I lead : a novel / by Keith Banner.—1st ed.
p. cm.
ISBN 0-375-40376-0
I. Title.
PS3552.A4948L54 1999   98-51916
813'.54—dc21   CIP

Manufactured in the United States of America

First Edition

ACKNOWLEDGMENTS

I would like to thank several people who helped me in the process of writing and publishing this book: Carolyn Ard, Elizabeth Arthur, Robbin Banner, Steve Bauer, David Bergman, Bill Broun, Andrew Cole, Michelle Cousins, Eric Goodman, Gail Hochman, Karen Johnson, David Lynn, Marianne Merola, Anesa Miller, Mike Perkins, Constance Pierce, Mel Plotinski, Brett Singer, Kim Strapulos, Victoria Wilson, Kim Wurzelbacher, Jim Zafris, everybody at Butler County MR/DD, and everyone at The Kenyon Review Summer Writers Workshop. A special thanks to Nancy Zafris, whose generosity and intelligence inspire and even at times stun me. A very, very special thanks to Bill Ross, who has always been there, no matter what.

PART ONE

1
DAVE

Mom, Dad, and Troy are cleaning the living room carpet in our old house. I'm in one of my dad's old T-shirts, what I wear to sleep in, standing up on the couch, watching. Dad is mad because the carpet-cleaning machine they rented down at the store is making too much foam. White foam spews all over the yellow-green shag, and my mom and Troy, the neighbor's son who was going to help Dad move the furniture, are laughing, both of them, out of nervousness. Still in his work clothes, my dad gets angrier and angrier, a short, skinny guy sweating with a cigarette in his mouth as he holds on to the machine's hose.

He looks up at me. Looks right at me, clicking the machine off.

"What is he doing outta bed?" Dad asks.

Mom and Troy stop laughing. Mom's got that playful, after-laugh voice. "You said he could stay up, Paul."

"Shut up," Dad says, still looking at me.

I feel like I've been caught doing something, but also all I'm doing is standing on the couch in my dad's T-shirt and my socks. I was just watching the way the white foam keeps coming out, like a soft-serve pump at Dairy Queen, only bigger.

Dad comes up to me.

"Get your goddamned feet off my goddamned couch," he says.

But if I jump down, I'll get into the foam. He knows that. He's watching me. Even at six, I get it, that he wants me to jump into that foam so he can bust my hind-end for getting on the carpet he is trying to clean. It's a setup, my six-year-old brain says, and I look over at Troy. He is coming to the other side of the big couch where there's no foam. Troy motions for me to go over to him, and I do. He lifts me up. He's not that big, but he can lift me. I smell the sweat in his black hair and see the moles on his neck.

Dad says, "That's right. Take him in there to bed."

But I look up and I see Dad is looking at Mom, and he goes, "What? What? Why ain't you laughing now?"

I look at Dad's face while he flicks the stupid machine back on. He looks like he just got beat, but I don't feel like this is a victory by any means.

Troy takes me to my bedroom, gives me a tongue-kiss right after shutting the door. He does not smile. I go sit on my bed, being quiet, and he sits on his knees in front of me, kissing me again.

Then he says, "He put too much soap in that thing."

He rubs both my arms.

"You just put a little soap in that thing."

I lay back in my bed. Still on his knees, he stoops over and kisses me lightly, the way a dad might do on a TV show. Like, you know, I am being "tucked in." He stands then, skinny and a little taller than Dad, although he's only sixteen. On Sunday mornings when the old guy comes and picks us up on the church bus, it's me and Troy the first ones on there. We sit together up front, and Troy has his Bible, the one he won at Vacation Bible School for memorizing seventy-three verses, and he has combed his hair back with shiny stuff like a kid evangelist.

Now he says, "He won't ever get all that stupid foam up."

Troy covers me with a sheet. I stare up at him, feeling dumb, thinking about what we've been doing. In the garage by his house, on one cot, in silence, we lay together, and he holds me tight, like we are falling out of an airplane. Tight like he won't let go until we hit the ground splattering like a cartoon. He tells me over and over he loves me but if I say anything to anybody he'll have to kill me and then himself. He touches me, and I touch him, and there's this bird's nest I watch in the garage's rafters when we touch. It's like somebody has put it there for me only to see, made out of twigs, pieces of plastic, grass, colored yarn. The birds that made it have disappeared.

"Well, I better get back out there," Troy says, after kissing me one more time.

I know he loves me, but his love is like that bird's nest, something I can only look at, way up high, and his love being so high and out of reach makes me think that I don't deserve it. But I am glad that he has decided to let me in on it. I know he is crazy, even at six, I sense it in him, and part of me wants to keep him happy so he won't go completely crazy and hurt himself, or me, or somebody else.

Troy waves, flicking off the light switch. When he opens the door, I can hear my dad still out there with the machine, and my mom yelling above the sound, "Let's take it back to the store, Paul. Come on. Give up."

What happens sometimes now is that I don't know what I am doing at work, which could be considered dangerous, as I work as a meter-reader for Indiana Gas. I mean I go out and check on people's gas usage by observing the little numbers on the robot-looking meters out behind their homes. So I do this, and all day sometimes I feel this pressure. All the numbers blur. I go out and buy a little bottle of vodka and mix it with some OJ and sit in my truck and drink. Almost ready to go crazy.

I could blame Troy if I wanted. Sure. But he's gone. Might be dead. I could blame my mom or my dad. But she remarried and he's got stomach troubles. I could blame a lot of people. But mostly it's not about blame or nothing of the sort. I know that. It is about this sick feeling around noon on a Friday when I am sipping my screwdriver out of an old Wendy's cup that was laying in my truck, and I start remembering Troy one summer, me and Troy, going down a slide together at Meadowbrook Park and me between his legs, him holding on to me while we went down this curlicue slide hot from the sun, my legs burning off. Then we are bouncing in together at the bottom. Me laughing, but also knowing.

Vodka and OJ burns all the way down into my stomach. The CB in the truck goes off, the crackling dispatcher's voice. All these houses, I think, parked in the middle of a nice neighborhood, sun shining through trees, off clean windows. I turn down the radio, almost go to sleep. The fear gets loose after a few sips and gets elastic and forms itself into caulking that lines the little cracks in my skull. Shake it off, Dave, I keep telling myself, shake it off.

I think about the boy at church and I think about the one in the bathroom at Wal-Mart and I think about the one in the baseball dugout at Shadyside Park, the one with the long eyelashes and when I said I loved him he said, "Why?"

And I didn't know what to say.

I stop drinking, throw what's left out onto the pavement. I get back to work, forging some numbers, doing some actual meter-reading. I take the truck back in at two, tell them I got a dentist thing. Go on home, wait on my wife, Tara. We got a baby she drops off at her mom's when she goes to work during the breakfast and lunch at Bob Evans. Brittany. We got pictures in our living room, all over the place: Brit in her sunflower hat,

Brit in a stars-'n'-stripes ensemble, Brit by the baby pool out beside the house. Here I am fine. This is my home. This is okay. In the La-Z-Boy, I remember Brit's first birthday, a month back. I borrowed Bob's videocam, and I shot two hours of Brit in the backyard. Tara got mad, but I wanted the stuff for posterity. You know, Brit smashing cake in her hands, Brit crying from being so sleepy, Brit gawking at her presents with that baby look of not knowing what to do next.

"The fuel pump," Tara says on the phone, an hour later. "I swear to God, Dave. You gotta get this fixed. Can you go over to Mom's and get Brittany? Mom's got to go get her X rays, they think she may have cysts. I told you. Anyway, she doesn't have time to drop Brit off and backtrack."

"Sure," I say. I picture her in her Bob Evans outfit, her hair puffed-out sweet, her face made up, talking into the phone by the cash register.

"That guy at the car place said he'd ordered the pump, babe," I say, lying. I haven't got to that yet.

"Well, tell him to hurry up!"

I laugh at her a little.

"I will. I'll come and get you after I get Brit."

"Well, hurry. I feel so tired. Hurry."

But right after I hang it up, it gets me, that I need it. I need to do it. It's just like today, only worse, because I'm not on the clock. I always used to think it was love, but that's wrong. Once I wanted to tell someone and I tried to think who and I only came up with the police or a doctor. I imagined saying it out loud. I saw a policeman's eyes go *out*. In my mind I saw it like two fuses blowing right then, right when I said it to him. The burned fuses stayed with me for a long time, like the smell of smoke in your clothes after you go to a bar.

There's this public pool by the railroad tracks. I'll just go look. I'll go look and then I'll pick Brit up and I'll go get Tara at Bob Evans and we'll eat out and then go home and watch TV.

Yes. So I go by there. It's a pretty hot day, and I am thinking like a shark, knowing this, I know what a shark thinks now, I am doing it, but still it's like this is not happening. I sit in my car across the street looking through the chain-link fence at them. I have this category system of the ones who look like angels, the fat ones who are white as ghosts and sitting with their legs into the pool like old ladies, the athletic ones with almost empty faces like they are being formed even as I watch.

Then I see the one I have been courting in secret, without doing anything. He is seven, I bet. Last week me and Brit came down to the park across the street, and we got some ice cream from the concession stand. There he was in front of us. He didn't have enough money for his Popsicle so I pulled out a dollar for him, then got Brit a small shake. After that, holding Brit backwards to me after she took her sip, I turned around, and he was over by the trash can. I said, "Enjoy that." Smiling, winking. He was all alone there then in his swim trunks. He was that kind of child.

Today he has on those same trunks. He's got the blackest hair, shining. I'm thinking it is me back then and me wanting me is what I am feeling—to go back and be myself, and then I am Troy, or I am some other person who is innocent but about to do something bad, something people go to hell for.

As I walk into the boys' locker room I feel the old self peel off like old clothes and I am naked like a star athlete, but not really. I am golden shiny like a star, but not. I spy around, slip my foot up on a bench, untie my shoes real slow. Just a couple of boys. I know I should stop right then, go get Brit, pick up Tara. I imagine apologizing to Tara's mom for being late. "You go get your X rays right now," I would order, being stern to show I care.

I don't, though. I breath in the smells of wet concrete, sweat, chlorine, pee. I wait. For an hour. Some of the waiting I do in a stall, some of it on a bench tying and retying my shoes. I wait.

And then when he comes in alone and I am sitting there in the middle of retying my shoes again, I am tongue-tied.

I manage to say, "Hey, Bud."

The child looks at me deeper. He seems to recognize me. This is the point where our eyes lock, like he knows I have been waiting here for him for so long. I feel what I feel for him in the back of my mouth, in the muscles in my hands, in my chest and crotch. Sparks all up inside my body. Like my blood is turning into flashes of sunlight off chrome.

He tries to ignore me then, in his way.

"Looking good," I say, wanting to reach out to him. This is too hard out here in public. I got a system. I pull a ten-dollar bill out of my wallet, my hands shaking.

"Here."

His small hand takes the money, and I know he wants that money more than anything. I see him grip it tight.

"I want to see you again. Somewhere nice."

Some others come in, and I know I can't do anything else. Even in my disappointment, I feel relief. He runs off, and when I go to get Brit, there's no one there. I drive over to Bob Evans, and the manager on duty says that Tara's mom came and got her. I see the old car Tara drives, a 1987 Escort piece of crap, parked right under the Bob Evans sign. I want to cry.

I go on home.

"Where have you been?" Tara says, in a T-shirt and shorts, her hair pulled back. Without makeup she looks like a little girl, like Brit, and I try to make it like I'm pissed off, but really I just want to tell her I love her that's all.

"Work called me. Some pipes leaking out by the bypass," I say. "I was gonna go out and check real fast and then pick Brit up but it got complicated."

I see Tara's mom, a fat old lady with orange hair in shiny nylon sweats, pulling Brit out of her high chair in the kitchen.

"There's a new invention out there, David," Tara says, light-

ing up a cigarette at the dinette table. "It's called the phone."
Then she whispers, "Mom had to cancel her X rays."

"I'm sorry," I whisper back.

Tara just shakes her head, taking a big drag.

I stand there for a second, without anything else to do or to
think. I can't move for that time. I can't move at all, like I'm
froze, this statue waiting to be taken off. Then I notice Tara is
getting freaked and I smile.

"What?" I say to her.

"Nothing," she says. She keeps smoking, putting place mats
on the table.

I go into the kitchen. Tara's mom does not say anything
except "Here's your daddy" to Brit.

I walk over to hold Brit. She seems heavier than this morning even, growing all the time. She smacks her lips and she has
big, wondering eyes, like she wants to see everything in the
world right away. I hold her up close. I hold her and I smell her
head and then I kiss it right on top.

TROY

I thought of it like a spaceship. The place, in the garage. I tried not to think about it that much, but when I did it was our spaceship. Actually, of course, I thought about it all the time. I didn't tell this to David, the way I figured things. I kept talking to a minimum, as talking decreased the emotion. Talking, in fact, just did not make that much sense. I was sophisticated for a sixteen-year-old.

At that time, also, I was deep into God. I still am, when I need to be.

A spaceship had landed, and we had turned it into our club-house. I put the cot in there, stolen from our attic, and I had an eight-track tape player and a canteen filled with lemonade sometimes, plain tap water others. Often David and myself played restaurant at a small card table with two folding chairs, a bedsheet for a tablecloth.

"Yes, we would like two of your blue-plate specials," I said to the invisible waiter one afternoon. We had candles for light. Even in the daytime it was dark. My dad, before he died, had painted the windows in the garage so that no one could see inside.

David was laughing. He got the giggles from what I could

do with my imagination. I remember him as a perfect-looking child, although he was plain to most. He was the kid no one really paid that much attention to. This was his total MO. I was this type of child also. The one who always had crayons and watched too much TV, you know, not quite an all-out sissy, but not good for anything either, at least in the eyes of most people, most adults.

Playing restaurant one evening, I ordered swordfish instead of the blue-plate special. I remember David looking at me, as if I had just ordered up a big piece of God.

"Haven't you ever eaten swordfish, Monsieur?" I asked, smiling, and he shook his head no, his eyes wide.

"Wouldn't that cut your mouth?" he asked. He was serious, too.

I touched his mouth, rising from the folding chair. I got down on my knees beside him, on the oil-stained concrete. There were many spiders, and also I think some mice in here, and I did not like being on my knees. His face, however, was glowing, and I thought how innocent, how stupidly innocent, he was, this whole thing was. One time, when I was living at the Good Samaritan Ranch before I got adopted, the lady who ran the place, Meredith, blond, fat, always smoking those long lady cigarettes, she took us to a fancy restaurant. The man who owned it had donated a night of fine dining to the sweet orphaned boys at Good Samaritan. We feasted on a huge swordfish, with its head still on: nine boys and Meredith and two workers, all of us cutting into this big blue dead swordfish. It didn't even have a nose, just a long jagged blade, its eyes black, as if it were seeing into outer space.

I did not tell David this. No. I got down on my knees beside him, and I put my index finger close to his lips. I remember I was shivering. I felt the lips. They were warm, almost dry, but soft like orange wedges. I traced them, looking at him. I said:

"I would never let anything cut your mouth."

He did not know how to take that, so I told him how to take that.

"Smile," I said. "Come on. Smile."

David and I had our hair cut together about every two weeks or so. His dad took both of us. I think David's dad was trying to be a father to me too, as mine, both of mine, my natural biological one that I never knew, and the one who had adopted me, both were dead, and my mom was kind of a drunk. My mom, the one who adopted me, was a good sensible drunk, though. She stayed in the house all the time, drank and got really quiet. Later, when she stopped drinking, she would tell me her whole life had gotten fuzzy from the booze. Had gotten silly and fuzzy, until she thought she was only dreaming things up that did not really matter. Like vacuuming, she said. She used to vacuum when she was drunk, but at the time when she vacuumed she only thought she was dreaming of the vacuuming. I remember that: the sound of the vacuum, and her drunken pushing around of that vacuum, an upright sky-blue Hoover with a floral sack blowing up like infected lungs every time you turned it on. She was always turning that thing on, bumping it into tables and chairs. She would jerk the plug out of the socket, at times the socket's wall plate coming off. One morning I caught her sobbing drunkenly while she vacuumed. Pushing the machine all over the place, sobbing and sobbing. I'm sure she did this a lot.

So where was I?

David and myself getting our haircuts together. This was 1972, when many parents and children were experimenting with new hairstyles, longer for boys, but David's dad agreed with me that short hair was the way. I was into God, remember, and David and I attended Faith Baptist Church together, practically every time the doors were open. David's mom and dad did not go. They seemed to be glad that I had taken it upon myself to take David with me.

The barbershop had a pop machine with a little door you opened, and the pops were in handcuffs inside the door. You pulled your choice of pop through the handcuffs, and it was yours, replaced by another rolling bottle, locked into place by the cuffs. David, being six, found this whole process magical. Pop was only fifteen cents back then, and we would both go over and get our pop out of that old machine after having our hair cut—clean, well-groomed gentlemen getting our pops. All the old guys in the shop would watch us. I remember thinking they thought we were brothers. That I was his big brother, which I was, kind of.

I still remember the smell of that old barbershop, which as far as I know has closed down like much of small-town downtown America: hot electrical smell from the buzzing shears and the alcohol perfume of the aftershave, the creamy lemony smell of the stuff that Red, the barber, used to shave people's necks with, the smell of sweat and cigarettes and the slightly sickly sweet odor of pomade and something else, maybe the way old men smell when they don't bathe enough, almost fruity, almost not. I liked it all, however.

David's dad, short and a little round-bellied, skinny other than that, always in his gray-green work clothes, paid for both of us every time.

I remember once at the barbershop, David's dad saying, "Those two. Mutt and Jeff."

I smiled. I was in one chair, David in the next. Red was doing David. Red's assistant, his brother-in-law named Tom, was doing me. Tom had wet palms that brushed the back of my neck. I kept thinking of how I had been baptized a few months back, the pastor's hands on the back of my neck as he pushed me backwards into the water in the tank behind the pulpit, all the people looking on. Organ music, beautiful scary organ music. Tom the barber was heavyset and did not talk because Red was always the one talking, except when David's dad was talking. Red really did seem to respect David's dad, whose name was Paul. Paul Brewer.

Red said, snipping David's bangs, "Yeah, Paul, they look like, you know, the same person if you ask me. One six years old and one—how old are you, Troy?"

I got scared suddenly. I guess because I was so into Tom's hands on my neck like that. I jumped a little. The men laughed.

"Sixteen," I said.

"Sixteen," Paul said. "No wonder you're so nervous."

This got a big laugh. Paul knew how to make people laugh. This was his gift. People actually said that about him.

"Sixteen," Red said, whistling. "Damn, that is the age."

Tom grunted, "Yeah."

He brushed me off with a horsehair brush and turned me around. I saw myself in the big barbershop mirror. I was rail-thin, had short clean black hair. My lips were very red, my cheeks slightly sunk in. My eyes seemed glassy and spiritual, not an excited sixteen-year-old boy's eyes really, but the eyes of someone who knows something other people don't know and don't want to know. I'm not bragging, as having those eyes most often is a curse. A beautiful curse but still a curse. I practiced that look of my eyes in the mirror in Mom's bathroom, staring at myself to get the perfect religious gleam. Eyes close to crying but with no tears. Jesus had those eyes. I don't want to sound like a total flake, so I'll stop there.

David had brown curly hair which got buzzed off all the way. Mine was cut short but not buzzed. David happened to be one of Red's favorites because David was so quiet.

"Don't like them hyper ones come in here and run around like they ain't got no manners. Damn little retarded savages," Red said.

"Yeah," David's dad replied. He looked at David, and David looked back. I was the third person in this family triangle, I thought, and then I thought about how I loved David so much at times I wanted to kill myself. It came to me in a flash, and I had to look away. Love happens that way. All of a sudden, an embarrassing realization.

"Yeah," David's dad repeated, proud perhaps. "That one there is a good one."

David smiled then. It was the smile I got from ordering spaghetti and ice cream from the invisible waiter. A timid smile, but one that could break your heart, and send you falling down the stairs inside your head.

Tom took the sheet off me, after untying the top strings. He flung hair off me like a bullfighter trying to attract the bull in the ring. David's dad got up and took out his wallet. This was one of those moments when you have to be grateful without opening your mouth, so I looked at David's dad and tried to smile the same timid, innocent smile David had smiled. I noticed that David's dad did not like me smiling like that, like his son. He ignored me, gave Tom his two dollars, gave Red his, and then Red took the sheet off David. Very ashamed suddenly, I knew Paul Brewer did not love me. He just liked me, and this would have to be enough. I saw David's legs, little feet that did not touch the footrest and had been covered by the red-striped barber cloth. Red shook and shook the cloth out. I wanted to grab some of the cut strands, to take the hair from the floor that had been cut from David's head, but not now, not now, and I flushed red as a beet. Imagining myself down on all fours getting his hair, and the men laughing and some of them would threaten to kill me, seeing what I really was.

Paul picked David up and put him down onto the floor, saying, "Come on, you two. Let's get on home. We'll see you later there, Red."

We walked out. I watched David's head. The white scalp shaved to perfection as if by a doctor of scalps. When he was born, I bet David was bald. Or like that: white scalp with a dusting of baby hair. My vision turned from David's head to the shine off cars in the street. Anderson still had a downtown then, a 1972 leftover from the hustle and bustle of the postwar. Red's shop was right next door to the Paramount Theater, but I can't remember what was showing there at the time, maybe it was *The Godfather*. Still, there was that huge glorious marquee and also the great Chinese place next to that.

David sat between Mr. Brewer and myself, in the great big Impala. We rode past Delco-Remy, still doing gangbuster business back then, spitting out parts for huge luxury cars, another 1972 leftover from the fifties. Past the half-built mall, on out into where the fields started, past the interstate and then back around to the bypass, where David and his mom and dad lived three houses down from us. There was a huge used-car lot on one side of the street, the longest row of chain-link fence I have ever seen, and right across the way the gas station that my adoptive dad, Louie, used to own but was now closed up.

Louie used to wake at four every morning and walk to the station. He died of a heart attack walking one April morning. I was the one who found him, and I remember seeing him on the gravel beside the pavement and thinking that he was waking up too early, and was too damn tired and just collapsed. Then I got it. Bald and old and his face, even though he was dead, was still that painful scarlet from his skin problems. I went over, and I said, "Dad?" For several moments I remember thinking that people would think I had killed him. It was still dawn-dark when I found him, as I was going to go to the garage where David and me spent our summertime, in order to do some of the secret things I did back then by myself.

David, myself, and his dad rode past the place where I found my dad dead, then down to School Street, our street. Seven houses all together. A hippie lived in one house, and he had a green peace-sign flag instead of the American one flying on the pole in his front yard. Our house was yellow brick with a carport, the garage behind the house with a gravel driveway up to it and painted-over windows, and the big door itself would not open so David and I always used the side entrance. David's house was white-sided with black shutters and small, two bedrooms, a kitchen, a utility room, a living room, and a bathroom. No garage or anything, hardly a yard. Built on a slab.

David's dad dropped me off, and I looked at David and I said, "I'll see you later." He knew what that meant. This was the second year of our affair, but it would be the last summer we would have together. At that time, of course, I did not know this.

"Okay," his little voice uttered.

David's dad said, "You mind babysitting tonight? His mom works tonight and I got a union meeting."

Mr. Brewer was smiling. His smile was not loving—it was an asking smile. You know your place, the smile seemed to say: the adopted freak of a boy who went to church too much but who was very trustworthy and kind and loving and maybe just a little slow. Not slow enough to make him dangerous to others, however.

I smiled back.

"Why, sure," I said.

"Three bucks," Mr. Brewer said.

"Sure," I said.

David's dad's smile increased. He nodded his head. He and his son drove down to their house.

. . .

I guess I'll tell you that I lied a little about my mom now. My mom, the woman who adopted me. She wasn't that bad of a drunk. She was just drinking then because Louie had died only months before. Like I said, this was 1972. She was forty-seven years old. She only had me left, just as it was only her and Louie alone before they got me from Good Samaritan Ranch, when I was eleven. Meredith, I remember, sold me to them. White slavery it was not, but still the thing was foster before Louie and my mom got me full-fledged, only a year before Louie died. I loved Louie, don't get me wrong. He was a quiet, sensible guy. He loved me like a father is supposed to, stern and a little self-righteous. Plus I was his namesake. That seems to be the reason I got adopted. They wanted someone to carry on the Wetzel name, but they didn't want to deal with a baby. So they got me, this eleven-year-old, to bear their name.

No, Mom was not really a drunk all the time. She got sober a lot after Louie died. She had to sober up to go to work at the Holiday Inn, on the buffet for business travelers. We would eat the stuff businessmen did not eat, as she brought it home in old cottage-cheese and margarine containers: green beans, gravy, roast beef, macaroni and cheese, and peach cobbler. If we couldn't down it all, she froze it. She was a hard worker. She believed in God, but did not go to church as much as I did. She watched Billy Graham and Oral Roberts and Rex Humbard on Sundays. She had a big white Bible she marked up like a scientist with red pens.

When I got home after my haircut, she was still in her white polyester uniform, which always made me think of her as a nurse. She dyed her hair a red-brown, and it was glowing in the pulled-curtain light. Auburn hair like that glows at certain times in the afternoon, as if lit from within. The afterlife hair of Patsy Cline. Inside, our house was decorated in the white-trash 1972 fashion of houses in Anderson, Indiana: yellow sculpted carpet and bright floral-print fabric furnishings and maybe a vinyl footstool and dark Formica fake-woodgrain paneling and these plastic gold-painted candelabras and frames Mom bought at Home Interiors parties that she went to with David's mom at different white-trash ladies' homes all over Anderson. There was always the smell of Holiday Inn buffet mixing in with Lysol and the minty sadness of mothballs. Mom was a big believer in mothballs. She said one time she almost got attacked by moths in her youth. Big moths, she said.

I loved her very much.

"Look at you," she said.

Ron Ely as Tarzan was on the big TV console we had—record player on one side, radio on the other, TV in between. The speakers were covered in hard itchy fabric that one time I touched with my tongue out of boredom with the radio side playing Elton John's "Don't Let the Sun Go Down on Me."

"David's dad took us," I said.

"You and David?"

"Yeah."

I sat down on the couch and she said, "I got lasagna. You want lasagna?"

"Yeah, sure."

She did not move, though. I looked on the little floor lamp beside her chair, that had a glass table connected on top. There were Oral Roberts pamphlets from the mail plus a tall tumbler. I knew if I smelled it, it would be vodka mixed with Fresca. Fresca was the color of fog. Vodka mixed in cut the color. I didn't move either.

"You and David spend a lot of time together."

Tarzan hit the water. Gigantic elephants were screaming horrendous screams. Mom had put Shar, our little toy poodle, in the bathroom. Shar was barking and scratching.

"Not that much," I said, trying to sound bored.

"He's nice," she said.

She sipped. She sipped, and I thought sometimes she blamed

me for Louie's death because I found him when I was going out to the garage behind our house that April morning to jack off. I was in pajamas. I never jerked off in our house. It was like my one rule I could follow that made me feel less guilty for breaking all the others. The Eleventh Commandment: Thou Shalt Not Jerk Off Thinking of Little David Across the Way Inside Thine Own House. Anyway, I saw Louie lying there down on the street like a derelict. I ran to him. You know the rest. I'll try to stop going on and on about it. That face, red and splotchy, like a painted-on mask, the open eyes he had in death, not creepy, not shocked, but open eyes that seemed almost like he found out how innocent he could be right at the end.

The ice in Mom's glass clinked at the sides. It was the sound of every dead summer afternoon: dog scratching at the door, ice clinking, Tarzan in a waterfall yelling. I closed my eyes, as if in prayer. I heard Mom get up and move slowly to reheat the lasagna she had brought home from the Holiday Inn. I heard the TV and the dog, and when I opened my eyes, I was afraid that Mom was thinking about David and myself, suspecting me of doing what I did with David.

I got up, and she was putting the lasagna from the container into a pan. She was bent over slightly. She had on her glasses.

"I'm babysitting tonight. Three bucks," I said.

"David?"

"Yes."

"David," she said, as though she were thinking.

"Yes, David."

She turned the oven on. The kitchen was tiny. On the fake-brick wall by the oven were mushroom placards and a recipe for praying to Jesus.

She sat down at the dinette table with her tumbler of vodka and fog. "I think I'm going to go to bed. You can eat without me, honey. I'm going to bed."

I heard her let Shar out, and then she whispered for Shar to go to sleep with her, in the back bedroom, yellow walls with a sewing machine the color of pearls and her bedspread of green vines and red flowers and the pictures on the walls of irises and daisies and Louie in the army and the dresser of ornate wood covered in old Holiday Inn uniforms and name tags and hair-spray cans. I saw this in my head, like I had memorized what her bedroom looked like for a test. Heard her door shut.

I only ate a small portion of the lasagna. Just two mouth-fuls. In an hour I was going to go.

Go where I was needed down the street.

Like I said, I did not know this would be our last summer. I did not know that in close to one month I would be banished or what have you. Back then maybe I did feel the strange dread that people like me feel, the dread that what I am doing is not right in the eyes of people who don't think very much, and even I know it's wrong, but so is everything else. That's a bad defense, and I have spent my life since School Street following that kind of logic, the dumb logic of a pervert. Which is what I am, so just let me get that out of the way. A forty-one-year-old pervert who lives in Muncie, Indiana, thirty-six miles from School Street. Thirty-six miles in twenty-five years.

I don't want to cut myself down, though, as I'm sick and tired of that. I won't bore you with that kind of a pity party now. Life now is about working the second trick at Sunny-haven Nursing Home. It is about this small apartment, about my computer and my new kind of life without the pervert part, only residues of pervertedness remaining. A new, clean, and highly sanitized way of looking at life, and partially living it. I'm not Catholic, but right now I could compare myself to a priest or a nun, I imagine, take your pick. As my new life is about erasing myself very slowly, until finally all I am is the memorized version of myself, who I was, who I wanted to be and I was, and the blanker I get, the better person I become now.

I help the needy. I eat inexpensive groceries. I have hunkered down. So I sit here, trying to tell whoever you are out there what it was like, 1972, that summer, that last year, maybe the only year, I think I was actually alive.

3

DAVE

Bob and Stanley and me are going to play golf, 7:15 tee off, Meadowbrook golf course, just about six miles from where I used to live on School Street. Now we live over on Reservoir Drive, pretty nice neighborhood they built back in the fifties for people who worked at Delco. Anyway, it is a cloudless day, and I woke feeling pretty good. Coughed a little, looked over at Tara. She had on her red see-through nightie. In the mall they got a Victoria's Secret, and she made me go in with her when she bought it. She said it would be sexy for us to buy it together. It was me following her from rack to rack, her pulling off different ones and me blushing like an idiot. Right then, in bed, waking up and seeing her in it, I got tickled, and remembered how she wanted me to go into the dressing room with her, and we almost got into a big hairy fight when I wouldn't.

She stood there in the Victoria's Secret, people everywhere. There were Cupid posters and big placards of sexy women in underwear with angel wings on the pink walls. The smell of new nightgowns is like the smell of a clean unfurnished room.

"You *will* go in there with me," Tara said, in jeans and a sweatshirt, her hair pulled back. She had on lipstick, but that was it, makeup-wise. This was about three weeks back. It was before the boy I mentioned previously. I was feeling pretty good about my life.

I laughed.

"I can't go in there," I said.

She laughed, whispering too loud, "Yes you can, honey."

"No."

"Yes." She got stubborn-eyed, playful.

I looked around. Some of them were smiling, but most thought we were just trashy, showing-off kind of people. I didn't like that.

So too loud I said, "No."

Tara said, "Fine. Dave. I was just kidding. God, you are so stupid."

Yes I was, I knew. I saw her walk back and I walked out into the mall. I walked into the mall and I stood there, and I promised myself to take things with a better attitude or I would lose her. There was this dumb fountain out there in the mall proper, this old green fountain of an abstract sculpture dripping water down into a pool filled with pennies, and so I took some change out of my pocket and I made a wish. I wished that me and Tara could be like we used to.

Well, my wish kind of came true last night. I made like I was totally into it. Part of me was. It was Friday night after I had fudged things by not picking up Brit and making her mom miss her X rays. I went out and got some chicken and came back and we ate. Then Tara's mom left and I put Brit in her bed. Amazingly enough, she fell right off. Me and Tara watched some movie she had rented the night before with Whoopi Goldberg in it. It wasn't that good, and she flicked it off.

"I'm sorry I jumped on you," she said, just out of the blue.

I felt like I was the one who should apologize, I always feel like that with Tara, but then I decided to let myself off the hook, as it would be better for her. I didn't even see the boy in my head then. I promised myself to get back into regular ways. Normal life just sounded good.

"I'm sorry I did what I did," is what I told her.

She took my hand and guided me into the bedroom, and then I got naked, and she got into the nightie. The one I was looking at right then upon waking. Red, lacy, and see-through. I don't think it was that trashy. It was like what a husband and wife use. I remember last night kissing her and closing my eyes. Then the boy's face and arms, his rib cage coming through his skin, his legs and swim trunks came at me. It gave me the electrocution feeling that I didn't want. I pushed him away, and in that struggle I got hard. I won't go into any more details. She loved me, though, loves me, and this is what I needed to know this Saturday morning.

I looked in at Brittany, who was wide awake just lying there in her baby-bed. Blond hair, just that face. I picked her up and we went into the kitchen. I slid her into her chair and made some of the cereal stuff. I wanted the intimacy of feeding her. There's nothing like that. She made noises as I drank my coffee and looked at the paper we get in the morning. Then I looked up from the news at Brittany and she was spitting onto the tray. I gave her some more food. She liked that.

"What a girl," I said.

I was clean right then. Perfect. I had a golf game to go to, and after that me and Tara, Brit and my dad and her mom were going out to eat. After that was the next day, Sunday, when me and Tara, Tara's mom and Brit and maybe even my dad would be going to church. Then came Sunday afternoon where you just lay around the house with your family. Which is what all of America does and being in on that national pastime, the after-church nap time and baseball watching and eating of pot roast, this gave me cleanliness. It was like I canceled the TV show in my head. The one starring the child in the locker room. I could hear my voice, though, talking to him, saying stupid stuff. My

voice gets low, like an electric razor. Then I think of Troy and
the way he used to talk to me. I try to cancel him out too. Troy
bending down to me as I lay in bed, or in the garage on the cot,
or when we would pretend to be in a restaurant with lit candles. His voice inside my head coming back out through his
mouth.

Brit starts crying a little.

"Honey, what?"

But she stops, looks at me. I know she's taking a dump.
Even though that's a little vulgar, it makes me happy. Tara
comes in then, kisses me on the mouth, puts her hand on Brit's
head. Tara has perfect fingernails, painted frosty pink.

"Saturday!" she says, her voice still hoarse from being asleep.

"Yup," I say.

"You feed her?"

"Yeah. That cereal."

"Good."

I like it when Tara is like this. Easygoing. She gets some coffee and sits down. We have our normal conversation. Just, you
know, normal everyday bullcrap that gives you a reason to live.

"Mom says she wants to go to Cracker Barrel."

"That's a good place."

"Yeah."

She's feeding Brit some now.

I get up. "Cracker Barrel it is."

Tara laughs. She has on her Chinese-looking robe. I always
think of movie stars when she's in that thing.

"Your dad is gonna say Ponderosa, you know that."

I laugh. Dad always wants to go there. It's like he thinks
that's the only game in town. Ponderosa Steakhouse. I see him
in his chair in his trailer, putting his feet down in the recliner
and going, "Well, if you all don't want Ponderosa, that's fine. I
can eat here. I got that Lean Cuisine stuff."

Plus his stomach. Last week he found out from one of the

doctors that he's going to have to go to Indianapolis for some tests. Sounds serious, but he says it's ulcers. Dad doesn't want to talk about it and we don't.

I laugh at my dad a lot now. I used to plain ignore him and prior to that, as a kid, I feared him. He's close to sixty, and he's been left behind by Mom, who lives in Ohio with her younger husband, and they own two video-store places. Dad stayed in Anderson and took early retirement because he didn't want to be laid off. Now he does all the same stuff he did when he worked except the work part, even wearing his uniforms and going to get coffee and donuts at Phillips downtown with the people who still work. Sometimes he even goes to work to hang out. It's not embarrassing, I don't guess, for him. It's his life.

"Well, either way," I tell her.

"My mom's cysts and your dad's ulcers. Damn," Tara says, standing up.

"I gotta go take a shower. We're teeing off in a half hour."

"You and golf, Dave."

She kisses me again. I try to give her a sexy-man smile. I imagine that's how a sexy man would smile, lazily, Kevin Costner-like. I smile and go over and Brit's crying again.

"I think she pooped," I say.

"Well, I guess that's why you went ahead and changed her right?" Tara says, laughing.

"Yeah, right," I say, responding to her sarcasm.

"Dave, you are a piece of work, honey." Tara pulls Brit up and walks down the hall to change her. I stand in the kitchen for a second or two, ashamed of myself. I should have changed Brit. I know that. I should have done that, I say to myself over and over for a brief period of time.

Bob and Stanley are drinking McDonald's coffee out in the parking lot. This is one of those public courses that aren't well maintained. We don't have to pay big dues, though, and once or twice a year, me and my buddies come out and do the real hard maintenance because Mack, the guy who owns the place, is seventy-nine and has some bone problems, among other things. He hires a teenaged boy to do the cutting, but we'll do the intricate putting greens stuff and the landscaping. It's only nine holes anyway. We play eighteen by doing it twice.

"Dave, Dave, the golfing machine," Bob says. He is a big cutup. This morning he's wearing a Hawaiian shirt, bright green pants, and white golf shoes. A show-off mustache hangs over his top lip. He's skinny with a fat face, which gives him a total comedian appearance.

"Bob's already at it," Stanley says. He sips his coffee. Stanley is close to fifty-five, and he's a veteran and all that, a get-along kind of guy. Boring. Kind of like me.

Bob and Stanley have those elaborate two-wheel carts to pull their bags around with. I just have a strap. Forget about carts at this place. It's like a workout carrying your clubs. I can already smell that good peaceful smell from all that grass on the course, the wet dew and mildew of it. Dark dirt seasoned up with a little fertilizer gives off a smell like dirty clothes, only nice because you know it isn't actually dirty clothes.

"How's it hanging there, Dave?" Bob goes. He gulps the rest of his coffee. I wish I had some. I had a cup before at home, but now I feel a little sleepy.

"Oh, just hanging fine, man," I say.

"'Hanging fine,'" Bob mocks. "You got a funny way of putting things. *Hanging fine*. I'm hanging long. I'm hanging heavy and long. Heavy and *looong*."

We laugh, out of courtesy. The guy doesn't know when to quit. By the end of the day we'll be kiddingly telling him to shut up. And he'll get PO'd, but then laugh himself out of it.

We walk out past the still-shut-down clubhouse 'cause Mack doesn't usually get up until ten in the morning. He lives inside the clubhouse with a Korean woman named Greta. He tells everybody he purchased her through the mail, but we know she met him at a mixer at the VFW. She's half his age but gets along with everybody.

The clubhouse is a long ramshackle trailer-building, and what I mean by trailer-building is that it started off as a trailer and then Mack built onto it outwards, until it turned into this long tunnel filled with pop machines and old trophies and tables and chairs and then in back there was a kitchen and a bedroom, and a shower room with a commode that Mack had put in. The windows of the built-in part aren't glass, but the see-through green fiberglass people use usually as shower doors.

Me and Stan stay back, Bob running ahead of us with his pushcart, pretending to be Chevy Chase. Who knows what's in the guy's head?

"How's Tara?" Stan asks.

"Doing pretty good."

"Yeah, I've always liked her. You're a lucky guy," Stan says.

"I know," I say. We walk on, nothing else to talk about.

Bob is teed up at the front, and the golf course, though small and kind of crappy, is heaven at that moment. Fifteen after seven, Saturday, July the twelfth. I keep thinking of heaven. It is like all that green, all the different kinds of green, tree green, rough green, putting-green green, the green in the fairway and the green fiberglass behind us and the green that fringes the putting greens, and then all the blue of the sky waking up, and the orange light on the green grass, and the sun sprouting out like an eyeball that has been washed carefully in a doctor's office. Sparkles everywhere, in a way. I like the clean green stuff, this feeling. I always try to get this at home and sometimes, many times, I do: green tranquillity. I even like that word.

After Bob tees off, he says, "Motherfuck!" He is in the rough. But what's new? He'd rather go long than straight, won't turn in his driver for a three wood for nothing.

"This game is gonna make me into a goddam serial killer," he says, kicking at grass.

We laugh.

Stanley's up next. His is a pretty good swing. He goes on through with it and then doesn't say nothing. It lands right in the middle. This is a par four to start, so he might do some good.

You really do have to start off good. I'm thinking that as I tee up. Man, this is the feeling. I got the driver in my hand. I'm looking down. Nothing in my brain but that silver club and that white ball and me. Then I rear back, thoughtless. God is like that, always thoughtless. No thinking. I go through. There's this whack I get into my arms, like I am hitting everything that scares me, that makes me sick, everything is getting hit out of me, beaten in one simple clear stroke. Like an exhalation running. And the simple connection of the club to the ball, and the ball in the sky.

It gets a nice bounce.

"Thank you, Jesus," Bob says behind me. He whistles. "That's good. You are almost on the goddam green."

I get bashful when complimented. I look down at the grass.

Bob goes, "Trade you shots."

I laugh, almost crying. I'm flattered and out of breath, even though I know this is a crappy course and nobody gives a crap what I do here—still I am emotional, and still I think I'm okay.

We play on through and people show up, people we all know, adding to the good feeling. I'm having one heck of a day. Three birdies, four pars, only two bogeys. Stan is doing a little less well, and Bob is just plain bad. He's got double bogeys and triple bogeys. He makes jokes, which makes it a lot better. We go on up to the clubhouse around ten a.m., sit outside on some rickety old lawn chairs. Greta comes out in her nightgown and bathrobe, drinking coffee and smoking a long brown cigarette, I think they're called Mores.

"You all do good?" she says.

Bob goes, "Dave here is exceptional, Greta. I kid you not."
I just sit there, taking it in. I can smell my own sweat in my clothes. It isn't a dirty smell because I used lots of deodorant.

"He oughta go pro," Bob says.

"Yeah, big pro in Anderson, Indiana," Stan says, looking at me.

I laugh. "Hey, Bob, I ain't that good, okay?"

Bob nods his head and lights up. "I'll be your agent or whatever," he says.

Greta stands there for a second and then says, putting out her cigarette in a nearby standup ashtray, "It's a nice day. Nice." She has pretty features, delicate, almost like Tara. She goes back in and comes back out, scooting an old folding chair to our table with her pack of cigarettes.

"So did you really do that good?" Greta says, smiling right at me.

"I guess," I say.

Her smile goes from interested to sexy, and I get a vibration from it that scares me and makes me tired at the same time. Tired of people always looking at me.

Bob says, "Fucking super-stud golf pro." He starts wheezing from laughing too much.

Greta winks at me then, one hand putting a cigarette into her mouth, the other one touching my knee real soft and playful under the table. Automatic, I jerk away, hitting the stupid table, making a gong sound. I feel dumb and used-up suddenly.

"Damn," Bob says, laughing more from my little stunt.

Greta pulls her hand back. "I'm sorry. I didn't know you were so jumpy."

I smile, redfaced, rubbing my knee, "No, no. Too much coffee."

The sun is hot on my forehead, and I put my hat back on. Stan comes back now with pops for all of us. He is so thoughtful. Bob and Stan start talking about Greta's new car, the Neon out front. But I get stuck on her touching my knee, that feeling of her trying that on me, and me being so freaked. Which leads me right into thinking about the child I was pursuing. This is too secret to be thinking here, out with people I know, and my stomach goes down almost to the bottom of the earth. I get terrorized, but I got to maintain in front of them. I think about that show I watched as a kid, *The Incredible Hulk,* when that guy started feeling his clothes ripping off from his muscles growing and turning green: I feel like that almost, as I sink closer in seeing the boy I was pursuing hurt bad in a basement. I see me saving him just before he dies. This gives me such a rush of feeling that I go deaf and mute. I have saved his life. No one loves him, but I have saved his life. I get all sentimental inside. I think of him with his hands tied behind his back and his mouth taped over in a basement. I would never do that to him.

I remember then how one time my dad whipped me outside our house, me up against a tree and him with a switch. I was ten or eleven, and we were living closer out to the country by then. He had caught me getting money from my mom's purse, and then he just took me outside not saying nothing, with that stupefied and angry face. He pushed me up against a maple, like a cop frisking somebody. I stayed there while he went and got himself a switch. Just stayed there. I could have run but I did not. He kept saying, "You little goddam thief," his voice full of pure disgust. I was getting lunch money from her purse. That's what the money was for. I told him that, but then I started crying. When I started that, he went ahead and pushed me outside to the tree. And then I just shut down, let the crying take me. I had shorts on. He whipped me into welts and a little blood. I screamed. My tongue and lips touched the bark.

Later that night when Mom came home from work, I was

sitting in my bedroom. Dad was in the bathroom across the hall shaving 'cause he was going later that night to a union meeting. Mom walked past, and I wanted to tell her that Dad tried to kill me, lying like that to make it more dramatic. But if I told her that he switched me, I knew she would just look at me, worn down and sick of me and him both. She would go, "What did *you* do, tattletale?" and I would have to tell her I was getting lunch money out of her purse (which she did not take with her to her job because a lot of people there had sticky fingers). Mom would go, "I would have given it to you when I got home anyways." Like I was stupid for getting into it with Dad. And really I was.

So I just stay in my room, the welts losing their burn. Mom walked past, and Dad kept shaving. Even if I knew how silly it was, I wanted to tell her that Dad might kill me.

There are people out there who would rather kill that boy, my boy, than love him, I think, sitting out in the sun at the golf course. This seems so incredibly vile that what I want, to love the boy deeply, seems small and beautiful. Today, anyways. This mixed in with the fact that I promised myself to stop. Yes. I'm going to stop.

"Dave?"

Bob and Stanley have stood up.

"Yeah?"

They have their club carts, and the whole thing.

"Time to start all over again. You having a daydream?" Bob says, laughing. "Dreaming of shooting birdies?"

"I don't got to dream about that," I say, all smiles.

Bob and Stan laugh, not expecting me to brag.

Greta looks at me.

"You getting a big head on you," she says, grinning, tapping out another cigarette.

.   .   .

Mack looks at my score card after we get done. He's got some oxygen in a tank with a tube that hooks into his big nose. He's bald and short and full of stories. But he looks at my card and he says, "Let me frame this."

"Sure," I say. I got three birdies out there, an eagle, and no bogeys. I'm tired and feel really good.

Stanley had to go because he has a second job at some superstore, security-guarding to pay for his daughter's college. So it's me and Bob and a few others, around one-thirty. Greta has changed into this purple two-piece bathing suit and high heels, makes you wonder if at one time she worked in the exotic-dancing industry, and Mack is behind the counter at the old-fashioned cash register, taking in his oxygen.

"I ain't seen nobody do better here," Mack says, putting my score card into his shirt pocket. "You want a beer, you guys?"

"Nah," I say. "Got to get home."

"Pussywhipped Brewer," Bob says.

Everyone laughs.

"Yeah, I'm pussywhipped, that's it," I say, smiling like I'm proud of my pussywhipped status, and maybe I am. Maybe I want them to know that I like my wife. I love my wife and my kid.

"Well, next time you're here, this thing is going to be in a frame up front," Mack says, touching his shirt pocket. On the flimsy walls are all kinds of certificates and score cards and even an autographed picture of Bob Hope, who Mack saw in the forties at the Paramount. All in gold frames, like artifacts.

"I'll see you guys later," I say, and Greta is outside when I'm leaving, smoking again.

"You got plans tonight?" she asks.

"The whole family is going out tonight," I say, my golf clubs on my shoulder.

She walks over in her high heels. She has the blackest hair, and she looks up at me 'cause she's a little short, even in the heels. "Your wife's lucky. You got a kid?" She smiles and then I smell alcohol coming out of her mouth, a sweet fume of it.

"Yeah, little girl." I'm squinting my eyes.

"Little girl? How little?"

"One year old."

She licks her lips and laughs lazily.

"Little girls are so precious," she says, and then goes past me back into the trailer clubhouse.

For a moment I feel like I have been touched by Greta again, like she wanted to flirt with me again. That panic returns. But then I see by her going back inside that she understands I don't want any of it. I feel good about her understanding that I am a one-woman man. Straitlaced and nose to the grindstone. This was my day here, this was when I got the best score of my entire life. This was when people thought I was a good family man and a good golfer and just a good all-American guy. And this made Greta really think about me. She's thinking about me now. Thinking about me and fantasizing maybe. Who knows?

I walk off and get into my car and drive home.

4

TARA

Finally making the bed at two-thirty in the afternoon, I can hear Mom out in the living room doing baby talk to Brit, her voice smoky from her menthol cigarettes. As I shove a pillow into a clean case, I think how I ought to quit smoking. Some nasty habit I picked up from her. I remember as I slide another pillow into another case how I used to steal all Mom's cigs. She'd ask me about it, and I'd just lie like a rug to her, trying to look innocent as Little Bo Peep.

There. Bed's all done. I go out and Mom's got her measuring tape around Brit's neck. I have dirty sheets in a bundle.

"Six inches round the neck," Mom says. She insists on plucking her eyebrows till they look sketched on, and then there's the eye shadow, the color of Zest deodorant soap. I stop and think then, how much of a bitch I can be.

"Six?" I say, getting nice.

"Yes, ma'am."

Brit hiccups, lying there on the couch.

I'm still holding the sheets. Mom's measuring Brit's arms, stooped over the couch, in another one of her famous wild-colored jogging suits. They're so comfy, she tells people in her smoked-out way. Plus the hair, red like Ronald McDonald's. God love her.

"What kind of outfit you gonna make her, Mom?"

"You know that little girl they had on PTL, Tom and Anita's child? It has gold piping and pleats."

Mom's examining more. I cannot stand that Praise The Lord cable channel. Way too sickly sweet, and everybody shows off on that thing. The preachers are sissified, and the women are all trying to be either Kathy Lee Gifford or Barbara Mandrell.

I go through the kitchen, down to the basement. Just that naked lightbulb down the stairs. Dave promised to fix up down here. Whatever. I put the dirty sheets and pillow cases in, and can smell our bodies off them for a sec. There's other whites, so I add them, put the soap in, turn it on. Old washer purrs, like a sick cat. The basement has one of those basement smells, dirt and cold water. In my mind, though, Dave and my smell comes back. Last night, me in my nightie. Good God! I promised myself all the time I was putting that thing on not to be ashamed. This is what a healthy husband-and-wife relationship can be. I was still ashamed, no matter how many *Cosmopolitan* articles I read, and I got kind of bitchy with him trying to stay unashamed. We needed *something*. I kept telling myself that that day we bought the nightie at the mall, that day we got into the fight because I was forcing my sexy agenda on old Dave. Sometimes it's like he really just wants to be a kid. Looks out at the world like he has lost his mommy in the supermarket. When he gives me that look, I could kill him.

Down here with the washer going, I get the feeling that I mistreat Dave, but also that he wants me to. Someone you love wanting you to hurt them is the worst feeling in the world, unless you're some kind of sicko. We loved each other last night, though. We did. You cannot fake that. His eyes going teary when he was up inside, kissing me like he was trying to go through to the other world where you don't have to speak to communicate. I felt like I was the one and the only. But it was not that nightie. That stupid thing. God no. It was me. He loves *me.*

As I go back up the steps, Dave is walking in with his maroon golf bag, holding his spiked shoes. "Man, I rocked that course today," he goes, smiling like a winner.

I flinch a little, this hate coming back. Mom's got Brit on her lap. I like it when he is happy, I do, but I have to get through this feeling first.

"That's good, Dave," Mom says. She's still probably pissed about yesterday, missing the X rays, but she's being all wide-eyed with him. She likes to talk down to him. It gives her a secret pleasure.

"Yeah, let's see. Nine birdies. Five pars. Only three bogeys, Mom."

He puts his golf bag down, looking suntanned and fine. All-American—his hair is thinning out just a little bit, and he is getting a spare tire, but otherwise he's a good-looking man. Big eyes, with dark lashes and ears that stick out just enough to make him look alert. I remember seeing him in the halls at our high school, him in a Rush T-shirt, jeans, hiking boots, long hair, those eyes. I did not know then that I would be here now, God knows, but still I'm a little glad.

"Hey, babe," he says, pitching his voice low. He comes up and gives me a kiss in the hall off of the living room, then pulls back and sits down next to Mom, sliding in. Mom gives him Brit. What a damn fine daddy. Really.

"So is it Cracker Barrel?" he says, lifting Brit up, blowing his fart-frog noise on her tummy.

"Sure," Mom goes, smiling. Her smile is slightly dumb because she's never liked Dave really. One time, when we were first engaged and I was going through Professional Careers Institute to become a dental hygienist (did not make it, too many open mouths—plus this teacher had it in for me), Mom says to me before he was to come pick me up: "He's creepy. Are you sure he ain't retarded?" I just looked at her, like she was being an idiot, and she went, "Well, he is." And I said, "If you say another word, I'll just kill you, that's all."

Now she's all Miss Congeniality with a little icebox mixed in. I hear that damn washer pounding.

"I like that little country store they have," Mom says. "I need to buy a gift for Ladies' Fellowship, and that's just the place to get a gift."

Dave says, "I'll tell Dad on the phone," looking at me.

"You know what he'll say," I say.

Dave laughs, gives Brit to Mom, goes into the kitchen.

"What time?" he says from in there.

"Five-thirty. We'll beat the rush," I say.

"I don't know if I'll be hungry at five-thirty, Tara," Mom says, all serious.

I grab Brit.

"You will be, Mom."

Mom grunts. "You have had the attitude all day."

I ignore her. At times you just have to. I take Brit to the kitchen. Dave's on the phone with his dad, his voice trying to go even lower-pitched.

"What about Crackle Barrow. I mean Crackle—I mean . . ."

Dave laughs like a little boy then, on the phone with his dad, losing it. I have Brit, but he looks at me, his eyes glossy-innocent, and all of a sudden his not being able to pronounce Cracker Barrel right scares me. I smile and kiss Brit's cheek.

"Crackle . . . Shoot."

I can hear his dad yelling through the receiver.

"Calm down, Dad," Dave goes. He looks at me and winces. "Crack. Er. Bare. El. There."

He's listening. Mom comes in, spying.

"No. No . . . Dad."

He puts his hand over the phone.

"He wants you-know-what."

Mom whispers, "Not Ponderosa."

"Yep," Dave says.

Mom rolls her eyes.

"The man's sick, Mom," I go. I nod at Dave.

"Okay, Dad. Ponderosa. We'll pick you up."

Mom says, washing her hands in the sink, "I guess they have chicken."

It is a deeply worried whisper. Me and Dave laugh at her and his dad. He comes over, smelling golflike: grass stains, leathery odor of dried sweat. I kiss his warm mouth with Brit between us. She cries. He takes her.

Dave's dad lives in a trailer, on the other side of a Marsh Supermarket, the trailer park and parking lot split by a deep ditch filled with brown rocks and water. It's a good solid trailer. Despite his temper, you have to like Dave's dad. He's one of those people so stuck in a rut, it's beyond his comprehension to even go to the bathroom outside of his place. He drives long distances just to pee. I knew from the get-go he was not going to have any of that Cracker Barrel dreaming.

The trailer's silver and white with tinted windows, cinder blocks for steps up to the door. Inside it's just packed with furniture from the old house. Dave's mom did not take anything with her. She left Dave's dad right after Dave graduated high school, got her own apartment on the other side of Anderson, opposite Dave and Dave's dad. Like once Dave matured it was time for her to leave him, even though they still lived in the same town and all. Dave gets a little sore about that whole thing, how she avoids him, how she's snotty. She met Jerry, her husband now, at work, in the City Building, almost seven years back, when she was temping in the Sewer Department as a receptionist. This tall guy named Jerry Forkheimer of all names, from Columbus, Ohio, coming in to complain for his dad who was too sick to.

Dave and I go up to the door to get Dave's dad. Mom and

Brit stay in the Grand Prix. As soon as Dave knocks once, Dave's dad is out that door, going past us, like he'd been waiting for a real long time. He is in a pair of polyester dress pants, a beige dress shirt, and white dress shoes you can tell he hardly ever wears. His eating-at-Ponderosa outfit. His eyes look weird, tired but wild. Lost some major weight too. You can tell by the way his white belt is tightened up, the end of it dangling from his last loop like a dog's tongue when it gets hot.

"Ready," he says, racing ahead of us.

Dave and I look at each other, like we did when Mom was washing her hands back at the house, as if to say look how our parents have turned out, just look. Then Dave grabs my hand. On the way back, we get a view of Dave's dad, my mom, and Brit in her baby seat in the back of our car, Dave's dad and my mom kind of scrunched up together, their faces looking pissed but trying to get along.

Dave is still holding my hand. It feels like the gravel under my feet goes through the soles of my shoes, and the sky is bright and hot, beating down. Dave says, before he lets go of my hand, "Family."

A joke almost, but is he choked up?

Mom goes, soon as we get back in, "You two lovebirds, holding hands."

I just smile.

"Look at them, Paul," Mom says. "Did you see them hold hands?"

"Why, yes I did, Miss Martha."

Dave's dad has a beaten-up voice, a little sadness in the way he says everything, edged off with a slightly smart-assed tone.

Dave starts it. We are off. Mom's White Diamonds nauseates me in close quarters, and Brit might have pooped back there. I listen to Mom and Dave's dad complain about being old on a hot day such as this. We go past a garbage dump, trash as high as the great pyramids of Egypt, the sweet overripe garbage smell getting in through the AC vents. Dave turns the radio to country.

Halfway there, we get stopped by a train. Brit automatically starts whimpering and fussing. Dave looks sweaty, the train rushing past. There's a public pool shining across the street, kids splashing in and out of the water. I won't let Brit get into one of those pools. People pee and everything, and I'm sorry, no amount of chlorine can make that clean.

Dave's dad says, "Hey, Dave, you doing okay at Indiana Gas?"

Dave doesn't answer. He's watching the train roar by. It seems to be headed toward that pool almost, like hell on wheels. The country music goes off to commercial.

"Dave, your dad said something to you," I say, and I see him snap out of it. He honks the horn, maybe accidentally.

"You guys," Dave starts. "You guys wanna go to the show after we eat?"

"Brit may get cranky, Dave," I say. But I feel like I just peed on his parade, so I add, "She might sleep through one. You never know. Brit can sleep real heavy sometimes."

Dave smiles. The train keeps going. Kids splash and walk around.

Dave's dad coughs, "Goddammit, I said how's your job going, son?"

"Fine," Dave says. "Fine."

As soon as we see the train's end, Dave pulls up behind the guy in front of us, real slow. It's an Escort, like the piece of crap I drive to work.

"Did you tell that car guy about the fuel pump?" I ask.

Dave keeps getting closer to the car up there.

"Yes," Dave says.

"Well?"

"He'll get it done next week."

"So the damn car's gonna sit there all week?"

"I'll get it towed, Tara." His voice cracks.

"Whatever," I say. I am over it.

Dave's dad from the backseat: "What fuel pump? You don't know nothing about fuel pumps, Dave. Maybe I can help you there."

Dave's dad's voice sounds judgmental, like he knows there's no way in hell Dave could fix that car. Dave is almost running into the guy up there, but then the guy pulls out too. We go over the tracks. Ponderosa is about six or seven blocks up.

"What fuel pump?" Dave's dad repeats.

"Everybody just shut up!" Dave says, furious. When he gets mad like this, I just want to kill him. I mean out of nowhere, but I kind of understand too. Dave's dad used to beat him pretty good. He was an okay father, Dave says, but he used to beat him. That was the way back then.

I look into the rearview mirror. Dave's dad is looking at Brit. He's touching her chin, and she seems to almost be liking it.

Dave has on his blank-mask face. He's driving too fast.

Mom goes, "Slow down."

I go, "Mom, be quiet. Just be quiet."

I turn the radio off. Dave pulls into the Ponderosa. The bushes outside are scorched, and the black-tarred lot has litter all over it. It's one of those old Ponderosas, with a barn-shaped building, a big sign out front that says, FREE TRIP TO MARS WITH EVERY T-BONE. Dave gets out and then opens Mom's door, and she gets out real slow, like it is hurting her to move. Or like she is showing Dave for telling us off like that. I don't know who I'm madder at. Dave's dad gets out, looks all pissed but sad. God, I could pull my hair out. Why is family so hard? I want to ask somebody smart that. Einstein or whoever. I unstrap Brit. Thank the Lord for small blessings: she has not pooped all over herself.

Dave's already inside. I imagine him not wanting us here, like he just wants all of us somewhere else. Well, sorry, Dave.

It's a long brown tunnel up to the front where the trays are, and the air in here smells musty and burned. Brit wants to get fussy. Mom and Dave's dad go up and get their trays, and some fat girl in a green jumper is taking their order. Dave gets a T-bone, and Mom gets chicken, of course. Dave's dad orders a T-bone. I just get their Grand Buffet and Sundae Bar for Brit and me.

"She can eat off my plate," I almost-whisper to the fat girl, who has got pretty cat-eyes.

"We have kid's meals," she says, snotty.

I ignore her. I can't deal right now with anybody's attitude but my own.

Dave gets a big piece of cake out of the dessert case, and Dave's dad does too.

"I'm paying," Dave tells all of us.

Dave's dad says, "Let me get mine." Jaws set tight.

Of course, you don't hear anything from Mom.

"Dad," Dave says. His voice is grave, like he is talking in court. "It's on me."

After I get a high chair for Brit, we all sit at a table by the salad bar, then go and load up all our plates. Brit seems happy at least, not a care in the world. I feed her applesauce. I think this is why God made kids, so you can look at their mouths eating applesauce you are feeding to them and forget everybody else's BS.

"What they mean by free trip to Mars?" Dave's dad says, mouthful of something. Trying to be cute.

"It's a joke, Dad," Dave says, laughing, buttering his roll. So superior. Oh so superior, that Dave. "You know. A joke about that landing on Mars with the truck-thing that sends back pictures?"

"Oh," Dave's dad says. All he watches on TV is *Gomer Pyle* and *Wheel of Fortune* and *Jeopardy.* Then he has to get a jab in: "Don't get smart."

ι looks miserable, but she's eating. I keep feeding Brit. ιaks and chicken arrive. I keep messing with Brit. Wipe ιth and give her Jell-O and pudding and a little soup. ιιιe waιls in here are covered in cowboy and Western decorations and there's a dusty forgottenness to it all, like nobody really knows the stuff is there: a pair of chaps, whips, old-timey handcuffs, guns and holsters. The Ponderosa in Muncie is newer and has kelly-green and mauve booths and pictures of beaches and rainy days on the cream-colored walls. This one is just crappy. But Dave had many of his birthdays here. That's what Dave's dad is talking on about now.

"'Member? You were ten and we brought you and your friend here and we got a cake at the store, and candles, brought it all here, had your party—"

"Yeah," Dave says. He is not smiling. Dave's dad just wants to remember your tenth birthday, Dave: Good God. Then again it's okay. Dave is mellowing, becoming boylike. I get a dreamy quality to my thoughts, like Dave turning into a boy makes me turn into a girl. Mom goes up and gets some fresh fruit. More people are coming in.

"What did he get for his birthday when he was ten, Paul?" I go.

Paul looks sick, I'm sorry, I have to say that for real now. He says he's been vomiting a lot more. We don't want to talk about that, but red meat is the last thing a sick stomach needs. Anyway, Paul keeps on eating like he is trying to forget how bad it feels to eat.

"One of those ten-speed bikes," he says.

"You didn't bring it in here?"

Brit spits up. I wipe.

"Yes ma'am, we certainly did." Paul smiles like how proud he is. "I went out to the truck and wheeled her in here. People looked, but boy was he surprised!"

Paul laughs.

Is he dying? I mean he's skinny, and in here I can tell he's got ashen skin. Dave wants not to talk about it, but right then when Paul smiles you can see his skull like in a horror movie. You can almost see what he is without the skin and the voice and the hair and the manners.

"I rode that thing all over Anderson," Dave says, digging into his cake. He's happy, thinking of his bike. I pull Brit up from the high chair and hold her. She's doing fine. Mom comes back and eats her cantaloupe, then says, "That chicken was excellent."

In her jogging suit. I love her. She wants to hold Brit. Dave and Paul talk about how the bike fell apart.

"It wasn't that cheap," Dave's dad says, sulky or maybe just acting sulky.

"Dad, the darn thing was from Kmart," Dave says, laughing.

"No, it was not from goddam Kmart, Dave. I got that at Sears. Why don't you get your goddam facts straight?"

Dave just whistles and laughs, like how crazy it is, what his dad just allowed to come out of his mouth. Dave's dad winces some more, looks around. I get up, all dreamy still, people at tables talking about their own private matters. I get a cup for ice cream. The machine hums to life when I pull the handle down. Ice creams spills down into my cup in a graceful line. I think of Dave riding his ten-speed and I think of Paul dying. It is cancer, is it not? Has to be. Nobody says anything, but . . . I think of me in a red nightie, and I think how I did not put the sheets from the washer into the dryer, and I wonder if Brit will go to college, and I wonder if Dave really loves me or if we are just too desperate to see . . .

The ice cream tastes like soap, but it melts down my throat. Dave is sipping his coffee, telling his dad about his golf game, Mom playing kissy-face with Brit. I look up and see that the dining room is now all the way full, not a table or a booth empty.

As if by magic, all the other people just suddenly appeared, like nothing, like everything.

Like cancer, like birthday bikes, like babies.

Dave thought Brit might like *Hercules,* some Disney cartoon, but she is just screaming. I knew even before we got here that it would be me having to come out here into the lobby and rock her and carry her around. She doesn't stop for three whole minutes. Finally, though, her fit ends, and after it, I walk around looking at the candy and movie posters. Brit starts gurgling, smelling good from the powder when I changed her. It is Saturday night at nine o'clock almost. I just want to go home, put her to bed, put the sheets in the dryer and go to bed myself. In one poster a giant lizard monster is in the fetal position across some man's face. In another a big gun is neon-purple. In another that Martin Short guy, what an idiot, has a hairstyle like a hyperactive girl in the Sunday-school class I used to assist in. I never taught, Mrs. Maloney does, but I used to help maintain order—before I got the Bob Evans job, and now I work on Sundays a lot, have to, that's the restaurant business.

When the movie lets out, Dave is all smiles. Beaming.

"That is a classic," he says, pointing back into the theater. "It's got everything."

Mom goes, wide-eyed and sincere, "I got hypnotized by it."

Paul looks very tired. He is not going to start any fights now. He's all out of it, like Hercules just beat him up. He tries to smile. "Not bad for a cartoon," he whispers.

We all walk out to the car. Dave drives his dad home first.

"Hope you liked Ponderosa, Dad," Dave says, laughing.

Dave's dad grunts his way out. I see that Dave is hurt by his dad not thanking him or whatever, but also Dave's jaw clenches back, like he expected his dad to do that anyway. Dave's dad just stands outside while we back out. Outside his own trailer, like a stranger. I wonder if he might have to vomit. You could tell he went to sleep during the show. He just stands there in the gravel, and I think now that we should have offered him to spend the night with us. It might be scary and lonely in that trailer, but asking that is not possible because Dave's dad has his pride, and Dave wouldn't want him there anyway, I know.

But still, as Dave pulls out, his dad looks to me like a deer out there on the gravel, one of the stupidest, one of the ones that get hit but do not die, that just runs off into the woods to disappear.

5

DAVE

I forgot my sunglasses, and there is this thing in my throat, like spit, like lightning. The last two kids are settled in the middle of the bus, in the same seat, twins, two girls in dirty dresses. Their mom's a drunk who scoots them out every Sunday morning in her housecoat, ratty-headed twins with jam-covered mouths. I push on past the mall and out to downtown, with its old buildings. The girls giggle. It gets lonely after the final kids get off. It's like I'm driving a house around, me this bachelor in his house on wheels or something. They had it painted this really ugly gold color with sparkles in it, this old used-to-be schoolbus, the Golden Chariot. Patterned after the one that took the prophet Enoch back up to heaven. Right now it's the only one we have at Norris Road Baptist Church that works.

The girls are jumping up now, in anticipation. They live in a small dirty house, the back of Weaver, right behind all the black-windowed warehouses. It's a house made of cinder blocks and wood, it looks like, no insulation, no siding. Somebody said their mom is a stripper at The Toast.

"Sit down, girls," I say, seeing their eager faces in the rearview. I wonder why they would even want to go home to that nasty place, but they do. Star and Lisa. Then I wonder why they don't have rhyming names. It seems like if a stripper had twins, she would give them cute rhyming names.

I stop in their neighborhood. You can just smell the poverty. It's like barbecue smells, mixed with dirty hair and the way an old car that hasn't had its insides taken care of smells. It is hot today and clear. They tiptoe up while I swing the doors open and grab the sack of suckers on the big green-colored dashboard.

Their tiny hands reach in, one at a time. The picture of their small hands taking Dum-Dums before they go back into their dirty house lasts while I back out. It has a religious quality. Small hands reaching into a plastic bag. Finding things. I back out onto the street, down the alley toward where the thrift store is and the old place that used to be Kentucky Fried but now is just a nameless chicken place 'cause they lost the franchise, whoever owned it. Somebody said somebody got a breaded rat in with their extra-crispy, and there went that store. I go down sun-hot streets, past used-car lots and closed-down stores and houses that don't look like they could house anything but vampire bats and crackheads. Urban blight.

The bus rattles all over, a big diesel one, and even though I drive it every Sunday a.m. and p.m. it always seems while I am driving it like it's too old and messed up to drive. Or that it has ghosts that want me to wreck. Kid-ghosts, gruesome-faced. I read a Stephen King book once about a little boy who could move things with his brain, or was it about a boy who came back from the grave, gray-skinned and evil?

The damn pool now. No train today. Yes. He's in there. Swimming. In the blue water, like a movie. I remember last night, being stopped by the train, how I wanted to die: the promise to myself has been made, and I feel it go down the drain, down the drain that is connected to my spine from my head, the promise draining down. I am sleepy. The pool passes. The boy does not. The boy stays. I think of Tara doing it to me in the bedroom the other night in her nightie. Think of Brit's face blown up like a flower growing in fast motion on a nature show. The boy does something else. He floats and then blossoms into my body. I think of Christ.

"Christ Jesus," Pastor Lewis says in his sermon, reversing the regular way to say it. "Christ Jesus will be coming in the sky, folks. Will be floating there, raising out His arms for the saved, the born again, to join Him. Cars will crash on superhighways as bodies rise up and rise up."

Pastor Lewis burst into tears after saying that part today. He's a big guy, and all into Armageddon. Some say obese, with curly hair going bald, waved back, and black suits and a red mouth. His wife is real little.

I drive out beyond where I live because if I go home now I'll just get peeved. Past cornfields and there's a dog outside an old farmhouse, big mutt on a leash looking like he is laughing but he is only hot. Roadkills are all over the place. What if the child left me? But he isn't even with me. He is always with me in a way, though. If the child left me, maybe my whole life would be worthless because I need the child in my mind to soothe me out of the boredom of my everyday life. This is upsetting to think, to say the least.

I pull into a long driveway, and I stop. This old two-story house, abandoned and burned up but still standing, is right beyond the gravel drive. I look at it for a second and think of it as a house me and him could live in. The little old burned-out house on the prairie, in the middle of nowhere. I'd have one house with Brit and Tara, and this one with him. We would paint it up nice, but still there would be no electricity or water. I'd bring out milk jugs of fresh water from home, and we'd use batteries and I would feed him food and candy and water, and I see him in the doorway when I'm about to leave. The boy is so sad. I realize this house would be like a prison. Without me. So I go back and we stay together for a little while longer.

I get home, and he's still inside me.

I go inside our beautiful little house. White-sided with black shutters, a good yard. Tara looks out the window in the living room.

"You parked that bus so nobody can get around," she says.

I bring the Golden Chariot home on Sundays, because I go pick up people for Sunday night service too.

"They can if they try," I say.

"You are impossible."

I go into the kitchen. The bus ride hangs onto my skin like chiggers. I see that burned-out old house, I see him standing in its doorway. When I am alone, it's when it happens. Then I understand that that old house is actually Troy's garage. Troy takes off his shirt in the garage. Troy takes off his underpants. His thing just hangs there like an arm without a hand. I look at it. I'm on that cot, on my knees and Troy is standing there saying not one word except, "This is for you," and I look at it. I have to look at it.

Geese on the paper towels' design. Sunflowers on the curtains. The linoleum is coming up by the back door like the dead skin off a sunburn. The phone is off-white. There's a big grease stain on the wall by the trash can. I see me hitting the ball yesterday, hitting it far, the impact of my stroke vibrating into my palms like electricity.

"Why are you standing there?" Tara asks, in the kitchen doorway.

"I'm hungry," I say.

"I made spaghetti sauce, but I haven't put the water on to boil yet because I didn't know when you would be back."

She goes and gets a big pot out and starts filling it up in the sink.

"Where's Brit?"

"Guess who?"

"Your mom's got her?"

"Yup."

Tara puts the pot on to boil. I leave. Can't look at her. I can't look anymore. So I go and shut the bathroom door. I do that pinching thing where I pull up my shirt and pinch what gut I have really, really hard, which makes a mark on my white belly.

I have been good. I have been very good. I have done the regular things. I drove that church bus. I played magnificent golf. Took my family out to eat and to the show. Put up with Dad's bullcrap. Went to church. Our church is white-sided with a small chapel, a gravel lot, hardly very much room with a coat-and-hat rack and a big map of the Holy Land and a table where you can pick up salvation tracts on your way out. And red carpeting.

The pinching gets blood. I clean it up. Spaghetti's ready. Me and Tara eat.

"Brit loves Mom," she says.

"Yeah. Pass me the Parmesan."

She does. I do not look at her. The table is wobbly. I think about putting a matchbook under the short leg. I think about Dad because this is what he would do: put a book of matches under the leg to stop it from wobbling. He looked dead last night, like he had run out of ideas. I remember then when he brought that ten-speed into Ponderosa on my birthday when I was ten, how he thought it was so great because he had done it. At that point I kind of hated him. The week or two before he had shoved me into a wall six times in a row in one night, saying I was not doing enough around the house. With Mom working, I would need to dust the furniture and do this and do that, and I told him in my pissant little voice, "Lay off, Dad." And he came at me, joking first, then serious, pushing me into walls over and over. Pretend-boxing at me, until I started bawling like an idiot. He stopped, ashamed I couldn't take it. "God, you are such a little crybaby." Then there is the ten-speed at Ponderosa Steakhouse for my birthday, me and Todd, this friend I had, sitting in a booth with Mom, while Dad wheels it in. People all around laugh, and then comes this pressure for me to be grateful when the sight of him giving me something like that made me sick. Mom sat there with her cup of coffee, trying to smile, looking at me, as always, it seems, not wanting to put up with the bullcrap between me and Dad. After sipping her coffee at Ponderosa, she says, as Dad puts down the kickstand in the middle of the dining room, "See? He got you a bike."

I eat, drink Kool-Aid, and have a piece of peach pie with frozen yogurt on it. Tara cleans up.

"I work today," she says from the kitchen. "Molly called. I'll go in at two and get off at six. Just a short shift. Molly said something about the car still being out there."

I sit down, then stand up.

"What?" I ask.

"We need to have that Escort towed, Dave."

She's wiping her hands on her shirt.

"I'll take you to work and see if I can't rig it up to get it started and drive it back."

Tara gets pissed. "David, it is *dead.*"

"I know," I say, moving toward her. I grab hold of her and she tries to shake me off, but I start to laugh and nuzzle her neck, which smells like sweat and tomatoes.

"Get off me," she says.

But I kiss and kiss that neck. I bury my sorrows in it in an invisible way. This is love, I think. Love is burying your sorrows in your wife's sweet neck. That feels like love. I kiss again. I kiss and kiss.

"Stop it!" she says, laughing more.

We go on over to the couch, and I kiss down to her boobs. I kiss them, then her fingers, each one. There is fire inside me. I feel the church bus ride again, the vibration and pull of it. The Escort I might could get started by uncapping the carburetor and tricking it with a swallow of gas. Dad used to do that.

We get up. Tara has a red face. She looks all around her like she's lost inside. When we go on into the bedroom we are as quiet as church, two people doing it the natural way. Love is doing it the natural way. We don't get naked all the way till under the covers. I ain't hard, though. She grabs my thing, plucking at it. In my closed eyes the boy is swimming naked. Troy's thing in my tiny boy's hand. I feel it like a club made out of warm clay. I feel him shiver like he has come out of his skin. The boy swims up and out onto the concrete. Wet and naked the boy looks at me and I am naked and we look like Martians in another world. He tries to run from me, but I cannot let him.

At the last it's her. Tara. I see her face. She has the face of an angel working hard, as we do it. The love is bright, back here in the natural world, and when I go off inside her I see my stuff swimming up toward her egg like a sex-education cartoon, but still this is sacred and I thank God for her.

She gets into her Bob Evans outfit after taking a shower. The outfit is like a square-dancer's uniform. I get into my under-pants and things, and I think about changing my clothes to shorts and a T-shirt, but that would only make more dirty laundry, so I slide back into my shirt and pants and even my necktie from church. When I pull on my clothes, I remember the pinches I did and I'm glad she did not see them. She looks around at me now, putting her earrings back on.

"Why are you wearing your tie, honey?" She laughs that way she does, like she cannot believe me sometimes.

"I don't know," I say, playing it dumb.

"Men," she says, still laughing. I like it when I am classed like that, like her laugh. I'm doing good. A-OK. Outside it's hot and clear still, sunlight in tree limbs almost the color of molten iron and honey mixed up together. She gets into the Grand Prix and I follow, passing the big gold bus I parked at the back of the neighborhood.

"She may stay all night with Mom, I don't know. Have you talked to your dad since last night?"

We are out on the main intersection before I answer.

"No. He didn't come to church."

"He was looking pretty bad." She's sliding some lip stuff on her lips with her pinkie finger.

We don't talk anymore. Not about anything. There's the old Escort beneath the Bob Evans sign. I park and she says, still angry about the whole Escort problem, "It's dead." This is a whisper. She flings her purse over her shoulder and walks off. I get out, realizing I forgot to bring the damn gas can, but I figure I ought to try and start it.

The damn thing starts right off. Like nothing. This makes me laugh out loud. Pure magic. I push down hard on the gas, keep it going, smells burned but still it's going, a major triumph. I feel powerful, my head no longer aches, and I sit there in the driver's seat letting it rumble on, blue smoke coming out the tailpipe. I let up off the gas all the way, and it still goes. I go in and tell Tara. She's snapping on her name tag up at the cash register.

"You are kidding," she says. Then she looks scared and embarrassed, like I'm mad at her because it started. I am not mad at all, I want to say.

"I swear to God, Dave, it was dead."

"I got the touch," I say. Not bragging, just joking, really.

She laughs at me, and suddenly I am just this guy who fixes cars by sitting inside them.

"You got something," Tara says.

I smile and tell her she can drive the Grand Prix home.

"I'll try to make it to Sunday-night service," she says, but I know she won't.

Outside the damn car is *still* running, and then I am off, feeling like I should have taken a shower. All restaurants out here, and I-69. Plus the horse track, with cars all over its lot. I drive to the pool because I am happy. I drive the piece-of-crap Escort there, stop in front, stop there. I pull on my necktie knot, tightening it.

I am triumphant. The swimming pool gives off a silver radiation, like a spaceship. I get this image, staring at the splashes and skin, of a big metal space station just sliding into earth.

Then I see the boy. He is walking in the grass, right beside the fence. I turn the car off. Rise up like I have hypnosis going. My mouth fills up with spit. There is not a word for what he does to me. I keep thinking of Jesus's Second Coming, of Jesus floating in the sky, of blue smoke and of a little boy skinny as pipe cleaners, delicate as something made up in your head to be beautiful, and that's it. Jesus coming back isn't scary to me because He would stop the world right then and He would stop me. Like when the bomb got dropped on Hiroshima and people were just standing around outside. Their bodies got nuked, but their shadows were scorched into the ground. We saw that in a movie in high school.

The boy is walking toward the locker room, and there I am close to the front. He has got a cut on his foot. I am seeing him bleed. I thought that I was a ghost then, brought back into real life by the smell of his blood. But then again I was always with him, even when he did not know it. I was following him, walking through walls to get to him.

Me in church clothes standing there. He looks up at me. I stare down at his foot.

I say, "Oh my gosh. You've cut yourself, Bud. Oh no." I was slowing down my voice to prove to him that he meant something to me.

"I know," he says, slow-voiced too.

"What happened?" I say, people screaming and splashing in the background.

He looks at me and then gets it, that I really want to know. Nobody else wants to but me. So he takes me over to this broken bottle in the grass by the fence, on the other side of the pool.

"That's what did it," he says, all cute and serious.

Little thing just walking in the grass because the cement part was too hot and his feet were burning off. So he cut his foot on that glass bottle there, shining in the sun. Little drops of blood on the concrete.

"I'm going to take you and get that fixed up, Bud."

Even though he seemed scared by me, the boy smiled and allowed me to lift him up. For all anybody knew at the pool, I was his dad. First I stop off in the locker room with him and put toilet paper on his foot. The blood glows through the white toilet paper. I carry him out to the car. This is the justice of stopping myself, for when I stop myself I can give up and get what I want: him, with a cut foot, in the car with me. This is why I tell myself to stop, so I can give in eventually.

The car starts, like it knows if it doesn't I might crack wide open, my blood turning automatically into fire.

I go to the Super X drugstore and buy peroxide and cotton and bandages. I smile at the old guy cashier with a beard. I think he thinks of me as a sweet man buying clean things. Then there is the lady at the Motel 6, looking at me like I am a dope pusher or a sex fiend. She has a baseball cap on, spider legs for eyelashes. She takes my credit card, saying something about luggage. Any luggage? I don't know what I say in return. But I leave with a key.

The boy waits in the car while I do all this, then I drive back to where the room is and then I carry him into the motel room in secret.

I take him into the green and white bathroom first off. Begin to wash his feet, especially the cut one. I wash the cut one very carefully. I wash the cut and his toes with soapy water in the white light, him standing on the sink, dipping his toes toward me. There we are in the mirror, it is not weird at all.

This is a painting of us in a museum. I think he likes what I am doing very much, in fact. I am just careful enough to let him like it. I realize too the Jesus aspect in this. I work the soap into a lather. The boy is quiet. Quieter than a cloud or than clothespins or a car dashboard in winter.

"Yeah," I keep saying. "Oh yeah. We'll get you fixed up."

The peroxide, after I pour a little on, bubbles around his cut, bubbles and bubbles. I am so hard I feel like I could cut myself off from it and it would land soft on a pillow, its own dreamy thing. I cannot let him touch it.

I call him *honey* several times. Once inside the motel room, I start calling him that, instead of *Bud*. It just comes out natural. *Honey* this and *honey* that. Out in the bedroom, the TV happens to be on. Something on HBO with Sylvester Stallone. I keep the room dark, but it is not hellish, no.

I bandage his cut, and he is still in his swim trunks. One last time I look at him in the mirror after I dry off his feet. His face is serene, his black hair still a little damp, his skin glowing half red and half brown from being out in the sun.

Me and him walk out, and we sit together on the edge of the bed.

"My name is Dave," I whisper, as we watch people get shot.

"Nathan," he says.

"Nathan," I say. "Now that is a name."

I am not touching him. At all. Nathan is the sweetest name. It's almost the same when spelled backwards, and this goes through my head several times: "Nathan" and "Nahtan." It is so easy just sitting in the AC, hanging out with him, quiet, the movie going, me re-spelling his name until it spells my name in a way, like "Nathan" spelled backwards is my name spelled forwards. We sit there and watch explosions. I think of how me and Troy used to sit and watch TV all the time.

"What did you buy with the ten?" I say.

"I got an Uzi water gun," he says, not taking his eyes away from the screen.

"Wow," I say, laughing a little and crying. "You shoot people with that?"

"Just water," he says.

"How's your foot, honey?" I ask.

"Fine," he tells me. He keeps it propped up kind of cute.

The credits are rolling, right after a big building blows up. Standing, I am crying but smiling. The crying scares him a little. Adults only cry on TV in his world. It reminds him, I bet, how serious situations like this totally are. But again, "serious" isn't something this is about. This is sposed to be fun, sposed to be about him and me getting to know each other, the end.

I say, standing there in front of him, "Honey, I want you to stand up on the bed like a big boy."

Seeing him, his ribs glowing through his skin, sitting there like he is in a library with no lights on, so well behaved, his foot Band-Aided, it is perfect. Even though I cry silent like that, my voice is still low-pitched. I think I was pretending to be a veteran baseball player. I don't know. But then as soon as I ask, he moves. Just like my puppet. He stands up on the bed.

"Yes," I say, like an exhale of breath that I had kept in all day.

The room goes all dark as I have reached backward and shut the TV down. I stand back and ask him nice if he would not mind pulling down his swim trunks.

Nathan says, "Why?" His face does not change. He just wants a straight answer on that.

This sends something through me. My heart shrinks up into a very small stone. I look at him in the dark, his face glowing, like cobwebs lit by a flashlight.

"I don't know," I say. And I didn't know why, I did not, or I did but it could not at that time be put into real words. So I look at Nathan's face, and he looks at mine. My crying stops. He has a small nose and thick eyebrows and he seems not to like being here anymore.

I laugh, to take away from the seriousness.

"Don't do it," I say.

I start laughing harder and harder. *Get ahold of yourself, Dave.* But I feel like the voice in my head is only joking with me and that kind of joking hurts me, like I am tricking myself over and over, endless: torturing myself with my own voice. Can you keep mocking yourself this way and stay sane?

"Don't you dare do it," I say.

What did my laughing do to him? I don't know. I guess it scared him, I guess it made him think of how laughing and crying can often go together in a crazy world. I remember how Troy used to not cry in front of me out in the garage, but sort of hum, on his knees, like he was praying to the god of bees, and the humming turned gut-sounding after a while, like the sound of his voice was actually the sound of the blood going through his veins.

I pick Nathan up then and hold him up like a little baby, my arms sort of hurting.

"You," I say, laughing more.

Then I put him down on his feet on the floor. He looks up at me.

"I wanna go," he says.

"Well, I don't blame you for that," I say. "Not at all, honey."

I go over and smooth the bedspread from where he had been standing up on it. Smooth it with both my hands, closing my eyes. The material is like satin, but has many snags from hangnails. He goes and turns the TV back on, sits down on the other side of the bed. I open my eyes then and stop smoothing out the spread, looking at the silhouette of Nathan's face in the TV light. I think of what is inside that head, and how I am some man in the dark of his mind walking around smoothing out his footprints behind him. It is like he'll never know where he has been because I am doing that.

"Well, honey, you just wanna stay and watch some TV?"

I laugh then. Softer. Sit down beside him. He looks up at me, his lips parting slowly.

"No," he says, but also it is like he is trying to be nice, 'cause he does not move. I slowly take his hand in mine. We hold hands for a short while, watching HBO.

Soon after that, I take him out of the room. On the way back, we are both very quiet. Nathan just sits next to me, and then this is when I have the realization that I can do whatever I want to this little kid. Anything I please. It scares me deep down knowing how much power I could have, scares me where you have the fear of rats and snakes and high places and drowning in deepest water.

Of course as soon as Nathan gets out of the car, I get out and go to him. This time it is a twenty-dollar bill.

"Buy something nice," I say. "No squirt guns, huh?" I laugh. "Hey, Bud." People are passing by and not paying any attention. I am his dad dropping him off or picking him up.

"Hey," I say, bending down to him. "Do you know your address?"

"Yeah."

"You mind telling me?"

He has the twenty in his hand. Grips it. This is what matters, he must be thinking. A twenty to a kid who is poor is like the world. He needs to tell me his address so he will not get into trouble and lose that twenty. That twenty is his.

"Fourteen seventy-five Hampshire Drive, number twelve," he says.

"Oh yeah, I know that place," I say. I stand up. "Yeah, that's over there by the bank I go to. That's right."

He nods his head.

"Well, Bud, I guess I'll be seeing you." Smiling, I step backwards to my car. He knows I will be back to get him. I can tell by the look on his face. He knows that, and with the twenty-dollar bill in his hand he gets on his little bike and pedals on home by himself.

I am alone then. In my car in front of the public pool, I feel down there. My thing is wet. I look around at the outside world, shining on a summer's day. Trash glitters on old picnic tables and in cans beside the pool. Kids are jumping in and out of the water, like the water itself is accepting some, rejecting others.

Back home, I go to the shower. Right away. The water very hot.

In the shower, I am who I have always been: I am a man in a shower in Anderson, Indiana. The soap in the dish attached to the wall is broke in two, soft and gooey, the color of vanilla ice cream when it melts down to a delicious soup you can either drink from the bowl or spoon directly into your mouth.

PART TWO

6

TROY

David has kindness going for him. A six-year-old boy being kind is odd, and it is beautiful, like a butterfly in an elegant animated cartoon talking in an extremely soft and high-pitched voice. His face has that delicacy. I am not going completely sickening, so please bear with me. He is eating with his mother this Saturday evening. He is passing her the salt. I sit there, not eating, as I gagged on Holiday Inn lasagna just minutes ago. I am just waiting for my babysitting stint to start.

His mom is bony, tall, has an angular face. She is mysterious and proper, but also likably down-to-earth. She works as a clerk at a motel on the interstate, but dresses like a legal secretary. My mom told me she went to secretarial school. Even so, she has trashy habits: smoking and not keeping the bathroom clean and getting the giggles at times. She and I often get the giggles together, as if I am her girlfriend from down the street, even though I don't think I act real effeminate. Especially around Paul, though, we giggle. He is always getting pissed off. Plus she's always kidding me about being religious. I smile like it does not hurt.

David is quiet now. He eats a cut-up hot dog, dipping each cut into catsup.

His mom says, "You sure you aren't hungry, Troy? There's plenty."

"No," I say. "Thanks, though."

She laughs. "You are way too skinny, honey."

I smile, gazing at David. He has stopped eating. This happens to be the boy I love, I imagine telling his mom, almost like a joke. I imagine her jaw dropping. But what if David told her? Would she do anything? When I see the three of them together, Paul does all the talking usually. She shuts down, even shutting down for David, as though it's just too hard to be around the both of them at the same time. David sits on his knees now, and I smile, remembering our jar of lightning bugs, our play restaurant, our drawing in the living room the other time I babysat while we watched *Sanford and Son* and *Hawaii 5-0*.

His mom says to me, "Let him stay up late if you want."

"No," I say. "We'll be going to church tomorrow."

She laughs again. I hate her guts all of a sudden. I wonder if she thinks I really am a big sissy, a fairy. They called me that at Good Samaritan Ranch, but that was no big deal. We were all fairies. Meredith did not like that. She wanted us to go to sleep at night. You can't keep nine boys living together apart like that though—can't keep their hands from exploring; it is nature. I am not going on about that. No one wants to hear trash like that, except everybody. I sit here at this godforsaken computer, typing it all in, letter by letter. Part of me will type in two boys, one kissing my "wiener" (that's what we called them), the other my asshole, myself eleven and beautiful, them thirteen and fifteen. Faceless, of course, like angels, and the time four of us did stuff up at the lake on an outing, that time in the stinky bathrooms with the toilets full of shit and blue deodorizer: myself and three others completely pornographic. I am going to sit here right now and give it to you, spelling it out correctly. I'll use spell-check. 1. We kiss, four at a time, everywhere. 2. We fuck awkwardly, in a scaredy-cat fashion, little wieners growing out, fingers and tongues, all that, in the damp and pissy place.

3. We laugh and we grunt and we laugh and we scream. 4. We don't stop. We can't.

I can't stop sometimes. I don't want to. I do not have to. This is who I be. This is the world of the broken-down molester. Also I have my imagination. You can't get rid of that, unless you resort to electroshock. This is how I have grown up, realizing that what you do and what you think have to separate completely, or you will lose it all. Back then, as a sixteen-year-old, however, I was devout. I thought devoutness and Christian purity would protect me, help me separate what I did from what I thought. Nope. Wrong. Without the purity, however, I would have just gone after David like a wolf. With it, with the devoutness of an orphaned teenaged freak who memorizes Bible verses and who can't go to sleep and/or eat a meal without saying his prayers first, I was shiny and lit from within. David loved my Jesus, my light, and he loved me, and I loved him. That was all.

To be honest, he happens to be the only person I think I have ever truly loved.

David finishes eating back then, goes out into the living room to watch the rest of *Hee Haw.* His mom is in the kitchen, too tall to be doing dishes, but still she does them. I realize she hasn't really said one word to David during the meal, just talking to me. I go in and stand behind her, watching both David in the living room enjoying the TV and his mother in her skirt outfit, her hands deep in greasy suds. I am between them and feel as though I am the only thing that could ever make them both happy at the same time, as though in the end all that will be left is me and him and her, an echo of that feeling I had earlier in the barbershop with David and his dad, who has already left for his union meeting. David's mom tells me now that it's just Paul's excuse to go out, the union meetings, to go out and get plastered with his buddies.

"Union meeting," she says after turning around and finding me. "Ha. Just him and two other fools drinking at some scummy bar." She dries her hands with a paper towel, then goes to her purse by the light switch on the counter.

"I won't be home till morning," she says.

I am standing in the middle of the kitchen with my hands behind my back, in long pants and a T-shirt my dad used to wear with STP on it. My hair is perfect I know. I am so pleased to be here. People in Kornfield Kounty are saluting the hometown of Hoyt Axton. *Salute!*

"So I guess you'll stay all night? Paul will be out all night honky-tonking."

She takes a compact out. Looks at herself. For white trash, she is very professional. I am white trash and very clean and organized also. Try to be grammatically correct. People think just because you are low-income that you automatically have cheesy ways. I remember being called white trash by some foster-bitch I had prior to Meredith. This big fat evil lady who gave the social worker Hostess cupcakes and iced tea and loved her check more than human beings. I was found, by the way, in a Laundromat when I was one year old. Abandoned by some other fat lady who I guess was my biological mother. A baby on an orange plastic chair at the Laundromat, late afternoon. Imagine the dryers going, all the gum stuck under the folding tables, late-afternoon sunlight shining upon the linoleum floor.

"I can stay all night." I am smiling. She laughs.

"What makes you so good, Troy?" She snaps the compact shut, looks at me.

I look down, embarrassed.

"Well, I'll see you tomorrow, then. I'll get home before you guys go to church."

Carol Burnett with black hair: that's her. Comical and friendly and a little goofy, but also a sad self-consciousness under all that. She kisses my forehead. We both go out into the living room, and I sit down next to David on the couch. On TV, four fat men in bib overalls stand beside bales of hay, singing "Amazing Grace." David's mom gets down on her knees to kiss David, still not saying anything. David laughs a little, very sweetly, as she whispers something. I laugh too, even though I didn't hear.

At the door, David's mom looks worried, but then she turns around and leaves anyway, almost as if she were about to tell me not to hurt David, or not to love him. Did she notice my extreme happiness? This was my guilty conscience, I'm sure. I mean I had one back then, a big one, which had to be camouflaged with John 3:16 and good deeds, the silence in the garage. Like David's father, his mom probably sensed the creepiness coming from me, that hunger to be left alone with him. Some things you just don't want to think about, though. Some things you ignore, as they could end up screwing up your whole life.

That night I was going to be good. Sweet and kind and good. His mom closes the door, and we sit there. He looks at me and smiles.

"You are looking particularly lovely this evening," I tell him when *Mary Tyler Moore* comes on. That theme song makes me feel drunk. There is a specialness to 1972 Saturday-night television. A dull excitement, like before school starts, and that song gives me that emotion, and I think of tomorrow morning, dressing David in his bedroom. Both of us waking up naked in the garage, where we will wind up no matter how sweet and how kind and how good I'm promising myself I'll be: *You're gonna make it after all . . .* A sad lush feeling and I fall down on the couch, after getting up just so I could fall down, my head snuggling itself onto David's lap. It has gone dark in the living room. His quiet means this is okay. That's my translation. The quieter he gets, the more okay everything I do is.

I close my eyes.

"I want to play hide and seek," I say.

"Okay," he says.

We leave the TV on. I lift my head slowly. "You go hide. In the house." My voice goes singsong. "But you got to take off your clothes."

I smile.

Don't think you don't want to see this. Okay, the other thing, about the rollicking exploits of the pornographic eleven-year-old at Good Samaritan Ranch. I lied. It was just once or twice, and it was not sexy. It was dumb, awkward, and scary. In the bathroom, with Meredith asleep. I loved it, but not because of a forty-one-year-old pervert's interest in the sick and the vile. I loved it because it was me, what I was, what I was with another child: afraid and scatterbrained and almost crying. Felt up. A tiny finger in my mouth. Afraid of something in my butt, bleeding, an older boy's dull stupid whisper: "Shut up. *Shut* up."

Nothing is buried here in the soft dirt of my imagination. It's all lying out there, uncovered. My memories reek. I see and feel them more than I see and feel the present most of the time. I see these idiots on *20/20,* just suddenly BOOM discovering they were "abused." Bullshit. They cling to those memories. They need them to remind themselves how alive they once were. Their sad, pale little faces, as they confess to Barbara Wawa how one day when they were walking in the woods, it all comes back wham-bam-thank-you-ma'am. Memories don't go away, and then just come back because you smell autumn leaves. They become *you.* They turn into flesh and eyes and stomachs and . . .

Memories don't hide. They seek and find you and turn you into the person you have to be.

Like this: this is not a lie. David taking off his pajamas. I must describe him. Naked boy in the TV light. Holding himself there. Bony and petite. I am naked too.

"Go on. I'll count to twenty."

He runs down the dark hall out of the living room. I have shut the front door. It is steamy hot in here. I am not thinking of anything, just this game. While in the process of my pursuit I'm just a little kid too, after all, unaware, but there is a part that sizzles and kicks off and on like a machine. The part that knows how I am ruining David's childhood. I stand and count in the dark TV-glowing heat anyway. To twenty, like I promised. Then on my way. Being naked in a house is like being an extraterrestrial investigating a new planet. Your feet feel the texture of the floor, every floor-type you walk on, little grains of dirt on cool reptile linoleum, the bear-scalp of a carpet. Your skin feels the different air in each room: window open in the kitchen, the windowless damp of the hall.

It's a small house, so there aren't many places to be hiding. I call out his name. There is no sadness now. It is his house, but I am finding him in it, like a naked baby abandoned in a maze. A baby that does not know it is naked, but likes knowing someone is looking for it. I don't turn on any lights. I go into his mom and dad's room, slide open the closet door. The smell of his mother's perfumed clothes, a nest of dress shoes, a strange fishy stink from somewhere. There's a shelf above the rod the coat hangers are on. I see movement on this shelf.

He must have climbed up there, a monkey. I push his dad's uniform off an old dinette chair they have in here, take the chair to the closet, and stand on it. Wordlessly I pull away a blanket, a shoe box of curlers, and an old fan. I see him at the back, curled up tight. I think of a kangaroo's baby in a pouch. David is smiling, being caught, his face rising. I climb awkwardly into the little space, bending into it like an illegal alien into a cubbyhole. Our bodies touch, mine hurting from being so bent in.

I slide the door shut with my toes, very slowly. We are in darkness, hot, touching. We stay like this. I imagine Nazis touring the house with flashlights. David tries to talk. I hold his mouth, intertwining with him, sweating and holding him, in the belly of a whale, in a spaceship orbiting the sun, in a box being shipped to a place neither of us know.

· · ·

Mom, of course, didn't expect us at ten-thirty that night, David carrying a bag of his stuff which I helped him put together. She is up and watching TV, after having tried to go to sleep, and she has made herself some of that world-famous Holiday Inn lasagna. Always a late-night eater, she is in her housecoat, sitting in her chair, Shar right beside her. We come on in, me behind him, pushing.

"What are you boys doing walking around in the middle of the night?" Mom asks. She puts her plate down to the floor and automatically Shar goes for it, but Mom does not notice. She looks worried, like I'll be the one who ends up getting into trouble no matter what happens. Like she knows something. Maybe she does. For all I know, maybe she does at that time, although it would be later that summer when all hell broke loose. Right now she was suspecting me of being a freak but not wanting to face up to it, as she loved me. She always loved me. I know that deep down.

"We're gonna sleep out in the garage tonight, Mom," I say.

"Oh," she says. Shar is licking that lasagna, as though it is just the most wonderful thing on Earth.

"That's okay, isn't it?" I ask.

She looks at me, eye to eye. Her worry seems to increase, seeing me standing next to David in her living room. David is a little Christian soldier with his overnight bag. His hair all chopped off, buzzed and giving him the look of a child that does not know any better. I think of only twenty minutes ago how David and myself were intertwined together at the top of his parents' closet, as if it were the only thing we could do. Sometimes it truly felt like he was leading *me*.

"That's okay. You gonna ride the church bus?" Mom says, finally recognizing that Shar is feasting on her lasagna on the floor. She gets the plate and sits up, not saying anything about it.

"Yeah."

"All right."

Shar jumps up and saunters on over to David. Shar starts sniffing at the bag, probably thinking there is more food in it. A nosy timid bitch with a bark bigger than her bite, Shar stands there sniffing in a pathetic way, and David bends down the little bit to pet her. Shar really digs that.

"You doing pretty good, David?" Mom asks, holding the dog-licked plate.

David looks up. "Yeah." He continues petting Shar. All is okay. Mom is lightening up. Her face seems to absorb some of David's natural sweetness.

"You got your hair cut today too, didn't you?" Mom asks.

"Yeah," David says.

Mom walks into the kitchen and gets both of us Tootsie Rolls out of a fruitcake pan she keeps on top of the fridge, which she thinks nobody but her knows about. Her hair is a mess. She looks like Shirley MacLaine after a tornado, only with a big gut and minus any corrective surgery. She gives the candy side by side, opening her palms and there it is. She is smiling and must be drunk still. I like her this way.

I remember when Mom got so sick, about ten years after this, in 1982, when she had the first signs of the cancer, how she got uglier and uglier till it was a joke between her and myself. Mom was never vain, and even though she got bulbous, stooped over, and scaly, and even though she started losing her hair, she was always cracking jokes. I was there to get them. That was our relationship. From 1984 on, she was in and out of hospitals, and then in '92, she passed in the nursing home I am currently working in. Working there keeps me in touch with her. Don't ask. Right now I don't know if I should even go into it or not. I mean I started working there at Sunnyhaven Nursing Facility while she was still a resident. Got the job so I could be near her, plus we had no money coming in. Now I'm a five-year veteran. Working there, I dissolve. This is my tendency now, just to dissolve into a happy camper, silent as some new angel in a book. Old people don't make me sad, as they are filled with needs they cannot hide, and in this territory I can flourish. No one, not anyone, can hide from me, and in fact most of the time people are looking for me at Sunnyhaven, asking me to work extra shifts, asking me to change their dressing, asking me if I might not mind reading them this article in *Reader's Digest* as they left their glasses somewhere. I clock in and just throw myself into it, toward the people, like they might like to eat me up. Giving people baths and feeding them and wiping their butts and keeping them, all my patients, keeping them clean and comfortable, and I have even inherited my mom's knack for the wisecrack which she developed the closer she got to dead. I'll be working and I'll go up to someone say like Mr. Moore, a ninety-three-year-old guy with emphysema and no kids even left and all kinds of other miserable problems. I'll go to him, and while I'm doing his Ensure into his G-tube bag, I'll go, "Shaken or stirred, Monsieur? With an olive? Without?"

Okay.

Wait.

Tootsie Rolls.

David chewing on a Tootsie Roll and petting Shar in our 1972-smelling kitchen. Yes. Then Mom comes over to me.

"Is it okay for him to come stay all night with you?"

Worried in the face, but sweet. You do not know how much I hated that worry. Also, however, the worry grounded me and kept me from going off into flights of total fancy. I knew her and she knew me, and maybe, like I said, even back then she knew what I was, like I said. Maybe.

"Yeah, Mom. His mom is working nights and his dad is out drinking." I say the drinking part to make her feel guilty about her own drinking so she will just shut up.

"Oh," she says.

"I left a note too, just in case," I say. My voice goes a little whiny. The note stated:

*Me and David are going to sleep at my house. That way
we can catch the church bus. He will be back tomorrow
after church. I took his toothbrush and everything. See you
around one o'clock tomorrow.*

I signed, *Sincerely, Troy Wetzel.*

Mom says "Oh" again, looking at David. He is still petting
on Shar's ears. He stops and looks up, chewing on the candy,
brown spit gathering at the sides of his mouth.

"You like staying out in that garage?" she asks.

I feel protectiveness rising up in my body, forming harsh
words in my brain, but I keep it inside. I always find that I want
to answer for him, even when he is not in the same place that
I am, as if I have psychic abilities, constantly feeding him his
lines in a school play, wherever he goes. Whatever he does.

"Yes," David says. This comes out polite, small, beautiful.

"Well, okay," Mom says. She stands there a second. Then
she walks over and picks Shar up.

"I'll see you in the morning," she says, walking toward her
chair with her dog.

David and myself walk out to the backyard, the water-
melon-smelling grass covered with dew, our feet getting wet. As
soon as we get into the garage, I padlock the door good and he
goes over and he sits down on the cot, still chewing on his
candy. This makes me wonder, as I see him do it, if he ever was
not polite and small and beautiful, or if now I am just making
him that way to turn him into this little saint. Did he ever say
no to me? I think he did. I think it took about a year to get him
to this point. When we started, he used to be hesitant, and he
would whine, and I would have to remind him what would
happen if he did not stop that whining. This included hurting
him until he died, and then me dying too. This sounds much
more evil than it was.

It was a very serious game. When he got scared of me but

then went ahead and did what I told him anyway, I knew he knew that it was a game. Deadly serious yes, but also he could escape at any time he chose to. But this was a six-year-old child, you're thinking. A six-year-old child I manipulated. I know that. I was sixteen, though. So fucking what? I was sixteen, and I had it all figured out, including annotated Jesus parts.

This does not matter sir.

I know. Or maybe your thinking is slightly slanted? Anyway, I give up. I gave up long ago. To discuss morality at this juncture just interrupts what story line I have going.

When I first saw him, I wanted him, and that first time I took him over to the garage that summer I was fifteen and he was five, when I introduced him to what I would do, he kept trying to pull away from me, me holding his little hand and him wanting to leave and me bursting into tears and finally holding onto him and him screaming and me covering his mouth in the garage. "Shut up or I will hurt you, okay?" My voice, the voice of a sick individual. I held him and held him and told him I loved him and broke him down into my little lover. I broke him. But maybe, I can hear myself think even now in my apartment: But maybe he needed to be broke.

So Troy, the sixteen-year-old molester this time, me, I light candles, then flick off the flashlight I brought. In the candlelight, David looks like I have made him up. There is something sugary about his ghostly appearance, as though he is an angel made of glow-in-the-dark sugar, if there is such a thing. An angel on a box of cereal, with a glow-in-the-dark prize inside. A glow-in-the-dark whistle.

I don't go near him.

I stand and light more candles. I go over to my eight-track player. I find the tape I want. It's the Beatles' White Album. I stole it from some flake at Good Samaritan. He had all these tapes, and I got the White Album and *Revolver* from him. Now ceremoniously I push in the chosen tape and click it to our special song. Number four on the second side. It is called "Mother

Nature's Son." I sway a little as it comes out, looking at David, who sits there and does not move, but then he gets up and goes over to our table and sits.

Obedient, he recognizes the drill.

I go over and give him my Tootsie Roll, the song playing. He takes it. The song has such a sweet and haunting melody. I got up just now and put it on, to go along with my never-ending story. I am listening to it now, listening to it then, listening to it forever and ever Amen. It is a sickly sweet McCartney tune; nonetheless it has a terrifying loveliness. I try to push all the feeling back into its special envelope, but little songs like this make me rip the envelope, as if expecting a check for a million dollars inside. Little songs bring it all back. I feel a wave of nostalgia or something else purge through me, maybe spirituality, and there David is, eating the candy at the table where we played restaurant, where we colored witches in the *Sleeping Beauty* coloring book, there David is, blank-faced, David polite and small and beautiful, the son of people who I don't know really, but maybe, like me, David was adopted, which would make everything make sense, why we were connected like this, maybe he too had been abandoned, maybe the both of us were abandoned in the woods by Mother Nature after she pushed us out, not at some scummy Laundromat (poor poor pitiful me) or on the steps of the courthouse, but in the middle of a woods somewhere at night, on a warm and starry night: that's what music like this can do to you.

I step over to David as he sits at the table. I direct him back to the cot. I strip before this child. I don't say one word, except that one phrase that I say.

"This is for you."

The old lady at church has felt cutouts to portray Jesus stories. All the kids, before they go off to their respective age-based Sunday school classes, have to report to the multipurpose room in the back, a cinder-block wide-open place with folding chairs and a podium, the place where the ladies of the church present their suppers and celebrations.

We all of us sit there, us kids, that Sunday morning, watching the fat old lady with her felt cutouts get everything ready to tell her special story.

David doesn't sit next to me. We are in our age groups. There's only like sixteen or seventeen kids total. The church we attend is falling apart, everyone complaining the pastor, a Bob Newhart–looking guy named John Greene, has no charisma. He is on his way out. Anyway, we all sit and wait for the lady to get her easel with the felt background set up and her box of felt cutouts put in place. I am next to a girl named Terry Phillips and a boy named Darrel Houston. Darrel smells of aftershave although he does not shave, and Terry has on a dirty dress. These are poor kids I'm with, poorer than myself even, kids the pastor and the deacons go out and find standing around outside Boys Clubs of America, or in parks or libraries, asking if they want to join them at church, to learn about the Lord Jesus Christ and then get a bag of candy for coming. I feel mighty superior to these wannabes. There's David across the way with two other boys.

David looks tired, poor thing. He has on a bow tie I put on him. He looks like every little boy who was ever meant to be on the cover of a book of Bible stories, praying with his eyes closed, devout and quiet.

The lady has high hair, coiled and architectural. There's no windows in here, just pale yellow cinder-block walls, shiny linoleum floors, gray folding chairs, fluorescent light shining down on us. A big black upright piano off to the side and bulletin boards on the walls, one still showing Fourth of July stuff (a cardboard cutout of Uncle Sam and Jesus leading townspeople in a parade to celebrate the Birth of the Nation and possibly Christ triumphant over the communists). The other two boards have names of people who don't come anymore and a big poster of Jesus on the day of Rapture, floating in the sky in the clouds and people climbing an invisible ladder to get to him, to escape the chaos depicted down on Earth with exploding cars and looters and animals escaping from the zoo.

This lady, named Claudette Cunningham, begins by saying, "Quiet down, children."

She has a southern accent, and has been with this church since she moved to Indiana from Alabama twenty-six years ago. She tells everybody that. Her dress is a blue print, like Aunt Bea's on *Andy Griffith*.

"I have a Bible story for all of you."

She's a fake old bag, I know that even back then, I'm sharp enough to sense that in her, but we are in church, and in church at least you can pretend to be civilized. That happens to be the Grace of God.

"This is the story of a little man who wanted to see Jesus real bad. He was a short little thing." Mrs. Cunningham laughs, putting a felt tree on the blue and green backdrop on the easel. The tree is black and looks almost scary. She puts the felt man in a dress next to the tree, and then follows that up with Jesus and a crowd of people following Jesus.

"Now this little man's name was Zacchaeus, and he had been so excited about Jesus coming to his little town that people were thinking he was crazy. Well . . ."

Mrs. Cunningham put Zacchaeus way back of the crowd, and she went on.

"Well, he could not see Jesus and was having just the worstest luck. He tried to climb up on top of people and they just were getting madder and madder at him for being so stubborn, so the man finally just gave up."

She made her face go all sad, and she then smiled abruptly, scaring some of the younger ones. She was good at this. Show business was in her blood.

"Then it hit him. It hit Zacchaeus that he could at least see the Holy Savior way up that old sycamore tree here. So

Zacchaeus climbed that old sycamore tree. He climbed and he climbed and he climbed and he climbed."

Kids laughed. Next to me, Terry groaned like she was being sarcastic, like this was not groovy enough for her. I wanted to tell her a thing or two. How this sweet old lady, even though she was a little silly, had been going to this church for almost three decades. She deserved respect. Back then I was humorless. I was caught up in a vacuum of Christ and good intentions that did not allow me to see the humor in things. Even now, though, I love a good Bible story.

Mrs. Cunningham showed the felt Zacchaeus climbing and climbing and climbing the tree, and then she said, "He got to the top, children, and could see Jesus shining and shining and telling the gathered a sermon. It was a beautiful sermon. Jesus told no ugly ones. Of course. But it was just a wonderful inspiring sermon, and Zacchaeus got all interested in it and so interested in fact that the branch he was leaning on started to crack, and he did not hear it."

She pushed the felt man to the edge of the tree.

"The man fell and fell to the ground. Right in front of Jesus. It was embarrassing, I can tell you that. People was laughing and making fun of Zacchaeus, and although he was not physically hurt, Zacchaeus was emotionally embarrassed. But you know what Jesus did, children? Do you know?"

There were a few no's from the kids. I was one of them, the only one from the teen section.

"Jesus picked Zacchaeus up in his arms. And he told the people around him to quiet down. He looked at Zacchaeus, and Zacchaeus looked at him."

She made the felt figures look at least approximately like what she was saying.

"And Jesus told Zacchaeus, 'To see me, you have risked life and limb. You are faithful and filled with the spirit. I would hope all believers would be like you.'

"Well, this made Zacchaeus beam with pride. Just beam."
Mrs. Cunningham smiled for a little bit. Then she said,
"Now the moral of this story I just told you children is to
always keep that excitement about Jesus. It is an excitement
about being alive, children. Always climb that old sycamore
tree to see Him. Have that spirit."

She smiled again. I was smiling. *I* was beaming. I looked at
the felt figures and I thought of last night when David and I
had been at the top of the closet, then in the garage in the light
of candles. I had won David after a year of beautiful struggles,
of desperation, of climbing and climbing and climbing. I saw
the holy glow of that felt-board story, our story told that way,
little figures cut out of felt of David and of me, up there, in
front of the children watching. I saw our story as a Bible story
told by an old lady with high hair. I felt the holiness in my blood-
stream, as though I were on holiness drugs. Knowing something
is wrong does not matter when you see it flooded in the light of
God, when you experience it in the innocence of church. You
can direct your thoughts and feelings toward a special goal of
cleansing—of changing what you do to help yourself feel good
into something otherworldly, an activity of angels.

I looked over at David. He had on that blank face, that
mask of a child who is confused and stupid with hurt, the hurt
I had caused him. This face, too, was connected to me through
love. The face, the soul. Whatever you want to call it. David
stood, but then a boy next to him took his hand as all the kids
were told to hold hands when they went to their classrooms for
Sunday school. The teenagers did not have to do it. When the
boy grabbed his hand, David looked like he was afraid. Afraid
perhaps that I might get jealous. But then I smiled and nodded
my head. This was okay. Holding another boy's hand in church
was okay.

I pictured him being led off to our place, like he was being
led back to me, back to me to whom he belonged.

7

DAVE

I have to take Dad to this hospital in Indianapolis to have tests done on his stomach. He can't drive 'cause they have to give him stuff to make his stomach muscles do something or other. Sorry I can't be any more specific. Dad keeps everything top secret. It wasn't until yesterday that he asked me to take him today. I freaked, not knowing if they would let me have it off. They did. I got some pretty good bosses in the main office. They understand.

But also I freaked because Dad even asked me. I figured he must have been scared. This made me feel like I knew more than he did, somehow, even though I knew absolutely nothing.

The bosses I got, though, back to that, are just normal guys in neckties. Me and Bob and the others call them Neckties all the time 'cause they'll come out to look at what's going on in the shop, and try to fix a broken truck with neckties hanging down. The one that supervises almost all the meter-readers is Kent, and he's about ready to retire. He's all the time asking me about Dad. They've known each other since high school. Kent's the one I asked for the time off, in his little cubicle in the main office.

"So is he pretty bad, Dave?" he asked yesterday morning when I requested to have it off.

"I don't know. I do not know. He won't tell us nothing. Not a word, but this time when I go I'm gonna ask the doctors, you know? Even if he tells me not to."

I smiled. Kent smiled too.

"He's a stubborn old guy, huh?"

Fat, with a crewcut, Kent had a clipboard on his desk. He was doing some checking of what was on the clipboard with what was on his computer screen. Maybe checking up on me, who knows? So I acted like I was not noticing what was on the screen. But also I thought what if Dad knew what I did, cheating on the paperwork, drinking on the job. Chasing after a boy on the clock. Just thinking that made me angry at Dad, wanting to hurt him somehow, physically or mentally, even while I got scared as a little kid would of his dad.

"Pretty stubborn," I say, empty in the stomach.

"Well," Kent says, turning his eyes away and laying the clipboard down on top of his desk calender, "you'll learn. Once you get past a certain age, Dave, stubbornness just sets in. Like hardening of the arteries."

Kent laughed. His laugh was not very friendly, though. It was a would-you-mind-getting-out-of-my-hair type of laugh. I stood in the doorway of his cubicle a little bit, while he stood up and opened the blinds on the one window he had access to. His cubicle was pretty small, and the walls were made of old burlap-covered sheets of drywall on wobbly platforms. On one of them he had a poster of a bulldog with a rose between its teeth.

"Well, so it's okay for me to take him, then?" I said.

Kent looked at me, shocked. Shocked and kind of pissed maybe.

"Oh yeah. I thought we were finished. You don't need my permission to take your own father to have something medical done. You got the sick time. Go."

I nodded, walked out, kind of pissed off myself, out in my truck, with my daily computer printout list of meters to read.

It seemed to me that Kent had been rude. But I let it slide, thinking of last Friday when I pulled the fast one and clocked out early after kind of spending the day with the boy.

Then there was Sunday when I took him to the motel. The boy. Nathan. I had just had three days straight of the good life, of just clocking out of my own head and doing my damn routines. But now after my little run-in with Kent I felt this feeling come back, which I squelched automatically. I went and did my job hard. I read meter after meter, until I was almost dizzy from the little black-on-white numbers. I looked at my watch after traveling around and doing my job like that. It was only eleven, and I had done everything I had been assigned, almost.

I was in a really ritzy neighborhood now, looking around outside my truck. I bought a pack of cigarettes on Sunday night after church. Know I shouldn't, but I smoke out here in the new deluxe neighborhood right outside of where they had just put in the racetrack off the interstate. This, the shiny side of Anderson. PARADISE HILLS, big brick gate says. They're developing their butts off out here. Roadkill everywhere from where they were tearing down woods with bulldozers, and the possums and raccoons and skunks don't have any place to go but toward the road. The houses are all castlelike, but made of the latest suburban materials, brick and that new kind of vinyl siding, with dirt for yards and Hondas in every driveway almost. Hondas or those minivans that resemble shuttlecraft. Pools too, built-in and above-ground both, all gleaming that same swimming-pool color. My and Tara's house is too small, it hits me. Way too small. I make close to twenty thou a year, and we've been saving. We got two thou put back, with her job and stuff. It's never been our dream to live out here, though, because it's all too brand-new. Too antiseptic, you know? Looks almost flimsy, from being so brand-new. I want a big nice house, old Victorian fixer-upper. Imagine yourself coming home after work with a mission of doing the pipes or sanding the floors, painting, refurbishing, etcetera. Just sinking into that constant work with a payoff at the end being a great place to live that you yourself put your whole body and soul into. That house and you and your wife and kid, all of you on the same wavelength somehow, happy and settling into one another, old-fashioned like that. Sounds pretty good to me.

These all look like nobody's dreaming about nothing inside of them. They just sit there in the hot sun like restaurants not opened for business yet. I smoke and I dream of our old house. Then I think of Dad in his trailer. How he stood outside of it last Saturday after we ate out and saw *Hercules* like he did not want to go in. When he dies, if he dies, he'll leave behind only that trailer. We sold the house on School Street when I was eight, and then moved into that one house out in the middle of farm country. They sold that one after the divorce. Three years after we sold the School Street house, it blew up. Gas leak. The thing blew up. Left nothing behind, not even a smoldering teddy bear, just a concrete-slab foundation. It was not occupied at the time.

I smell roadkill somewhere, skunk. I go back into my truck, run the AC, continue to smoke, AC on high.

For the rest of the day I kind of ride around, and I don't think nothing serious. I drink some screwdriver to keep my nerves in one place. I drink and drive, but nobody notices.

The boy doesn't come back all that day, not really, until I get home early.

I'm driving the Escort to work now, due to me not wanting Tara to get stuck nowhere. As soon as I pull into the driveway and turn it off, I think of the boy next to me last Sunday in this very car, and how I got his address now. I told Pastor Lewis about it, about the address, not the boy, the other night when me and him and three others went out doing our visitation. Pastor Lewis calls it Outreach, but back when I first started going to church it was called Visitation, and that's stuck with me. Visitation, when people from the church go out cold into local neighborhoods and just knock on doors trying to get people to come to church. You gotta be friendly, you gotta be energized, you gotta *sell* church to these people. I told him while we were walking up a sidewalk in a poor section, half the houses looking vacated.

"I think I know of someone who might respond to our Outreach," I said. "A family that lives over in the Hampshire Apartments?"

"Well, yeah. That's way over there. Maybe next time, huh?"

I nodded my head. Pastor Lewis was breathing heavy right then. Fat as all get-out, but still he was a very serious presence and once you heard him, you forgot about the fat and paid attention to the man. Hearing that voice could make you forget the whole world, which was a major reason why people liked him. He always went with me on Outreach. He said he liked bouncing ideas off me. We would meet up at the church, people going out, and then pair off into teams of two, taking one car each team out into the neighborhoods of Anderson, like missionaries. Pastor Lewis said all the time he likes my go-get-'em attitude. My serious follow-through. My dedication. I mean I have been driving that church bus since I was twenty.

But anyways out in our driveway Nathan's ghost is in the seat next to me, and for a second I can feel him begging me to stop. This is a Wednesday, a church night, but I don't think I'll go. I don't think I could go anywhere right now. The begging me to stop has thrown me off, has scared me too much.

I haven't done anything to him. I have only helped him. I helped him. I helped him prevent infection in that motel room. And I stopped myself.

So I get out then, and I notice the yard is all scorched grass and litter, the heat now a fever taking over the universe. In the quiet of the house, I make our bed 'cause Tara didn't have time this morning. Then I go into the kitchen, start washing up dishes. The begging, his begging, pushed me on.

Hell, no. Don't beg me to stop, Bud. I don't want you. I was just playing around, Bud. I didn't even want to know your name, Nathan sweetheart. I would never hurt you, not in a million years.

Nathan's face, the one I imagined he had on, the boy's face begging me to stop made me go weak and made me feel sick.

I go get Brittany at you-know-who's. Tara's mom has Brittany in some new dress-thing she has made her, gold material, like a little-girl circus costume.

"What in the heck is that she's got on?" I say, laughing.

"I'm making it for her based on this little girl on PTL," Tara's mom says.

Eye contact with me must just piss Tara's mom off. I chalk it up to mother-in-law/son-in-law relations all across America. I took her baby away, you know, *that.*

"Mom, that looks like—that looks like you're trying to make her grow up too fast with that thing," I say, laughing more. But my voice cracks, and I feel tears heat near my eyes inside my face.

Tara's mom laughs at me. "What is *your* problem?"

She still ain't looking at me, but out of the corners of her eyes she is a little. Like she wants to catch me doing something.

"Take her out of that thing," I whisper.

"What?" Tara's mom goes, shocked. Maybe she heard me, maybe she did not, and either way she does not want to fool with me.

I back down then. The feeling, or whatever you want to call it, goes out like a flat tire in me. Brit is just lying there, kicking her feet up. Grunting, Tara's mom takes her out of the outfit and puts her back into her play clothes and I pick her up, smell her.

"You better get some help dealing with your emotions," Tara's mom says, but it is kind of like a joke.

"What?" I say, laughing. "You think I'm crazy, Mom? Crazy, me?" I laugh like a pretend lunatic, holding Brit. Brit gurgles.

"Get outta here," Tara's mom says, laughing under her breath.

Tara's home when I get back. We eat. She's glad I made the bed and washed the dishes and that I don't feel like going to Wednesday-night service. She does not like to go anyways, and so she's got tranquillity written all over her face, and she's in her comfortable sweats. It's just okay to be family right now. We're struggling, but we are gonna make it. We eat and talk about things. It's like why not? Why can't we do this all the time?

Right after supper, we watch one of those talk shows where people get all bent out of shape with one another. On there is this gay guy who dresses up like a woman as his career and is in love with this other gay guy. The two of them are on the show holding hands, while the sister of the one who dresses up like a woman yells at them.

"Good Lord," Tara says, half-laughing.

They all three are yelling, and the people in the audience are shouting, and the host, some lady with blond hair holding a microphone, seems to have lost control of her own show.

"I love Gary!" says the cross-dressing one. "Gary is my husband." He is currently not dressed as a woman, but looks sissy in a frilly blouse, his face all pale. His skinny boyfriend Gary just sits there beside him, looking like your average, everyday humiliated homosexual, redheaded in a plaid shirt and corduroys.

"It makes me sick!" says the fat sister with rotten teeth. The audience goes wild again.

"That is just perverted," Tara goes, laughing in disbelief, sitting on the couch with her legs up under her. "I mean why go on national television and humiliate yourself like that? Good God. This is trash."

Tara goes quiet to listen, shakes out her hair a little. Brit's over there in her playpen with some toy that makes a screaming sound.

"I know what you mean," I say, and I ain't spoiling what we got going here tonight by even going near what I do, what I think about doing with Nathan. Thinking about going on national TV with my own sick little story, I keep my eyes on the screen as the sissy one starts snapping his fingers at his fat sister's face. Then his fat sister just reaches across and slaps him right in the face. I tune that out. I can hear in my head Pastor Lewis's message from April or was it May about how the gays want to take over our schools. He is hoping to start a Christian private school in Anderson, so that parents will at least have a choice away from the public schools, and then he showed us on the overhead (it was a Wednesday-night sermon and they are more casual and he usually uses visual aids then, like he's teaching a class), and up there on the overhead was a statistic about how many homosexuals had died of AIDS in the last decade.

"Death begets death," said Pastor Lewis, and people nodded. People coughed and nodded. There were a few amens.

Later that same service, since this was a real hot topic, Pastor Lewis showed a videotape made by the Christians for a Better Tomorrow. It was about how homosexuals were taking over politics and education. It showed homosexual gay-pride parades. These people were just freaks, I'm sorry. They were in leather belts around their privates and rings going through their things and men dressed up like women and women like men. Some women had their boobs hanging down, with shaved heads. The pastor stopped the tape and apologized into the microphone about the boobs.

"I'm sorry about this being so graphic," he said, his voice sounding sorry and breathy.

Pastor Lewis turned it back on, and then there was this whole section about this organization called the North American Man Boy Love Association. I remember that. Some of them were marching too. Men with boys, marching down a sunny street, holding rainbow flags. Men holding the hands of boys, marching toward the end of that sunny street.

Of course it hit me, of course. I ain't gonna say it didn't. I am not that stupid. Although at the time I was not doing anything. Last May or April or whenever it was, I was clean, I was living the goodness of my life, and so my history was involved, but not the present day. This is the way you have to get by, Dave, I was telling myself, trying not to see what was on the TV but seeing it anyways. The way you have to get by, Dave, is by forgetting things. So I forgot things. I mean I knew deep deep down what I remembered, but sitting there in the dark church watching that video with the scary music and the pictures of those people in those parades (is that all these people did is have parades all the time?), I got angry at them. I got vicious thoughts going about what punishments they might deserve, even though I knew it was me I was directing the anger toward, me and them both. Me and them together in some sick parade, but also even that kind of offered comfort, in a way. Marching down the street in Anderson, Indiana, me some naked freak smiling like a crocodile, whooping it up, holding a boy's hand, and the boy just happened to be naked too, and yet I knew it was all over, and we were, all of us, being marched off to wherever freaks like us are made to go.

I remember people were in an uproar after church that night. There's this deacon named Cal Jacobs, a skinny tall guy who owns a hardware store, big in our church, looks like one of the Statler Brothers, and he said after, when me and the pastor and him were outside, you know, doing that after-church talking you do, he says, "Man, Pastor, that video."

The pastor laughed. "Pretty explicit, I know, but sometimes we need to be shocked."

"I'm shocked," Cal said.

I nodded.

Cal says, "I just wanted to you know—"

Cal beat his fist into his hand, and the pastor laughed and I did too. We laughed like if there were any homosexuals in our vicinity right then, we would have to let them have it. Maybe that's what the pastor had wanted by showing that thing: to get us stirred up so that we would keep coming back for more because he knew that this would do this to us. That what he showed us had made us love him, the pastor, somehow.

"Man," Cal goes, shaking his head.

He and me and some others played basketball some week-nights in the winter at the old elementary-school gym. Cal was always walking around naked in the locker room like he was showing us his stuff to let us know he was this big guy. But you had to respect him. He owned his own business. He had a pretty good sense of humor. He was always the first one to vol-unteer, and I'd be second. But we never really talked to each other or nothing outside of church.

"Man," he goes again.

"I know," Pastor said.

"I know," I said, looking down at the grass, at the gravel. At nothing in particular.

There have been four boys in all, total. Four of them. Four little boys. Well, five, if you count that one when I was teenager. I don't see any of them no more, of course. But when I did I was so happy that the sadness I have to live with now was just like a faint cloud, like a sadness seen from off the interstate, an aban-doned farm that you could barely make out. The happiness took over, the joy of coming into my own, knowing how rotten it is, but a happiness, a joy anyways. I think of fat people eating in the middle of the night, or dope fiends taking in their dope in a back alley, that kind of a smile coming across my face, lighting up my world brighter than reality.

No excuse, but when you are doing it you don't need one.

Three of them were strangers, and the fourth was a boy who moved away with his mom last spring. They could have told. Any one of them could have told. I figured if they do they do, and I'll just deal with it. I'll probably kill myself.

But I told them all that too. I'd kill myself. It would be their faults. Told them that in the same voice I used to tell them I love them more than life itself.

Brit's there now, in the TV, crying for her mom to help her get that icing off of her face. Tara bends into the picture and wipes, saying to me behind the camera, "Turn that thing off. Go inside and get me some paper towels. Put yourself to use." She was laughing, but I did as I was told.

Tara's laughing right now, right behind me, live and in person.

"What's wrong? Can't you sleep? Your dad?" she says, voice kind of hoarse from waking up. She's rubbing her eyes.

"Yeah," I say, flicking off the TV. I stand up and yawn.

Tara comes on over to me.

"It's just ulcers," she whispers.

"I know. I don't know. I just don't want to be in a car with him that long sometimes." I laugh, as though it was a real good joke.

Tara looks at me like she wants to discipline me. Wash my mouth out with soap. Sure I've told her what he did to me as a kid. The beatings, the yelling. I try to make it sound like I'm not blaming him for nothing, 'cause I am okay now, but still just telling her has that feeling to it: like I want pity. And Tara just doesn't do pity, sorry.

"Nobody has perfect parents, David," she says, philosophical and PO'd both.

I nod my head. Tara goes and takes the video of Brit out of the machine and snaps it back into its black case. She shoves the case back onto the shelf of the entertainment center.

"So he wasn't Mike Brady, excuse him," she says, walking toward me. I nod slow. Stand up, not thinking about Dad then as much as the boys I have pursued. Dad and them boys and even Nathan and even Troy intermingle, like channels on a TV colliding. A cable problem. I see in my head the cable being jerked out of the wall by me, me pulling and pulling on the thin black cable but it won't come out of the wall.

"Let's go on back to bed, Dave," Tara says.

That one at the Wal-Mart. He was blond. He looked at me like I was going to kill him. All I did was kiss. Down there on my knees, kissing. The one I did in the church bathroom, he must have done it before, because he kissed my thing and I did not want him to. He kissed it. All of nine. He wasn't smiling, but he did it. I wonder about the world sometimes.

Then I think of the homosexuals in a parade, proud of their depravity. That's a Pastor Lewis line: "proud of their depravity." It got stuck in my head one day like a broke record. I think of Troy, his black hair, the moles on his neck, and I remember me and him riding that church bus, that church we used to go to disbanded years ago and the church itself was turned into a day-care place. I remember that whole summer when all it was was me and him. Me and Troy and the garage and the whole summer was him loving me. That time we went to Indiana Beach up in Monticello. There was this dirty brown sand beach with fat people sunning themselves. Fat Hoosiers on vacation. The midway with its dinky dumb rides. And the smell of burning food. Me and Troy and Dad and Mom and Troy's mom. All five of us. I'm thinking about this ride before I fall off to sleep, next to Tara now: seeing me and Troy holding hands on a rackety old rollercoaster made out of matchsticks.

At the top is the view of that whole humid afternoon, the brown water lapping at the little brown beach and all those people getting skin cancer and me and Troy at the top, at the top, about to go all the way down.

Nobody screamed louder than Troy.

I have to drive the Grand Prix to Indianapolis, too afraid of the Escort. Going down the interstate, Dad listens to country, not saying nothing, coughing a little, dressed in black polyester pants and the beige dress shirt he wore to Ponderosa—me in jeans and a Garth Brooks T-shirt. After he grumbles a little, turning stations, Dad falls off into a deep sleep, his mouth wide open. The sun hits his bald head and seems to burn into his thoughts 'cause he kind of talks out loud in his sleep. I have to wake him up when we get to the hospital. It's great big. Big white concrete façade with sliding glass doors.

"Hey, Dad, I'll let you out here at the front."

He is lying back in the seat. His eyes open slowly, and then he kind of jerks.

"I was dreaming," he says.

"You ain't kidding," I go. I laugh, covering my nervousness. Now that he has woke, he looks sicker, just from having taken his nap in the car. Something in the way his face skin is pressed against his skull.

He gets out and walks in, disoriented. The sliding glass doors open. He walks in, like it's a big superstore and he is totally unaware where to go for a gallon of milk. I park in the garage part and walk in and find him sitting on a couch inside, down the corridor a ways.

This time I see he has blood on the edges of his mouth, just inside his lips.

"Dad," I say. Almost like I'm miffed at him, like it is embarrassing, this blood on his mouth. Quick, wipe it off before anyone sees.

I look around and people are gone, just this empty place

between the main waiting room and the front desk, a couch and a chair next to a pay phone. He must have walked here afraid to tell anybody, probably ashamed.

Blood starts leaking then out of his mouth with his spit.

"Oh God, Dad," I whisper.

I don't know what to do. He's collapsed now all the way. His body is bleeding inside. I see it the way a doctor might: blood flowing through perfect inside a healthy person, and blood bursting up like flames inside the sick.

I go get this midget kind of nurse, up by the front, and tell her, and it's amazing that he made it this far, isn't it? What was he dreaming of? Dying? In my car, dreaming while I drove him to the hospital. Maybe he was dreaming of Mom, when they loved each other maybe before I was born, or School Street, or me when I won third place at that track thing when I was a junior, running the hundred-yard dash but I gave it up the next year because I felt self-conscious about being in sports and plus I had a girlfriend who wanted me near her plus I was in love with her little brother and my thoughts were all scrambled and just plain (excuse my French) "fucked up."

Dad on a gurney in the elevator. He isn't talking. Ain't moving.

This is happening. This. I feel like I could walk away and still be here in the elevator with the short nurse and this intern named Dr. Calusinkinghom, from India, I guess. He's dark-skinned and young and has a voice that is both sad and urgent like a computer for the blind.

"He was supposed to have tests," I say in the elevator.

"For what specifically?" the doctor asks.

"For stomach problems."

"Yes," the doctor says. "He's unconscious now. He's lost a lot of blood."

"Yes," I say.

"A lot," the doctor says.

It goes on.

I fill out papers and Dad disappears into the hospital, into its secret mazes. I am in a chair surrounded by white walls, with a clipboard, filling out papers. It's like I have lost him by not helping him in at the front. I should have just parked and *then* went in with him. Escorted him, held on to his elbow, shown him the way even though I had never been here before myself. Then I see his bloody mouth again, like somebody punched him. Blood walking up his throat and painting his mouth from the inside. I picture him when he was my age, cleaning the carpet, foam going all over the place. I picture him mowing the lawn while I pull the weeds around the house. He would make me go without a shirt and I would get a sunburn every time.

I fill out all I can and take this to another nurse or receptionist or whatever and she interviews me.

"I think he's got insurance through his retirement. He took early retirement at work a year and a half ago. Took it instead of getting laid off."

The lady is pregnant. She has honey-blond hair. Her fingernails are painted perfect.

"Okay," she says. "Does he have proof of this insurance?"

"I believe it is in his wallet. Yes. Look we came here just for tests but then he started internal bleeding."

"Okay," the woman says, this time punching in things into a computer.

"Okay," she says again, still punching. And looking, squinting, in at her screen. I just sit there.

Then I am somewhere else entirely.

Thoughtless, going up and down an elevator and finding another part of the big hospital. Trying to get to Dad.

But then I'm a little boy all over again. I am lost in a mall. Remembering that feeling: winter night at the mall we went to in Indianapolis sometimes, with Mom off somewhere, and there's this great big cement turtle kids play on and I'm tired of playing on it and it's dark in the big windows to outside and Mom is not near. The first thing I think of is Troy, but this is after Troy has disappeared, the winter after that summer when I was six and he was sixteen. I thought: Mom has left me here because of what I did with Troy, they found out, and Troy is dead, and I'm going to be dead because my dad is going to kill me because Dad knows too. These are my little-kid thoughts. I have it all worked out, the way a little kid like me would.

I start running through the mall, my eyes streaming with tears. It's late. I can't stop crying. Finally I go into JC Penney, and I stop crying. Looking around at dresses hung up like headless women.

Right in front of me, some big man says, "What's wrong? Son?"

He's got a mustache. Tall as the Eiffel Tower.

"I'm lost," I say.

He picks me up. I wonder if he will kiss me.

"Well, what's your name?"

"David."

"David what?"

"David Brewer."

He takes me up an elevator and then to an office. There's a woman at a desk.

"This little guy here is lost," he says.

I nod.

The lady has a microphone she pulls out from her desk. She has a bird's nest for hair. Her dress is bright red.

"What's your name, honey?"

"David Brewer."

Suddenly my name is called out from the speakers in the ceiling, like God is calling me forward in a woman's voice. Her voice is both in my ear from being in front of her and in my head all over from the speakers. She tells my mom where I am. I wait, the man waits. He smiles at me without saying anything. There's this big artificial plant beside me. I hold on to one of the big leaves.

"There's nothing to be afraid of," the man says. He lights a cigarette and looks around. "Your mommy will come." He smokes and looks around. I don't want him to leave, even though I don't know him I want him to stay with me please.

I grab on to his leg then, and he laughs, shocked.

"Hey there," he says. "Hey there now, tiger, you're hurting me."

He keeps laughing. The woman at the desk looks at me funny.

Then I see my mom come off the elevator, looking mad but also like she's happy. Her face shines for me and for me only, and I know for like three seconds what real love is, what it can be. It's about being saved. It's about your mom getting off the elevator and saving you.

"David," she says loud. "David honey, I told you to stay with the turtle, honey." She looks around, obviously embarrassed by this commotion I caused. Smiling dumb and touching her throat tenderly, a nervous habit.

As soon as I see her, though, I start bawling. I can't help it. Cannot help it. That is my first response.

8

PAUL

They got me hooked up here on some good stuff. Well, that's okay. That's just dandy. Hooked up to the big bag of morphine dripping down the line, like the cord to a phone going straight to my veins. Plus some tubes. I'm all tubed out. Machines and tubes, the modern hospital.

Sunday, I think, and I'm reading some car magazine. Not really reading. It's hard to hold it, so I got it up on the tray in front of my face. Morphine makes me sleepy as hell. Sleep is like when glass gets real hot and turns to molasses, *that* falls down into my head from above: morphine and sleep. They give me my nutrients through this hole they put into my gut. White milk in a bag but not milk, thicker. A big nurse named Donna, God love her, sweet as all get out, comes in, fills me up with the white stuff. I can belch it up sometimes, but it don't burn. I can stare at the magazine, and I feel it inside me, like a wasp's nest, but then nothing but sleep. Then nothing else. "It" being cancer.

Oh, that day. That day, that day. Dave drove me here. Lord God, I was in the kind of pain makes you go unconscious. You don't want to know. I got bizarre in the head. I was thinking shit like about Irene, my ex, and about what if I died what would happen to little Dave. It was like I was regressing in my thoughts back to that time I had the kidney stones when Dave was real real little, and I was in the kind of pain makes you go unconscious with them stones right near my pecker wanting to come out. I made Irene drive me to the hospital. Didn't need to pay for a goddam ambulance is what I told her. All day at work, I felt the things kind of move, just inside me, but I kept it inside. Dave was in the backseat, and I remember he was scared due to my crying. I was screaming, telling Irene to go faster.

"Run that goddam red light, cunt!" I said. Now normally I wasn't a name-caller, but the pain was . . .

I fall to sleep, thinking this: me yelling "cunt" and crying. My face pressing up against the roof of the Impala's interior, my feet pushing against the floorboard. Sweaty like a pig. Put out of my right mind. And Dave back there crying.

They got me sitting up in bed this time.

I feel like a goddam dirty dishrag that's dried up on the side of the sink. My eyes are open barely. I wonder what time it is. If it's still Sunday. Don't want to ask nobody. Donna just gave me my feeding. Donna smelled like cinnamon perfume and cigarettes. What a lady. My nurse. What a lady she is.

"Dad?"

Then there they are, all of them: Tara and Brittany and Dave and Tara's mom, Miss Martha.

"Dad?"

Dave's voice is so soft I feel like he can't hear himself sometimes, like he says things to hisself and to other people but I bet he or them don't hear. My stomach don't burn. It just itches. Doctor said they will have to remove it. Cut my whole goddam stomach out. It's like a joke. Like removing somebody's head.

"Dad, you awake?"

Then I smile. "Hell, yes." It hurts to see.

"Hi, Mr. Brewer," Tara says. I've always thought she's good. She has that kind of a hardworking personality. She's got Brit. They ain't supposed to let babies back here, are they?

I can't really make small talk. Sorry. Feels like I died last week, like this is just some made-up dream somebody else has going. But it's all right in small little moments of time, like seeing Brit's fingers, small as baby worms, or seeing the sun hit old Miss Martha's dyed red hair, or Tara, seeing her chin crinkle up when she talks soft.

"You look better today than I've seen in a while," Dave says. He's lost weight, in a black suit, white shirt, red tie. His hair is a little long.

"The nurse said I could bring her back, bring Brit back here, Brit, so's you can see her, but now she's getting fidgety, of course." Tara laughs and moves Brit back up on her shoulder. She turns Brittany around, and Brittany is smiling and crying both. What a face. But then again I don't want to see it.

"Do you want to hold her, Paul?" Tara's mom asks.

I shake my head no. "Too many tubes."

Dave is over by the window now.

"You've got the view, don't you?" he says, turning and smiling. He doesn't want to know I'm almost about dead. That scares me to think it, but also I am letting myself know now, and that's good too. Before, all goddam alone in the trailer, sitting there, feeling it, getting up to go in there and puke my damn guts out: I did not want to know, couldn't. But now. It's all over, ain't it? Once they have to remove a part of you, once they start looking at you like you are special, once they allow you to bring babies into the hospital room. So. I wonder. What will it be like? I could ask God, but even now I can't muster up enough disturbance to believe. Dave was always the believer in our house, but I know I do—*believe*. I do, I think.

Brittany finally just busts out into full-fledged cranky baby crying.

"I'm sorry, Mr. Brewer," Tara says. She walks out with the baby and then Tara's mom comes over with a little wrapped box.

"Here you are, Paul," she whispers. "I got my X rays. I'm benign, but I know what you're going through. My brother had prostate."

She smiles like that is supposed to make me feel better. Dave is still by the window. Birds fly up and hover like they know him. I undo my gift. Slow, slow. It hurts to move everything. It turns out to be a wristwatch with Indiglo nightlight. It's very plain-looking. I take it from its box, and Miss Martha helps me slip it on. Does the mortician slip a watch off you? It feels heavy. Now what in the hell am I gonna do with a watch?

"Dave said you needed a watch," Miss Martha whispers.

"Yeah."

Dave turns around, comes back over to my bed.

"Mom may come in from Ohio," he says. "For your surgery."

"Good for her," I say.

Dave laughs. "She wants to, at least."

I loved her the best way I could, and that wasn't good enough, so the hell with her. She wants to come say she's sorry, huh? *Sorry* while I'm on my goddam deathbed. Let her. I'll let her apologize.

Miss Martha admires my apparatus.

"Looks like they got you hooked up to every tube and device they can think of," she smiles and says.

Like it is real funny.

"I'm almost about to die," I let out.

That shuts her up. Miss Martha, sorry for the attitude. Then again, I just want to go to sleep. Get away. Go on a vacation. Hot glass pours in, so hot it is cold: this is sleep, not death, but pretty damn close.

"I'm gonna be dead soon," I say, maybe almost singing, hell I don't know.

Don't give a shit about the Reds, about TV, or about my new watch. Just my life as it pertains to this feeling now of not knowing where to go next. I mean, after I'm dead. Hopefully I'll have to stand around in a line, in a real long line, for a real long time.

That night I wake up to Dave, who is still in his suit. The windows are black and shining back a reflection of the room.

Dave says, "You lost a lot of blood."

"What? You still here?"

Dave scoots a chair up. I look beside me and there's my wrist with a new watch on it. It ain't set right.

"Can you do my watch?" I say, barely able to lift my arm up. "Sure."

He finagles it off, like he is afraid to touch me. Stands up there and fixes the time right, then very carefully buckles the leather strap back onto my wrist. I watch his face. When he was a littler guy, he was quiet, so quiet it used to could make me mad. Seeing him watch cartoons of an afternoon after I got off work, little pale boy with his eyes wide open watching them dadgum cartoons. I was a country boy myself, grew up in Pineville, Kentucky, did farming, tended animals, so I wasn't used to a boy who chooses to be inside like an invalid. I'd get pissed just coming in the door.

Dave steps back. His face is so clearly serious.

"Tara and Brit and her mom went home," he says.

"Late."

I can't read my damn watch.

"Yeah. I'm going soon too."

"Yep."

I lay back and feel my body unlocking from itself. Skin and

flesh unlocking from bone. This unlocking scares me worse than anything else. I want David to hold both my hands. I have a craving to be held on to. It's my nerves too, coming apart. I don't say anything. This is the fear you don't know till you're here. Fear of closing your eyes, but there ain't nothing more you can do and you even want to close your eyes, that's the goddam fuck of it.

"Davie," I go.

He looks at me.

"Don't worry," Dave says.

I can feel myself slipping, slow like that molasses I was talking about: me melting into the hot vat of morphine and into the hot vat of glass. The only way to die is in an instant. That instant when the molasses goes to crystal, an automatic hardening, a see-through slice of sleep, which is a window, which breaks but doesn't shatter, breaks when you go through.

"Don't say anything," says Dave, but then again I'm almost back to sleep.

9

DAVE

Me and Pastor Lewis occupy the elevator up. About six p.m., a Thursday, and there is no real feeling left, as Dad got his surgery done Monday early. He's been up in ICU ever since. Pastor Lewis knows all this already. He stands there looking at the elevator certificate, a framed-like diploma beside the buttons. I called him last Sunday night after I woke up from this dream just drenched in sweat. I had just spent practically the whole day with Dad at the hospital. Tara didn't wake or nothing. But I was scared anyway because I thought the Rapture had come. And me and her were left behind. I mean I thought this truly. Felt it in my heart like pure pain.

I *knew.*

I got up and had this horror that made me not see Brit in her baby bed in her room. I mean in reality she must have been there. But I looked in on her in my dream-dark, and all I saw were the bars of her crib and the covers, an empty baby bed, and I just got this shocked thing going.

I started to call out Tara's name, but then I shut up. I did not want to wake Tara up suddenly. Did not want her to know that Jesus had come back, took the saved, left us behind as sinners. Like a thief in the night is what was in the Bible. A while back on a Sunday night at church maybe last year we saw a movie made in 1977 called *A Thief in the Night* that did not have Hollywood names in it as it was a Christian production. We were all excited 'cause it had just come out on video. It was about this blond woman who looked like Florence Henderson, and it was about her not getting saved but her husband did, and the Rapture happened. She was left behind in her 1977 suburban house in California or wherever, and watching that in church must have left a big impression on me, because the movie did not just stop with Jesus coming back as an abstract thing. It *showed* that day of Rapture, showed everyday life being interrupted by people shooting up into the air like angels off trampolines, cars crashing as their drivers were pulled up into the sky, planes as their pilots went, fires starting in kitchens as housewives were taken up leaving behind bacon on the stove, a policeman making an arrest whooshed away, the criminal escaping, and so on. Everyday life just shattered by Jesus, who was traditional-looking in the movie, brown-haired with a beard and bare feet in a blue and white robe in the blue and white sky, floating (you could see the cable hoisting him, but that was okay), floating and smiling as people shot up into the air towards him on that day of Rapture.

And I know how stupid this sounds now but right then, that night when I called Pastor Lewis, thinking of that movie, I was losing it all, thinking of all I had done. How my sin maybe had been spread out onto Tara, and this is why Tara was still here. The baby, all babies, would be taken by Christ during the Rapture, as babies were under the age of accountability. They are too young to know sin, that's why Brit was gone.

I walk around our house in total after-Rapture, this horrible horrible silence, not wanting to wake Tara. I wonder if Dad went up, if Mom did. It's hot and quiet as I walk in my underwear room to room, thinking of them taking Dad's whole stomach out, the whole thing, how does that work? Then though back into the nightmare that Jesus had come again, and me believing it to the point of going to the phone.

Of course what I did to those boys was in my mind. What I did. The life I lead, outside of being this so-called good Christian man.

So there's my face up to the receiver. There's me, frantic and terrified, pushing in Pastor Lewis's home phone number.

His wife answered. As soon as I heard her voice, I knew. I seemed to wake from the dream. Yes. I started laughing. I felt dumb and I felt drunk.

"Mrs. Lewis?" I go.

Tara is up now, rubbing her face. Looking at me from the doorway in the kitchen.

"Yes . . . Is this Dave Brewer?"

I laugh.

"Yes, ma'am."

Tara says, in a whisper, "What are you doing, David?"

"David," Mrs. Lewis says. "Why are you calling us at three in the morning, honey?"

"Is Pastor Lewis there?"

"He is asleep."

"Yes," I say and I bark out a bigger laugh. I laugh a little more. "I thought . . ." I start.

Tara looks at me like I am losing my damn mind. She comes closer.

"Go get Brittany. Go see if she's there," I tell her, cupping my hand over the mouth part of the phone.

"What?" Tara says.

"Get Brit."

Pastor Lewis is on the line. "David?"

"I thought Jesus had come again."

Saying it out loud made the fear come back. Mrs. Lewis and the pastor could be fakes. Could be total fakes, I realized. I mean I realized how stupid all my thinking on the subject was.

This whole bizarre incident. I mean I realized, so what if I was left behind? What could I do about it now?

"David. It is your dad, isn't it?"

Tara brings Brittany in. I don't know how, but like I said, my mind when I looked in on her had erased her. That my mind could do this was strange and kind of beautiful to me right then, as I got flooded with pure relief. Tara is holding Brittany and looking at me, looking quite pissed off. I imagine she thinks I've finally snapped in two, maybe something she's been expecting.

"David," Pastor Lewis says, his voice all low.

"I am so sorry," I tell him.

"That's okay. Hey, on Thursday when me and you go out for Outreach, how's about we go and see your dad first, around six, prior to Outreach? We'll go Thursday, me and you."

"Yeah," I say.

I hang up.

"Are you okay?" Tara says. She looks at me like she is trying to find a stain on my clothes.

I laugh again. Covering up.

"Dream," I say.

But I know dreams happen to sleeping people. Dreams have a peaceful quality. What I had just gone through wasn't no dream. It was like me breaking out of my life by imagining the most horrible thing on earth. It was me going crazy. Or was it me warning myself?

I saw the boy burying something in my head right then. Saw my boy, a seven-year-old with a too-big shovel in a dark park. Saw him awkwardly digging a hole at sundown beside a rusty slide in the play-sand. Saw that he was burying what looked like a cat but it was Dad's stomach. Saw his careful hands plop the stomach, a red-jelly sack, into the grave he had made.

Now what does that have to do with the Rapture? I thought.

I looked at Tara.

"You sure you're okay?" Tara said.

Brittany was crying.

"Yes."

"Maybe you need to get a sedative. Something to help you sleep," Tara said, turning around to go put Brit back to bed. She shakes her slowly and lovingly all the way down the hall.

I stood there a little bit, blank in the brain, my eyes hot. Then soon I went back to bed. Tara is already almost asleep.

But she says, "Whatever you need from me, you ask."

She closes her eyes, like she has shut down. Somebody took her batteries out. Somebody needs the batteries for something else.

In the ICU, Dad has been hooked up to even more machines. Life-supports now.

Right after the operation, the surgeon told me and Tara and my mom, who actually did come over for the surgery from Ohio. Dr. Zinn was the surgeon's name, and he looked like every surgeon on TV, salt-and-pepper hair, tan skin, clear brown eyes. He said in the little room off the surgery ward: "He must have had a real high tolerance level for pain. I mean, the cancer was in a stage that almost could have—excuse me—but could have eaten through to skin and muscle. That is pain."

The surgeon almost laughed. My mom looked at me. She was in a button-down shirt and khaki pants and sensible shoes, looking neat, clean, and organized, her hair cut boyish-short.

Dr. Calusinkinghom, Dr. CK for short, the Indian doctor who was Dad's doctor now, was there too with us. He said in his soothing way, "He will be on a feeding tube the rest of his life. The colostomy we might be able to remove eventually, but don't count on it. I don't know. Now it is wait and see."

Mom nodded, Tara too. I just stood there. After, we walked

out to the parking garage, and Mom told us she was going to drive back to Ohio. Like bye-bye, see you later, had a nice time.

"Don't you want to see what happens tomorrow?" I said, like it was a show on TV she might not want to miss. But I could tell she did not want to have anything else to do with this, as Dad had already burnt his bridges with her. So be it.

"I told you I would come over for the operation," she said, her eyes blank. She had a black Honda Accord. Nice. Her and her husband are doing quite well. They got two video stores they own now. It hurt me, though, like her leaving was her leaving me, not Dad on his deathbed. Selfish but true. I remembered how she left Dad that summer I graduated, how I felt stuck with him and his pissed-off sorrow. Mom on her own and me stuck with Dad, like it got reversed somehow. It was me who was supposed to leave and her who was supposed to stay. Then she stopped calling, got a life, and eventually I just had to leave Dad too.

Tara said, "We got room . . ."

"No thanks." Mom smiled, like Tara was just some waitress she had to put up with.

"We would love to have you," I said.

"I need to get back," Mom said.

The parking garage was echoing our voices. It was humid and dark, all these anonymous automobiles, all this concrete to keep them parked on. We went dead silent, looking around and then back at each other. I felt a crazy fear open up, but I pushed it back, scared that Mom had me confused with Dad, that she had grouped us together. A while back, she sent me this picture of her at a desk with a big old computer, half-glasses on her nose, a long line of adding-machine tape around her neck. She looked like an overworked character on a sitcom. That picture of her as an overworked business lady with just too many problems I would never understand, me this silly stupid meter-reading son of hers, that picture was her way of separating herself from me and from Dad, I knew. Maybe, I thought, she hated *us*.

That was the feeling I used to always get of course when I was a kid, that her wanting to get away from Dad was her wanting to get away from me, like if somehow I could have pleased Dad instead of making him mad, maybe then she would have stayed home more, or at least when she stayed home she would have paid more attention. Liked being there. Then again, maybe all she could do was just put up with us: me the little idiot getting into trouble, Dad the big idiot finding out. It was like a cartoon. Her too tired and too sick of the whole thing to help me out by stopping it.

I remember, too, her letting me brush out her hair when Dad was gone and she had the night off. How she would ask me to do it, and I would love to. I used a brush from the bathroom, her sitting on the floor and me up on the couch on my knees, her eyes closed as I pulled the brush through her short dark hair, splitting it a different part each time, seeing the white scalp appear like lightning in the night sky.

Now Mom stood there by her foreign car, jangling her keys. "Well, um," I said. Then I went to her and hugged her, telling myself to stop this stupid stuff, but angry too. I used to watch for her car, not Dad's, on those times Troy babysat me, Troy in the kitchen making instant pudding, singing Elton John, me waiting for him to come out so he could feed me the pudding like a baby. Dad was at a union meeting or he was working late, Mom at work or whatever. I was looking for her car, waiting for Troy to do what he did. I remember too that one time Troy counted to twenty and I hid, naked, up in Mom and Dad's closet, hoping somehow that Mom, not Dad, was in bed, in my little-kid illogical way, going into their bedroom to hide, hoping Mom, even though she had just left for work, was still in bed asleep, remembering other times crawling in with her before while she slept. But there was safety, there was comfort even in that.

And in the hospital parking garage, she hugged me back tight. I buried my head in her shirt. Tara stood back, like she knew this was something she could not share in. I pulled my head away and looked at Mom's face. It was this face I knew but did not know. Blurry but also too real.

"I hope he does all right," she whispered.

"Do you still love him?" I asked, out of the blue. What a dumb thing to say.

Mom looked at me like she was exhausted with this whole thing. "Do I still love him?" she asked, looking away from me.

I did not know what to say or do, kind of stuck there with her, arm in arm. When we had waited during the surgery, she let me put my head on her a while to sleep and that was when I thought about telling her about the boy and the other boys, so that she could help me find Professional Help. Or maybe so that she could suffer too. Tara had gone to see how Brit and her mom was. They were cutting out my father's belly because it was black with cancer, and I had my head on my out-of-state mother's lap, thinking about telling her how loving a boy was all that made me truly feel alive sometimes. Knowing that even what it did to those boys was a part of the pleasure, I was going to say. Not really. No. I thought about telling her about Troy too. Telling her all he did to me while she let him babysit me. Giving her a guilt trip. Throwing that onto her, even though I knew I was too chicken to even form the actual words. I felt love for her and also that I wanted her to pay me back something. Like she owed me, big-time. I stayed with my head on her lap though, and of course I did not say nothing. I wanted someone to take a picture of us with my stupid head on her lap. She smelled of fabric softener.

Now I went back to hugging her. I felt myself shutting down to a point. She gently nudged me off.

"Tell him when he wakes up, I'm praying for him," my mom said. She was crying. I wondered why. Was it because of Dad? Because of me?

"I love you," she said, but I knew she loved me the way you love people you used to know.

"I love you too," I said, knowing I loved her in the same way, but deeper because of all that was wrong with me.

Mom stood there. Tara came back. The three of us formed a triangle of silence. Then Mom invited us to come to Ohio when we got the chance. She got into her car. Drove off.

Tara said, "That was strange."

We went back in for a while, then left for home.

Now me and Pastor Lewis pray beside my tubed-up dad. Me and Pastor Lewis in the low-lit ICU. Pastor Lewis big as a house in a plaid shirt and big-man jeans. His Outreach clothes. I hear all the sounds of the machines keeping Dad alive.

I hear Pastor Lewis. "Lord, we're here tonight to ask you to bless what the doctors have done, to . . ."

I slide one eye open. See Dad's face. Lifeless as a piece of paper. His oily skin falls loose to the hospital pillow. That face, my face. Cancer is genetic mostly, isn't it?

"Lord. Let your grace . . ."

I can't listen. I keep looking at his skin. Wonder about all the stitches. I sat in a room with the doctor whose hands had been inside my dad's body. The surgeon talked to me after he put his hands inside my dad! That stomach I saw ate up like by gnats, millions of hungry and angry gnats.

"Amen," Pastor Lewis says.

He looks up at me. "He's gonna make it."

I smile. No he ain't, I think.

And then Pastor Lewis and me in my car. Driving to Hampshire Apartments. My idea. To go see the boy at home. To witness to him. Maybe to his parents. I have fears and not, because I know Pastor Lewis is my guardian and I know I am not gonna do anything. And really I am kind of excited. I want to laugh. Get rid of the Dad image in my head. Excited because I get to see him, my boy.

I get to see him, and I won't have to do a single thing but witness to him. But also to see him and to see his house. To smell it. It's almost like I am in a time machine, traveling back to see myself, not to correct the past in order to make a more perfect future, but just to see if I really ever existed that way, that size, that condition.

Pastor Lewis says, "Your dad's a survivor."

I nod. I see my dad coming up at me with his belt one night when I was, I think, four or five, for getting into his special cologne. I see him chase me round the dinette table. His face half-mad and half-laughing. *You get your little ass over here, goddammit.* His voice sounding caged-in inside the small house. Him laughing because I would not stop running. Mom in the living room watching TV, yelling at Dad finally, "Why don't you just leave him alone, Paul? What did he do?"

Dad stops laughing. "He spilled that goddam cologne all over the bathroom, Irene."

Mom does not say anything. I'm standing on the other side of the table, breathing hard.

"Well?" Dad says, looking at me but yelling at her.

"Well what?" Mom says.

"You still want me to leave him alone?"

Dad smiles great big, like once he gets her permission, it'll be over.

"I don't care what you do, Paul. Just forget it."

"You're the one bitching." Again he yells at Mom but looks at me.

"Paul, just forget it."

Then I am suddenly being grabbed, as out of nowhere he

reaches across the table with octopus arms and gets me, but he stumbles and I break free. I run into Mom in the living room, plow right into her, not crying. For a moment she holds on to me, and I love her more than you should love one person.

"Just leave him alone," she says. I can't see her.

But he grabs me from her lap.

"Let him alone," Mom repeats.

But he is whipping me.

Then I flash forward to him just the other day when we went out to eat, how he was so polite (at least for him), so beaten into by his fear that he was sick, a dying man, and now his fear had come all the way true. I am not happy, even though he caught me that night and whipped me, pulling me off Mom, laughing and yelling, "You thought you could outrun me, you little fucker?"

Mom gets up and goes, "Paul, you are gonna end up hurting him."

Dad whips me some more while she stands there, but then he stops and puts me down. I'm wobbling there. He looks at Mom. "I ain't hurting him. See? You okay?" He is asking me that.

I look up at Mom. Her eyes have turned into glass. She just does not want this in her life.

"Answer. Did I hurt you?" Dad repeats.

"No," I say. I go over and sit gentle on the couch, hurting but being quiet. Putting my legs under my butt.

Mom and Dad sit down then in the living room in their chairs, to watch *Bewitched*. That's about all we could do then.

"Your dad wants to live," Pastor Lewis says. His fat face is calming.

Right now there is a lack of any feeling, I want to tell Pastor Lewis. Not that I want Dad to die. Or not that I am in love with this boy. But about other incidents. How it all got started by Troy. Which would be a great big lie. I had it in me, and

Troy was there to find it. Inside me, a bird's nest like that one in Troy's garage rafters. A bird's nest where my stomach should be. I see the boy holding a bird's nest at school in front of the class for show-and-tell.

Pastor Lewis coughs.

"What?" I say.

"Nothing," Pastor Lewis says.

Hampshire Apartments are low-income totally. It's where trash lives, if you get right down to it, and me and Pastor Lewis walk up to the screen door after I park. Where Nathan lives is a town house near the front. His mom answers, tired-looking, with mouse-colored hair, kind of flabby but not all the way fat. A good face, like she's been through a lot and started out pretty doing it and this is what is saving her now. She has on a house-coat.

"Hi," I say on the other side of the screen. "My name is Dave Brewer, and this is Pastor Lewis. We're here to talk to you a little bit about our church, Norris Road Baptist Church, just down the road a ways."

Pastor Lewis is letting me handle this part, 'cause I made the referral to come here. Nathan's mom looks scared but also pleased somehow. Shocked a little.

"Well. I'm Elaine Marcum. Um." She looks behind her and around and then finally says, "Come on in."

The living room is beige-painted with old sunk-in furniture the style of the early eighties, contemporary, vinyl. Me and Tara had that when we first got married. She can't stand it now. The floor is linoleum all over with throw rugs on top. There's a man with a Fu Manchu mustache sitting on a recliner chair. He has tan skin and a tattoo and no shirt on, with a big belly.

"This is my husband Ronnie."

Ronnie does not look up when I introduce the two of us.

He looks mean. Like he whips children. I get that vibe right off. I wonder automatically where Nathan is. Where is he? Little thing.

There's a dinette set covered in what looks like bills and a phone and a calculator. There's a smell of fried food and cigarettes and also something sweet like cake just baked. Or powder, baby powder. And feet.

Elaine Marcum looks scared. Makes you wonder if she always looks like that. Ronnie looks like nothing, except mean and tired.

"Won't you all sit down?"

Me and Pastor Lewis sit down on the sofa.

Then I see Nathan hid behind Ronnie's recliner chair, in that place where kids go. Elation right off. I watch Nathan back there. That must be where he hides or where he plays. It's sweet, the places kids find in houses. Like they are always trying to survive doing that. I bet he wants to dig a tunnel back there.

Then Ronnie says to Pastor Lewis, "Where'd you all get my address?"

Elaine laughs, embarrassed. "Ronnie."

At that moment, when I saw him over behind the chair by the electrical socket, I was just trying to break out of my feeling. I got popped in the head with Dad lying there in the damn hospital bed, his mouth open, this mixing in with Ronnie's image of a redneck in a recliner. All the machines and tubes it took to keep Dad functioning and Ronnie's eagle-and-cross tattoo. I felt like everyone was looking at me but I was not gonna break down, no way.

But again I thought of Dad, of Mom leaving him, of Mom leaving me and Tara in the hospital garage, of Tara in her nightie, of Brit crying in her bed—all of that washing out, though, as soon as I saw him. Saw Nathan. Nathan. Good strong name. Seeing him made all the other stuff wash out. But "washing out" might not be the correct terminology. More like when I saw him my plight got so big all I cared about was Nathan, that small thing, curled up behind the chair.

This is when I said, "I just thought this would be a good place to visit."

I could not help it. I was not really crying, just my eyes going wet. I half-cry like that sometimes. Like I have been crushed, not by anything in particular.

Nathan's mom looked at me sitting there on her couch. She still stood by the recliner next to her husband, her son on the floor behind her and the chair. I felt the horribleness of what I was doing. Like I was showing off loving their son. Like I wanted them to find me out so they could kill me. But no. I loved it too. I had Pastor Lewis here with me, and all my sin and all my goodness were combined till I felt closed-up and slow, close to a retard. But also an angel. I was on display to them as a freak in a traveling freak show, but they did not know that quite yet and slowly they were finding out and yet by then I would already have what I want.

"Um," I go. "My dad—um—he just underwent major surgery."

The tears flow, folks. Flowing down, and I wipe my face. His mom comes over and for an instant I am a six-year-old being comforted by his mom, she leaning into me, sitting on the couch arm.

That is what it is! The whole thing. Boiling down to me wanting to have the same mommy as him.

"Hey," she says. "I know what you're going through. My grandma had a double mastectomy three months back."

I nod. I smile. I feel her sympathy mixing into my blood like a warm expensive drug. I am a child TV star in a serious TV movie about child neglect, but not. Stupidity has a dark shine to it, like night being lit up with flashlights and torches. Everything vague and a little scary. Shaky and half-lit. All I want is him. I could scream it right now if I wanted. To her, his mother. To my pastor. To his dad sitting there looking at me like he wants to whip me too.

Just scream to them: *Please let me have him!* I feel it deep. It's like somebody stuck something through the top of my skull. An electric prod. It strikes and stays. *Hit by lightning:* that's the freak-show sign around my neck. I imagine myself lit up and singed, black-cheeked and smoking, like one of the Three Stooges after the dynamite goes off.

All I want is to hold him naked in a real soft bed. Kiss him hard at first. (Reverend Lewis looks away—he knows, doesn't he? He knows or is too dumb to get it, and, yes, I really respect the man either way.)

Hard and mean, that kiss, then pull back to a soft suck. Feel that tiny mouth with my tongue. I want to see his closed-up eyes when I kiss him. I want to slide my mouth down. I want to slide my mouth down to every part.

"You guys," I say, "must think I am the biggest flake."

Pastor Lewis: "We maybe should go."

I stand up and help Pastor Lewis up from the couch. It's hard because he has sunk into the couch almost to the bottom, and I think he might be mad at me for being this way I was with them, with these people who might have come to church but now we weren't so sure after me saying that about my dad's major surgery. I see the night before Dad's operation. Sitting in our kitchen at the dinette table covered with dirty dishes after supper, Mom starts clearing the table, and I feel a charge of fear or love or hate, I don't know, but I was on the edge of screaming out to Mom, screaming out to her something mean and delirious, but managed just to bark, "Mom, me and Tara will get the dishes! You go in the living room and relax!"

Pastor Lewis took his Bible and walked over to Nathan's dad, who had stood up now. He gave the dad some tracts he had in the Bible, with the church address and phone number on them. Pastor's face was filled with understanding and apology. I did not like him suddenly, feeling him trying to suck up to those two, while I knew they were bad parents. Letting their child go to the pool on his own. Knowing that, I wanted to say something, but I just stood there.

"These may explain everything," the pastor said. "They have my number on them."

Pastor Lewis smiled. The smile again made me mad. Nathan's father took the tracts and put them in his back pocket.

I look back to Nathan, still hiding in that place only kids know about in a house: behind the chair, next to the electric socket. That's the only kid place in a house sometimes, in an apartment especially, outside of the top of a closet. Or maybe under the sink, where the pipes are, beside them.

I go over to Nathan and I feel the lightness of my step. Could I save him if his life was in danger? His parents hurt him. I picture his dad beating him with a belt. That's something I have promised myself I will never ever do is raise a hand to Brittany. But you could tell they were (or at least he was one of) those types. As I squat down to see Nathan at eye level, my hatred for his parents turns into that love of him, that feeling I keep going on and on about. My body turns into fire. The sun on vinyl seats is comparable to it, heating the seats till they burn your legs if you are wearing shorts or even if you are not.

"You can ride my bus," I say. I will cry again, if I don't stop. My mouth won't open all the way. I am dizzy.

"We'll have fun," I tell him.

We look into each other's eyes. This is what you are supposed to feel at one of those bars, those singles places, this is my affair, I understand: the excitement of reeling someone in, and being pulled back on. The excitement of knowing you will be lying all the time to your wife. Your home life could just be shot, but all you care about is the moment. Our eyes are looking into each other. Like a tunnel is about to enter another tunnel. Fish catching fish. But Nathan stops, looks away. Nathan does not want me. That doesn't matter, though, because a part of him does, the part I will have to bring out. Part of him wants me to be that way, I know this deep down, and this is what keeps me going. This is what keeps people like me alive.

But then, when we almost get to the point where we actually could do something, I will stop in the nick of time. You got to go this far then pull back for it to mean anything at all, and then after him, I will stop altogether.

I stand up after I shake his hand.

"We'll see," his mom says. Like she even cares about him. Then she comes over to me and puts her hand on my shoulder softly. "I got saved when I was a little girl," she whispers. "'Bout his age. I quit going. Now I work all the time."

I nod. "Yes," I say. "He could go, though. Kids need church." I smile.

His mom smiles. "I hope your dad turns out to be okay."

I smile at her. She walks back over to Nathan. Nathan's dad shuts the door behind us.

It was a humid night, and the dumpster was overflowing out by my car. We got in and I started it, the Escort. Thing still working.

"What happened in there?" Pastor Lewis says. He is looking at me like I just murdered somebody.

"I just got like, I don't know, kind of anxious and sad about my dad, so I told them."

Pastor Lewis nodded. I turned on my headlights.

"Do you think you might need help, you know, dealing with what has happened with your dad?"

I stopped from backing out then. I stopped and looked at my headlights shining on a dumpster, with three cinder block walls built to shelter it, and the dumpster had side doors that were open from having too much crap shoved in. I stared and waited, not knowing why. Except I might want to tell Pastor Lewis.

Just tell him, I heard myself say to myself.

Tell him, dummy.

I saw the shot-out segments of the policeman's eyes I had imagined before. I turned my head slow to see Pastor Lewis. He looked scared. Scared of me. I imagined myself spilling it. Just spilling it all over the place.

That little boy in there is the only person I can love right at this time. Love in a certain way, you see. I mean, Pastor Lewis, I love my wife and I love Brittany and I love my dad and my mom, and I love (of course) I love Jesus, God, and the Holy Ghost. Yeah, but I love that boy. It is wrong. I know. I could stop if I wanted, but I don't want to. I mean, I will have to soon enough. But why stop right now when it feels so good chasing him? I'll stop right when it gets out of control. Like right now it's not totally out of control. I can still sleep at night mostly, and with some medication (I am not gonna say "vodka") during the day, I can live through. And I know, I know I brought you here with me like a sick joke, on Out-reach Night, for pity's sakes! But I really do think Nathan deserves to go to church 'cause I have a feeling his parents are not good people. I had this—

But in real life I pull out. I get onto the street.

I say, "I might need counseling, Pastor Lewis. Yeah. This thing with my dad."

My breaking my silence relieves Pastor Lewis, and I realize I am relieved too, that I am away from that apartment, away from Nathan. But then I wonder if he ever goes by Nate.

Pastor says, as we pull into the church parking lot, gravel bumping up against the hubcaps: "Listen, David. I'll try to hook you up with a counselor I know. Good Christian. Okay? I think it was probably a mistake going to see your dad before, but still . . . How did you really get their address?"

I shrugged my shoulder and winced a little. "Just guessed. I don't know."

Is he suspicious? I kind of hope he is.

"Okay," Pastor Lewis says, smiling. He whispers to me then, "Your dad is gonna be fine. Fine."

"You think?"

"Yes. We pray and pray, and he's gonna be fine."

But what if your promise breaks, Pastor Lewis? I want to ask. I saw Dad tonight. He looked sicker than a damn dog, Reverend. Pastor Lewis gets out. Fatter than anything. Waddling over to his big Caprice. That's the car we all helped him purchase with money in the collection plate. Powder blue. People talked about that car for months, how it was show-offy and not a pastor's car. But I like it. Had no problem with the car. I like him in it. I like him driving away while I stay there.

I calm down. I get out to smoke in the gravel lot alone. The church shines from moon, white aluminum siding, silvery windows. I go and stand by the front and smoke, then walk back behind. Central-air box, natural gas meters, the woods behind, the rusty wire fence, the cement platform I poured along with Cal and some others for picnics and the basketball goal. Back here the church looks like a little country school. It's dark and it is hot. I imagine myself clean as this: the back wall of a church. Clean white cinder blocks, grass up against it, wet with dew. This is soothing, smoke in my lungs. The freedom of smoking and the freedom of being a pervert seem to collide. I dream about that boy. The dreams are sexed-up and silly. I won't describe them even to myself, except to say that they are so real I see them all day against my brain. The boy so beautiful he collapses into me, and then it's *me,* not him no more. A boy and a boy. A boy inside a boy. A boy "coming" inside another boy, like the boy will get pregnant if he is not careful.

I feel weak, standing behind the church. It's just grass and the woods and rusty fence and the cement platform, the basketball hoop missing the net. And birds somewhere, stars, sky. Tomorrow, I think, I won't even see him. But I don't know who I mean. Dad? Nathan?

I end up taking the next day, Friday, off. I just call in and leave a message on Kent's voice mail that night. Tara listens, sitting on a rocking chair in the bedroom in her red nightie, faded a tad from washing.

She was the one told me to do it. Take Friday off.

"Go play some golf. Give yourself a day to be alone. Then go see your dad. I think you are on the verge of losing your mind, honey."

Her hair was wet. Her face kind of lost. She looks upset tonight, like I've done something.

I call. As much to make her happy as anything else. Then right after we hit the sack, I think of what I told Kent. I needed a breather, what with my dad and all, I told him—and I saw myself through Kent's eyes, and it was a pretty good picture right then. A guy losing his dad to cancer having the foresight to know he needs a day to get his stuff together. To stay sane. Good worker too, calling and leaving it on the voice mail. He may be depressed about his dad, but the guy is responsible. We get three personal days a year, paid.

Tara wants to you-know. I get naked. But I can't. I cannot. She understands, what with Dad and everything. I kiss her deeply and stay naked. Then she backs off. She backs away. I can go to sleep then, after setting the alarm for 4:30 a.m.

"Why'd you set it so early?" Tara says, checking it after using the bathroom.

"I'm gonna go real early out to the course, just so I can get like nine extra holes in," I say, smiling. "A. Lone."

"What a day off, waking up with the chickens," says Tara. She hears Brittany then. She goes down the hall.

I close my eyes. I see that place behind the chair at Nathan's place. In my head this is where I fall to sleep, after I have been chased there by my dad with the belt. Sometimes this is the only place people like me can get to sleep.

. . .

That next morning when I get to the course, my stomach's got this swirl thing going off in it. I should not have ate anything, but Tara got up because she's feeling sorry for me, and she made pancakes. Smell of almost-burnt pancakes and syrup is still inside me, mixing up with the sound of crunching gravel under my feet. In the dark I go past the ragtag clubhouse trailer, the buildings built on, thinking about Greta and Mack in there asleep.

Off the green of the first hole, the interstate shines right beyond the trees. You can see a lightninglike smear of big trucks out there, truck drivers on speed probably going off to deliver whatever. Possibly dangerous chemicals. I tee up in the half-dark. I am down to business. Want to see the sun come up on the third hole. Want to see that sky color. Not a color, but like the bottom of the mother ship. An advertisement for heaven, or for space travel.

I draw back my club and ease right into the ball and whack it's gone. Good-bye. Everything is back to normal. I hear people sighing with relief, a choir of sighs, like in that movie we rented the other night, *Apollo 13*, all the NASA scientists at space-central after the astronauts land. Just everyone going "Shooooo." Wiping sweat with handkerchiefs. Hugging each other.

It is over. The boy is not near me no more. Out here I have distance. Just shut the door, leave me be.

I hit it on the green, first thing. The light is clearing. Mack has some old streetlamps up, halogen, most don't work, but the one by the first green is on, and in that light I feel protected. I put her in. The tiny tap of my putter on the ball just is like the sound of a perfect kiss. I start laughing at my thought as I go on to the second, where I mess up big-time. Get it in the rough, can't find the ball, and then I get this feeling like how dumb this whole game is. How incredibly stupid.

I find the ball, though, and get a double bogey but nobody is watching anyway. Nobody cares what I do. So I sing. I sing some song I heard on the car radio.

Third hole: I wait for sunup. I sit on the ground, smoking. This is my time of the day. This right here, enjoying something nobody else in the near vicinity is noticing really, everyone sleeping till they got to get up to face yet another ugly day, only it's a wee bit better because it's Friday. Third hole sunup. This is the place, on a little hill, with the trees spread out before me like angels, dark and a little stiff-looking. Not angels but broomsticks made to look like angels. Morning glories popping up like Barbie-doll parachutes. The sun appears above the branches, big orange ball, then blanks out, becoming a bigger color. I can't swallow when I see it. This is why God made eyes. I light another cigarette. I stand up and smoke and see the sunshine burning off the dew. The grass starts to go to haze.

Man, I'm thinking, I am *alive.*

Greta is drinking coffee up at the trailer as I walk up after eighteen. I may pull thirty-six since it's only about nine-thirty now.

"You were here early," she says.

"Yeah."

I remember her in her bathing suit two weeks back. How I had a good game, and she kind of came on to me. Today she's in her jogging suit and tennis shoes.

"You're addicted, aren't you?" She smiles. Her teeth are pearly white, her hair dark as the trees with the sun behind them. I can't really like her that way, but out here when I'm playing golf it's fun to pretend, to map out an affair with her, not a real one, but just this fantasy thing about a motel room. But this reminds me of Nathan.

"You bet I'm addicted," I say finally, among the sound of birds out here. "You got that right."

"You want some coffee? Just made some."

"Sure."

I put my clubs down and walk up the little asphalt path to the trailer. Mack is sitting up front by the old-timey cash register, sitting there with his oxygen thingy up his nose, the see-through plastic line going back behind the counter where the tank sits like his robot-pet.

"Heard about your dad," Mack said. "My heart goes out to you."

That about Dad scares me. I should not be here 'cause people are going to think bad things about me for not being by his side. But Greta gives me a cup of coffee. I sip and kind of just sit there. Dad will be fine. I'll go there tonight. This place, I think, is like *Cheers*. Somebody ought to make a show about a small clubhouse at a rundown golf course and all the zany characters strolling in and by. Call it *Fore!* Or did they make a TV show out of *Caddyshack* and I don't know it? But, of course, right when I think "zany character," Bob shows up. Turns out he took the day off too.

All is forgotten. You don't know what this feels like, being here. Being with these people. All is forgotten, all is forgiven. Nobody knows what they need to forgive, so it's all just forgotten.

"Look who's here. Hotshot. I bet they're missing both of us. Indiana Gas just cannot run without Bob and Dave. Dave and Bob."

Bob works in a different part than I do. He's on road crew and makes almost twice as much as I do. He lucked out when they were hiring. Still, he doesn't make a big deal out of it. He's cool about that, at least. Today he has on shorts cut too damn short, like short-shorts on a lady, a T-shirt that has the Tasmanian Devil on it, and a big cap. Looks like a cartoon, but I'm comforted seeing him like that. Greta gets him a cup, and we all sit in the trailer on old folding chairs, with the front-window air conditioner blowing.

Mack is staring right into me with his sympathetic bloodshot eyes. He goes, "I've been through a lot worse than your dad." His face is stone-serious, but his head is shaking as it does a lot now.

I don't know what my face looks like, but I am trying to take his sympathy in simple and clean, even as my teeth grind in the back of my mouth.

"Yeah," Greta goes, and she is concerned too. "Yeah, he's living proof," she says, standing up and going over behind Mack. She starts massaging Mack's shoulders.

"I wish I had me my own personal masseuse," Bob goes, and we all laugh.

Greta says, still doing Mack's shoulders, "Bob, what you need is a psychiatrist to massage your *brain*."

We all laugh louder. Greta looks down at Mack. You can tell she really loves him. She is helping him in his last years. She is helping him with the oxygen and sometimes when he pees his pants, I bet. That tube in his nostrils feeding him life, she keeps that going. She is protecting Mack all the time.

Bob goes, "Look at them two, Dave."

Greta keeps massaging Mack's shoulders. His head actually stops shaking, and it feels like me and Bob are interrupting something. Mack goes, "Oh yeah, babe. Oh yeah." Greta is not smiling at all. Her face is serious. Then she looks up and smiles. Her smile with the lipstick on the teeth hurts me. It hurts that she smiles and that I am this creep that chases a little boy.

The boy is in the past, as are the others. Remember that, Dave. As Greta continues doing Mack's neck, Bob tells us a dirty joke about Richard Gere and a gerbil, to pass the time. Bob laughs really loud about that joke. I wonder if Troy Wetzel was a "gerbil-loving faggot."

Is that what he grew up into?

Troy Wetzel just disappeared that August, 1972, end of summer. I forget the exact date. It was a Monday night, I remember, close to school starting. I will always combine the two: first grade starting and getting school supplies at T-Way, a crappy version of Kmart near our house, and coming home that night with my crayons and paste and little safety scissors, and finding out they had left. Vanished.

Mom said, "All their stuff is gone, Paul."

Dad said, "She's been screwy since he died."

Both of them looked at me. Sun had gone down. I had my school supplies, and this was what I focused on. I got sadder as the night progressed. Sadder and sadder. There was nothing left to do on School Street but leave, like Troy and his mom had done. I remembered three nights back when me and him were in the bathtub together, and his mom came in and there we were. In the bathtub together. Him sixteen and me six. How she stood there. In the doorway. She looked like she was going to scream, but the scream got caught in her mouth. Caught until she had to let the scream come out from her hands as her hands shook the right one pointing and she whispered in a loud way: "You get out of that goddam bathtub right now!"

She took me back to my dad. I remember not knowing what to say, just going home and watching *Horton Hears a Who*. A cartoon was on at night—that was great. But still I knew what happened, that we had been caught, and maybe I knew what Troy was gonna do.

And then he was gone. Her and him.

That night we saw they were gone, I got up and secretively walked over in my PJs to the garage behind their house. I looked at the door to it. I tried to peek in, but there was no way to see into the painted-over windows. But then I saw, taped to one of the garage-door windows, a small folded-up piece of paper, and I ripped it off. It was dark, and I went over to the chain-link fence outside of the used-car place, under a big light that had the shape of a helicopter on a tall stick. It was a piece of notebook paper with a drawing of a daisy flower on it. Each petal in a different color. The middle part was a peace sign, and there was a green stem coming out of a big red heart. Beneath that was "DAVID + TROY." I could read those names. But I knew even then I was sposed to throw it away.

I went and ran behind Troy's garage, to where there was this little creek, and I ripped it up and tossed the pieces of paper into the green water.

I ran back home. I got my school supplies out. I was crying but I looked at them, each new item a special magical object. Each special item was my piece of a new life: crayons, little pot of paste with a purple stick inside the lid to spread it like butter, them scissors with the green plastic handles, the little set of watercolors with a red paintbrush, big heavy pencils unsharpened. I worshiped these things in a way, thinking of Troy. Knowing then even in my little mind that I would never see him again, and that I would need now to start all over and learn everything anew, keeping myself quiet or he might come back at me. Mad as hell, out of love.

Me and Bob play eighteen holes together that day, and I stink. Bob keeps making jokes, and I try to play along.

"What happened, buddy?" Bob goes on the eighteenth, as we walk up.

"My dad had surgery on his stomach, okay?" I say, cracking-voiced. Like I was at little Nathan's house all over again. "Damn," I whisper.

Bob goes quiet. We walk back up to the clubhouse, and Greta is trying to do the books for the golf course. Mack is afraid they are gonna get audited like his younger brother who owns the pancake house in Detroit was. The green pages are fluttering in the wind across the table.

"I swear to God, this is like German," Greta says. "All these numbers . . ."

Her smile again chills me. I look away. Bob is apologetic for a while, buying me a beer. I drink it while Bob goes on about building this house out in the woods from scratch.

"I mean not just, you know, going to the lumberyard and buying the lumber, but actually cutting down the trees and shit. A for-real log cabin." Bob looks off into the distance, for dramatic effect.

We go quiet while Greta taps numbers into her calculator. Finally Bob gets up, saying he has to go buy some gardening stuff for the weekend. He comes over before leaving, smelling oniony from sweating, his breath beer-hot. He whispers in his loud way, "Hey I'm sorry about your dad. I think I might go see him. Sunday, maybe."

"Thanks."

He shakes my hand, and I watch him go off.

Greta gets up. I look up at her, squinting my eyes.

"I'm sorry about your dad too," she whispers. She walks to behind me and starts to massage my neck without asking. Just comes over and starts. I stiffen up in a spasm. Like her touch is painful.

"I'm sorry. I didn't mean to scare you. I forgot how jumpy you are," she says, stopping. She backs off. Her touch on my neck stays there. I get shaky from it. I realize I want her to strangle me.

Greta sits back down, embarrassed. "You got plans for the weekend?" she says, collecting her accounting ledgers, not looking at me.

"Probably just go see my dad and hang out at home."

Greta stands up holding all her papers, placing her chin on them as she holds them. She thinks I am some kind of freak, coming here with my dad in the hospital about to die. I had a pissy golf game, and I offended her. Right then I could go to bed with her, just so she'd know I am not a freak. I imagine her naked. But that doesn't stop me from thinking about Nathan, I imagine myself saying to Greta suddenly, careful to place myself as big old victim. I would get soppy with her. Tell her about my dying dad who used to beat the living crap out of me, tell her about Troy Wetzel, all that. Maybe she would take me into her arms like a mother, and I would have enough warning to know not to flinch. Maybe she would say to me, "You poor thing. Living with all that."

"Well, I'll talk to you later," Greta says in reality. She walks back in. Leaving me outside in the heat. I sip my beer. The grass is getting scorched, and I smell the sun cook it. Soon it will turn yellow like old newspapers. A desert made up of old newspapers.

It's two, and I don't want to go home. I go over to the home-decor place in the mall, to buy Tara this wicker basket flower-holder thing Tara told me about last month, thinking I would never remember. It ain't her birthday or nothing, but still: a present for my baby. And a present for my other baby at the Walt Disney store. I get her a Hercules doll. It costs like fifteen dollars and isn't big enough to do anything with, but still, like a souvenir for her. Like something to put on a shelf and to think of: that summer, when you were one year old and *Hercules* came out.

I take the gifts out to the car, and then I walk over to the General Cineplex just to see what's on. I ain't ate since breakfast and so I go inside and pay for a show. Buy a big tub of popcorn and a Diet Coke, and it's air-conditioned and nobody hardly is here. I get up close. I like this a lot. This feeling. Dark comes on like sudden clouds, and the previews hit me, and I am cozy eating my popcorn and drinking my diet pop and it's like there isn't a damn thing wrong with nobody.

It's weird, at the start of the movie, to see Nicolas Cage, the bad guy, shoot John Travolta's son. Right on a carousel. This big ticking time bomb in a little shedlike area in a mall, about to go off. The movie loses me because it gets sillier and sillier when their faces are shorn off and floating in little boxes, but the little shedlike place where the bomb is hid reminds me of the little gas-meter sheds I painted when I was in high school.

I was a junior, and I got hired that summer by Indiana Gas Company to paint the meter-and-pipe sheds that were all over Anderson. (This eventually led to the job I got now.) These are little buildings built to house pipes and meters that the gas flows into after coming out of the ground. Experienced people have to go out and monitor the flow every once in a while. Well, all these buildings were made of rusting iron and cinder blocks, the roofs wood covered in tarpaper. I got the job of painting each one. There was thirty-seven all total, and it took all summer. None of them were any bigger than a deluxe tool shed, so I could do usually one a day. I'd paint all day in the sun, getting a real good tan.

I was dating this girl named Trish then, and she had long dark hair like Crystal Gayle. She was skinny and pretty and went to horse shows, had this little brother, Danny. They lived in the posh (back then—now it's just another neighborhood) suburbs out where cornfields and radio station towers were. Anyways, I would go out and paint all day, and have lunch inside the sheds. I had keys to all these sheds, and inside they were gravel-floored and dark, with big rusty pipes the size of ditch pipes almost coming up out the ground, and meters and cobwebs and clipboards with plastic-covered papers and wax pencils next to them to write down the readings. So I'd pack myself some sandwiches and a big jug of water and some Fritos and snack cakes, and I'd have my lunch in there smelling of that awful enamel paint they made me use, all alone and cozy and feeling hidden from the outside world.

Then I'd go home after work, take my shower, and travel to the suburbs to see Trish.

When in fact it was Danny I wanted to see.

It happened slow. I did not think about it at first. At first it was me and Trish going out, and then I would escort her home. I would make a point of going past Danny's room. Secretively I would smell his room. Nobody thought anything. This was my first big love, the first one I pursued.

One night, Trish and me were planning to go to the June Jamboree, and I asked if we could take Danny along.

"Sure," her mom said, a stout lady who worked at Delco. Her dad did too.

Trish looked confused, but did not mind either, really. Maybe she wanted to be romantic or whatever. We had done it, of course, in my dad's Le Baron. She probably thought me being nice to Danny her little brother was just me trying to be seen as a sweetheart.

Danny was blond and short and had muscular features, even though he was not fully grown. He had thick, thick hair, and his eyes were blue, his cheeks sunburned. He was always getting into something, hyperactive maybe, and very healthy. I knew it was dangerous what I was feeling, but the feeling was never paired up with acting. Plus I was doing it to Trish, after working out in the sun all day. The sun burned away all my bad thoughts, but they came back as soon as I got home and showered.

We went to the June Jamboree, which was in Pendleton, about fifteen miles to the south of Anderson. Trish wore short shorts and her long dark hair pulled back into a long dark ponytail. Danny was in a tank top and gym shorts and tennis shoes. We rode rides and ate and just loved the whole thing. Loved it.

Fairs are like reasons to live for kids. Rides are comparable to little pieces of outer space brought down to Earth for their own personal enjoyment. Eventually Trish sat down on a bench because she was afraid of this one Snowball ride that went upside down.

"David," she said. "David. These rides aren't safe."

Her voice got pleading, while Danny pulled on my arm, and I gave her this helpless look, like Danny was making me do it.

We got on board, side by side. The ride started, and I let my hand rest upon his thigh near his crotch. He didn't say nothing. I let it stay there, like an accident, and the ride jarred, and my hand slipped up into where his underwear started. It stayed there, three fingers, and he looked at me, and he was not smiling.

He went, "What?"

I stopped. "Sorry," I said.

The ride went on. We got turned upside down several times, and then came to a dead stop. He got off real quick. We went home soon after. Danny left me and Trish in the car, and I kissed her on the mouth four or five times, felt her boobs. I went down on them and licked a nipple. She breathed hard. This was heavy petting, like we were doing it for a movie camera to show what heavy petting was.

I worried and worried he would tell. I worried while I painted the little sheds. I imagined hurting him into not telling, but the hurting him turned into doing other things to him. Pleasure things. Then one time at lunch I went over to their house in the gas company truck, an old crappy truck, not like the one they let me drive now. Danny was out on the lawn getting sprayed by a lawn sprinkler. No shirt on, in his cutoffs, his hair going dark when it was wet. I got out.

"Trish around?"

"She went to the mall," Danny said.

"Your mom around?"

"No."

He looked at me.

"You wanna eat lunch with me in my secret hideout?" I said.

I smiled. Then got worried that the smile would be taken wrong. I really did just want his company. I know what that sounds like, coming from someone like me, and it was a damn lie, but I was seventeen and back then I could believe the lies I told myself.

"What to eat?" he said. The sprinkler made a rainbow across the lawn. His face had beads of hose-water on it, dripping off his cute little nose.

"I got sandwiches and Fritos and oatmeal cream pies."

"What about ice cream?"

"We can stop and get some."

He ran in and back out, after putting on a T-shirt and his shoes. He was a little pudgy, and I guess food was his weakness. I was beginning to think sharklike then, to see where their weaknesses came from, and their weaknesses was like what the shark would smell: the smell of blood in the water. Little weaknesses. Ice cream. A fresh ten-dollar bill. Even quarters. Purely fun times.

We got Dairy Queen. Sundaes with lids, and we took them to the shed I was painting. It was in front of a ramshackle neighborhood near downtown, built on a side of a big closed-down warehouse, next to railroad tracks that weren't used anymore. Weeds had grown up, but still natural gas flowed through the shed's pipes.

"What's this place?" he asked me, as I parked.

"I'm painting it."

"For what?"

"For the gas company."

He acted like that answered his question okay. It was hazy, hotter than anything. We ate the ice cream first, as soon as I unlocked the plywood door, and inside it stank of the deodorizer put into the gas to make sure if there's leaks you can smell it 'cause natural gas alone doesn't have a scent. There was one window off to the left, but it was broke and had been fixed with plywood. Dark, with the door even half-shut, and the pipes hissing. We sat on the pipe joints and ate the frozen custard sundaes. Danny looked like he liked this secret hideout of mine.

As for me, I kept thinking of my hand on the Snowball ride, going up his shorts to the underwear, feeling the piping on his underwear, and getting that breathless feeling, that feeling that this was truly who I was, and finding myself was what my whole life was sposed to be about. Finding out that my hand up a little boy's drawers was my calling in life. I know it sounds stupid, but it felt not-stupid. It felt like these pipes in here had burst up inside of me and not gas but love had come out, just pure love that kills you, nondeodorized so you don't know it.

Danny kept kicking gravel. He ate one of my pimiento-and-cheese sandwiches and then was drinking red pop I'd brought along for him, as tapwater did not sound like a beverage a little boy like him would like. After, I took out my cigs and lit one, and I smoked, making it look like I was it. The one and the only.

Of course, smoking in here was prohibited, and we could have been blown to kingdom come, but I did it anyway.

Danny kicked little pieces of gravel, dangling his legs off.

I took a deep drag and breathed out and said, "You smoke?"

"Sometimes," he said.

I passed it to him, and he smoked, coughing his little lungs out, which made me laugh out of love.

I wanted a cot in here then. To lay with him on the cot and to hold him.

He coughed and he coughed.

I went over to him and got on my knees. The gravel hurt like hell. I kissed him on the forehead, pushing back his bangs.

Then I kissed him on the mouth. Deep, deep kissing.

"Stop it," he whispered.

I slammed the door.

I did not know if I was in my right mind, but I went to him in the dark and I held on to him so tight it was like I was trying to kill him and all's I thought right then was how big a mistake this was, which only made it that much more thrilling.

Danny started screaming.

I held on to him and then I let go and pulled off his shirt and he screamed, and he started kicking.

Finally I got him calmed down. I pulled back and he was in the corner. I lit my lighter. I held it up to my face. I was so scared I could not think right. Scared of him telling. I told myself I should have gone slower.

"You say anything and I'll tell your mom and dad you smoked," I said. "I'll tell them that and then I'll tell them that you wanted it."

Maybe I was just a kid then myself. But in the dark with the pipes hissing, he looked up and he said, "Don't."

He waved his hands in front of his face.

"Do you know what it feels like?" I asked him, the lighter going out. I lit it up again.

"What?" he said, half-whining.

"It feels like when you die," I said. I opened my eyes wide. I opened my eyes wide and I told him I would take him home, and I would never see him or his sister again. I gave him what money I had in my pockets. Ten dollars. I told him if he told I would have to do the killing part.

He was quiet all the way home. I dropped him off at the end of his street. He walked back on his own.

I went back and painted in the hot sun. I would not see him again, nor his sister, and for months I wondered if he was going to tell. His sister called me five times, and each time I told Mom to tell her I was not around.

"You have to fight 'em off, huh?" my dad asked one time, sitting in his chair.

I had just got home. Paint-speckled and sunburnt, I nodded my head.

"Where in the hell have you been?" Tara asks me as soon as I come in.

"I went and played golf and then I went to the show. My day off. I'm gonna go see Dad tonight."

She looks pissed.

"Reverend Lewis called. It sounded important," she says.

Brit in her playpen, the house all calm.

"It's almost seven, Dave," Tara says.

"I lost track."

Then I go back out and bring in the basket and the doll.

"For you, my dear," I tell Tara. She looks absolutely shocked. I love it.

"For you, my dear," I tell Brit, giving her the doll, after taking it out of the box.

She holds it, then drops it. Me and Tara laugh.

"There's no parts she can choke on, is there?"

"No," I say. I hold the box up and show her the writing: "One and up."

"I can't believe you sometimes, I swear to God," Tara says. She holds her basket like there's a Baby Jesus in it, and then softly puts it on the floor beside a magazine rack she got, antiquing with her girlfriends. She comes over and kisses me.

"Call Reverend Lewis."

I kind of get shaky calling him.

"Pastor?" I go.

"Dave." He laughs. The laugh is so beautiful and soothing, just what I need to make it through.

"Yeah?"

"Guess who called me."

"Who?"

"That Elaine. Elaine Marcum. You know. Hampshire Apartments? Last night?"

"Yeah."

"She says her son wants to go to church. Ride the bus. You got another passenger!"

Pastor laughs, like what he thought last night was nothing now that we had another Christian about to be born again. I wondered if she wanted him to go 'cause she herself had been saved, or—and this is what I wanted it to be—or if he had gone up to her last night and in his tiny voice he says, "Mom, I want to go. I want to go. Please."

PART THREE

10

TROY

This is Loretta Jones, let me introduce her to you. Her hair is long and silver, so thin it could be cobwebs. Her eyes peer out at you, half-open, lids fluttering from loss of muscle control. It is her face, the comatose, jowly face of an old lady slowly wasting away in a nursing home in Muncie, Indiana, that you must see. *I* must see, every day of my natural life. The face that tells me I am no longer who I used to be. That face with the moving mouth that says nothing. Loretta's fat daughters come in and try to get her to talk all the time, but she only peers back at them, through them, that dumb, dead-set stare doing all the talking: *This is what happens, girls. No matter how hard you try, this is what happens.*

Right now, in the midst of a quiet afternoon in Loretta's room, I am moisturizing her hands with Oil of Olay. Me, someone like me. Her hand bones slip, moving slightly under the thin flesh, bones I could break simply by pressing wrong while I rub in the skin cream. I am so careful—dreaming of this even while I do it—so careful that my skin tingles. My head aches from being this careful. It is a good ache, though. When I stop, Loretta's eyes are open wide, and just for that moment she has no fluttering problem with her lids. Her eyes are cut crystal, cupfuls of coffee, and even if she does only grunt, I can tell that she is trying to say something to me.

Something soft and probably flattering, something only she and I can understand.

Hard to believe that at forty-one I am now a full-fledged boy scout, is it not?

Dedicated to the point that the people I work with often question my sanity. I care for the old and the sick and the dying. I catch people in the twilight of their years, when they are becoming kids again, babies from being old and sick. Curling back into fetuses to die like the day they were born. I see it all the time, and it isn't mind-blowing, not even that sad anymore. Old ladies and old men in their beds, their mouths opened wide trying to get what breath they can, eyes shut tight against the strain of having to get through what's left of living.

When they piss and shit their mattresses, all I have to do is strap them into a convenient harness with a crankcase lift, and they are lifted up, as if by magic. I change the sheets under them, spray Lysol, their bodies suspended in air.

I see death all the time and spray Lysol at it.

It is quietly thrilling, being around death all the time. I have a feeling my reaction to it is a great big sentimental fucking cliché. Nonetheless, I'll tell you that the thrill comes from seeing something almost supernatural in the everydayness of doing your job. Like you clock in on the time clock up front, and then there it is: a whole warehouseful of people dying. Big deal. Then you start helping them through it, or toward it, like you are the last tour guide before they get on the boat to go home.

All this death is not a curse to me. It is a way for people to understand what they have done wrong. People like yours truly.

I'm not saying these old people are dying for my sins. What I *am* saying is that by caring for them I am not necessarily redeemed, but I am able, while doing it, to forget the first forty years. That doesn't mean I don't go home and jerk off to pictures of dirty little boys in dirty little books arriving to my apartment in brown paper wrapping like the butcher used to wrap up a leg of lamb. Little boys who like to take it all up their little butts, smiling like they love it. But while I do do that, I can come here after, and nobody knows the difference. Here. To my Sunnyhaven church, the church of the broken-down child molester.

I can come here, and I can wipe the shit from an elderly asshole. I can feed that open mouth without teeth. I can turn people over to prevent their bedsores from getting worse. I can, I am *allowed* to, wash that silvery yellow greasy head of hair.

I can feed Mrs. McGlothen in the Alzheimer's unit cafeteria (so named because the doors always stay locked on this side so no one can roam and get run over out on Route 9)—oatmeal sliding down this old lady's chin in the gray dining area, with empty tables and the sound of somebody's wheelchair bumping against a door somewhere.

Doris, a woman I work with and practically the only friend I have, is in here with me, doing the blood pressure of Mr. Torrence, a black man, but also talking to me, as we four are the only ones in here. Obese but still able to walk, Doris tells me about her and Lyle, her boyfriend, doing threesomes. They take pictures sometimes, she says. Doris in a white LPN uniform with a Santa Claus pendant on next to her name tag. Christmas happens to be a big thing for her. Christmas all the time. Her tree stays up all year round. What started as a joke became her Christmas-loving life. Christmas and threesomes.

She tells me, as I feed Mrs. McGlothen: "It was some guy name of Tony. He's a mailman. Lyle found him through the personals."

I look up. "The *Muncie Herald* personals?"

Doris laughs loud. She is doing Mr. Torrence's blood pressure over by the big windows. He goes through it like she is positioning his arm so she can paint his portrait, an old black man without eyes (cataracts replaced them), peaceful as a sleeping bird.

"No! We got our own newsletter. *Midwestern Swingers*. It's put out in Indy. Duh."

Dyed blond, golden brown from going to a suntanning booth in the mall, she tries to act like a suburban teenaged slut most of the time, although she is almost fifty. There is a special sadness to her depravity. I get that. Oatmeal splatters onto the floor. Mrs. McGlothen doesn't look happy. She is not as peaceful as Loretta, and her skin has a see-through appearance that I don't want to touch. Oatmeal sounds like a bug being smashed as she slowly rubs her naked toes into it on the floor. I finally get some into her stubborn mouth.

"Tony works out," Doris says, sliding the blood pressure cuff off.

Mr. Torrence gets up slowly, walking away like a ghost. Being blind has given him grace, and the Alzheimer's has given him silence. Silence and grace are a good combination.

Doris comes over.

"Oh, she is gone," Doris whispers about Mrs. McGlothen. "Look at her face." Doris snaps her fingers in front of Mrs. McGlothen's face. She doesn't move. Her idiot's stare remains. Doris looks up at me.

"Lyle really dug it," she whispers, being a bad girl. Winking.

I look at Doris, then at Mrs. McGlothen's oatmeal-smeared mouth moving slow, like a fish, a fish wanting more water, more something, more anything.

"Lyle and I are coming over to see you tomorrow night," Doris says, taunting me. It's a joke now, how my apartment is off limits, but she comes over anyway, and really I kind of like her coming over. I don't like Lyle that much, but still you need people like Doris in your life.

"We want to go to the fair," Doris says, grinning. She rolls up the blood pressure cuff, swinging the cord like a stripper's strand of pearls.

"You are going with us," she says, her face getting serious.

I don't know what to say, so I just nod. Then Doris walks off to do something else, leaving Mrs. McGlothen and myself to our oatmeal, our silence. When we finish, I go get a wet cloth. Mrs. McGlothen stares at me while I clean up the oatmeal from the table and floor, on my hands and knees doing it, not thinking of a thing, not even the fair, just the gray oatmeal on the linoleum. Her toes still squirming, Mrs. McGlothen sits in her chair like a queen of all she surveys, her eyes rolling back a little. I like her watching me, as I wipe under the table to prevent ants or roaches.

After that I go over, and with the same cloth I did the floor with, and still on my knees, I wipe off her toes. Mrs. McGlothen stops all movement as I do it, freezing into her moment of pleasure, like *Oh please do go on.*

Doris and Lyle are over here at my apartment right now. They are ready to go to the Free Fair. The fair is a sad thing, the fair makes me want to puke, the very idea of the fair, but Lyle and Doris sit on my couch which I just had Scotchgarded to protect against stains.

"Come on, it'll be fun," Doris says, dressed in shorts and a tight tank top, an outfit that obese ladies of the nineties should steer away from. Her smile saves her from being too grotesque, however—her smile and her face, which, despite everything else, is close to doll-like, almost Dolly Partonesque.

Lyle is tall, with long hair and a mustache that connects to his sideburns, but he doesn't have a beard. He's only thirty, and Doris, you can tell, is proud that she has a young lover. He looks almost like a stretched-out Captain Kangaroo, wearing jeans with his *X-Files* T-shirt.

"Come on, Troy," Doris says. She likes to think of me as her best friend, and when against my will she comes over to my apartment and we watch old movies together, she likes to talk, as I don't really talk back much. Doris is one of those people who likes to talk.

"Let me have a cigarette," I tell Doris, laughing under my breath, turning around in the swivel chair before my computer. I talk to Doris, but look at Lyle. Sometimes, when I am feeling full of pep and vim and a little frisky, I treat Lyle like he's my boyfriend too. He seems to like it when I start to get in sync with his and Doris's form of perversion.

"We are going to the fair whether you like it or not," Doris says, lighting up my Virginia Slim she just got out of her purse. "Vaginal Slime" is what Lyle calls them.

Lyle says, "Come on, Troy. You always come home and veg out."

I blow out Vaginal Slime smoke. Doris comes over to me and starts to whine in a little-girl way, which makes me angry. She swivels me slightly. I stop and look at Doris, at her pretty face, and despite everything else I love her. She's my contact with the outside world.

I'll puke, but I'll go.

"Sure," I say.

Lyle stands up and yawns and stretches, and his T-shirt comes up to reveal a fish-white stomach with hairy curls scattered across it. Letting his arms hang down like a chimpanzee, he looks at me.

"Par-tee!" he says, being half sarcastic, half for real.

What can you do?

Doris and Lyle are so happy I am going that I feel like they both need a slap in the face. I am not angry at them, though, just at the interruption, which makes everything seem stalled and stagnant all of a sudden. Like nothing fucking matters. I feel like going to work, where everything I do seems to have purpose. Doris's hair is a nightmare, a black-root jungle. Lyle

likes me, I think. Likes me like he isn't supposed to. He gives
me The Eye. I would like to show him my shoe boxes filled
with dirty pictures. Boys slim and pale, their faces blank, bodies smooth and nude, their stomachs inside probably empty.
What do you think of that, Mr. Lyle? He wears a wallet on a
chain, and now as I lace up my sneakers after turning off my
computer, I can see the beginnings of a big tattoo hidden under
his pant leg slightly.

Doris sings a Christmas carol under her breath.

My apartment is stinky, dinky, and crowded. Smells of old
clothes, old food, a dumb bitten-into life. The only clean thing
seems to be the computer on my desk. There's a unicorn poster
framed in chrome above it, the small TV, the stupid but precious knickknacks left from when Mom was alive, all dusty. It
is somehow elegant too, though, this place, dark with the
blinds always shut. My bowls of potpourri smell of burnt roses,
and the almost sickly sweet odor of Doris's and Lyle's colognes
colliding into one another. Lyle is fiddling with my keyboard.

"You on the Internet?" he asks, licking his mustache.

Shoes done, I look up at him. "Yes," I say.

Lyle looks up. Doris is by the door, getting her purse off my
dinette table. Lyle flirts. Again I want to show the demented
photographs a washed-up pervert keeps, or tell him what it is
like to be me in one hundred words or less. But not kiss him.
Nor Doris. I do not kiss anyone anymore.

Lyle says, "Being on the Internet is a trip."

I nod.

Doris says, "You can find playmates all over the place."

Yes, I think. I zapped myself into a chat room the other
night. A bunch of teeny-boppers. You do not want to know.

Then Doris and Lyle and myself walk out of my apartment
building into the hot Muncie night. Cracked sidewalks, big
beautiful trees, houses from the fifties. Dogs barking, cars
going past. Us three, this threesome. I'll have nothing to do

with this, I think, getting into Lyle's red jeep, into the back. We pull off. They must feel sorry for me. They think I am a shy and reserved bachelor, a homo, they think that—almost unattractive, but good enough on an off night. I'm clean. I want to scream, and I judge Doris and Lyle suddenly with a religious fervor. I am motherfucking Jerry Falwell in the windblown backseat. If they knew me really, they might be afraid, afraid of what I have done, what I am still capable of doing, but I have chosen not to do. In a way, I like pretending to be the lonely and naïve homo Doris comes home and tells Lyle about: maybe this turns him on, this flaky nurse's attendant in his semi-exotic, cramped one-bedroom apartment filled with Oriental knickknacks and unicorn posters, his fancy computer with laser printer, his ashtrays from Canada. This freak who speaks in an embarrassed whisper, smiling often. Maybe Doris likes me too. Like I am her son (although she is only nine years older). Or like I am their son they are taking to the fair, then later they will both fuck me with the tenderness of parents on Christmas morning. I am a sweet boy. I'm nice. I do everything they want. I am kidnapped and sweet for the kidnapping.

So I find myself at the Muncie Free Fair. The midway glows at the end of a bridge outside downtown. Orange, red, white, blue neon smearing and flowing, like electric eels and rock concerts and Las Vegas and like that time, of course, that David, his mom and dad, my mom and myself went to Indiana Beach in Monticello, Indiana.

I hear screams coming off rides as we get out.

Shaking his head back and forth, Lyle says, "We are gonna ride every ride they got."

Doris says, "Not that damn broke-down-looking roller-coaster we aren't."

She laughs her big fat ass off. Bending down, Lyle kisses her shoulder. The tank top she is wearing has spaghetti straps over the shoulders that make her upper arms look like huge mushrooms. What crazy kids, filled with a lust for life! What fun we will have here in the Magic City! Looking at the rides in the dark, I hear David's voice. Six years old. Twenty-five years back. David's voice in a Port-O-Let.

David is saying, "Let me go."

Little David just doesn't seem to get that I cannot do that.

Now Lyle is grabbing my hand. Doris has his. We walk together like that toward the front gates of the free fair. People must be looking. We are Dorothy, the Cowardly Lion, and the Scarecrow. Guess which one is which?

"Come on, you guys," Lyle screams, pulling us on.

I let go, but hold on to Doris, Lyle running in. I look over at her, and she is smiling.

"He is just a big kid at heart, Lyle is," she says. You can tell she loves him a lot more than he will ever love her. It is an instant of recognition for me, as if I can see inside Doris's feelings. I am her psychic twin, her emotional X-ray technician. I feel close to her in that, somehow. We are bonded together in that situation. We can only love people who cannot love us back, trapped, but getting along okay by ignoring it all, by trying to have some fun. She and I keep holding hands. We walk inside the gates, as if going to church.

Doris says, "See? Isn't this better than being alone?"

11

TROY

David, David's mom and dad, my mom and myself went to Indiana Beach on lovely Lake Shafer, up north toward the Dunes, as relaxation, as a treat before school started, as a family and their lonely-widow-with-an-almost-retarded-son neighbors. We went up in Paul Brewer's big Impala, what a car. It was one of those heavy gray salty days in which you get sleepy just picking your nose in the car, which little David happened to be doing. The landscape of Indiana was as flat as the floor of a basement. The gray scorched grass around the road resembled the overcooked vegetables Mom brought home from the Holiday Inn Businessman's Buffet.

This was early August 1972, and David and myself were hot and heavy into our affair. The garage was our church, our bedroom, our honeymoon suite. Our school. Since he was about to go into first grade, I was playing school with him in there now. I was, of course, his teacher. I got a coffee cup and drank Tang out of it, hating the taste of coffee at the time, and he would sit with old books I retrieved from Mom's dresser, math books from 1947, a reader from 1945, and some notebook paper. I sat at the table we used playing restaurant. It was my desk. Prim and proper, a gentleman scholar, I spoke perfect grammar, or tried to, no "ain'ts" at all. I purchased us a small chalkboard and colored chalk at T-Way, and I taught him how to write his own name. I taught him how to write my name. I taught him how to write his name and my name with a plus sign in between. He stared up at me, doing his writing, over and over and over, until I would get so damn aroused I could see stars.

One afternoon I went over and looked at what he was writing, over his wee little shoulder I looked. There it was, a document of our love. "DAVID + TROY" at least fifty times, all across the paper. I cried. Tremendous. A+++. I was his teacher. I was the boy pretending to have his degree in teaching and getting away with it, teaching the boy I loved more than pizza, more than girls, more than record albums by Elton John and the Carpenters. I grabbed the page after he was finished. I took my red magic marker I used to grade papers. I marked A+++. I drew a little flower with a smiley face in the center. You need to encourage good work.

He was so quiet when we played school, serious as a heart attack. Rivulets of sweat trickled down his little nose. He wanted to be smart so bad.

David asked me to teach him how to spell his mom and dad's names.

"Why?" I asked in my delicate fake-teacher way.

He looked up at me. Not smiling.

"'Cause," he said.

"*Be*cause why?"

"*Be*cause they are who I come from."

"No," I said. Not mad, just hurt. "No, honey." I went over to him, kneeling down before him.

"No. You came from God."

We arrive that hot day in August 1972. We get out in a gravel parking lot. There are piles of reddish dirt all over the place, little mountains, where road crews are making the parking lot bigger. We stretch. David's dad, of course, has on Bermuda shorts with dark socks and loafers, a blank beige dress shirt, T-shirt underneath, a baseball cap on his head. David's mom is taller than Paul, in pink culottes and white shirt. Mom has on a dress, with flip-flops and a big floppy sun hat. David and myself are dressed almost alike. White T-shirts. Blue-jean cut-offs. His sneakers are dirty white, mine blue, but that's about the only difference.

"Hot," Paul says, taking off his hat.

Big sign, you can see it from the lot, big rusty sign above the entrance gate:

INDIANA BEACH
MONTICELLO, INDIANA
BE SAFE AND HAVE FUN!!!

Underneath the words is an oversized blue parrot dressed up like a pirate with a peg leg, winking, perched on a riverboat that is undersized.

"I mean this ain't healthy, this hot," Paul says. His face looks worried, almost frantic.

"We can swim if we get too hot," David's mom Irene says.

We all wear our swim gear under our clothes. My mom has towels for all of us in her big purse. I want to hold David's hand. I don't, though. I have enough restraint, the molester's instinct to keep everything perfectly hidden. We will have a fun-filled day of fun in the sun, I keep promising myself. I prayed last night without him in the garage. Like Jesus in the Garden Alone, I prayed on the cot:

Jesus, let tomorrow be a day of great blessing. Indiana Beach sounds like a lot of fun. Please let me act right. Let David and myself be together for a good time out in the sun. Let us swim and eat goodies and just, Lord, let us have some fun, okay? Jesus, please don't let a car wreck or bad feelings get in the way. In Your Name, Amen.

It is so hot, profuse sweating feels good almost. Covered in that sweat, I feel religious suddenly, being here, in the hot crowds, all the nasty rides, nasty people. We walk into Indiana Beach. There's a fake saloon and a fake candy store and a fake grocery on this fake Small Town America street, with a big anonymous polar bear with a red hat and scarf walking around, a smile like the big bad wolf on its face. Its head droops down slightly. I look at David. He does not want to go near the thing.

David's dad and mom walk away from each other, but then back up close. My mom stays behind them.

At the end of the fake small-town street, we see the lake with brown sand and masses of people lying on it, the water dingy and foamlike, like the stuff that comes out of drainage pipes, a big slide above it all where kids go down into the water. Beyond the shitty beach is that midway of dumpy-looking rides, the screaming and the laughing and the crying. In the gauzy daylight, the rides have no glamour. It takes nighttime to make them look flashy and glamorous, and now they feel to me like candy ruined from being left on the dashboard of a car, gummy, discolored, melting. So darn hot, I must be thinking, "darn" the Christian for "damn," and I look down at little David.

"Come on," I say.

David and I run off together. No one says a thing. It must be they just want to die too, from the heat and the cheapness of the amusements and the lacklusterness of a good time. *It ain't Disneyland,* all three of the adults' faces were saying when we got here, Mom and Irene and Paul. Maybe that's what David and I were running from, that constant disappointment adults face the world with.

To be here. To wait in line for the Scrambler at Indiana Beach!

I keep hearing a voice in my head, repeating a Bible verse I was memorizing as I was doing back then even without a contest to enter. Filling up my brain with holy words. "And Enoch walked with God: and he was not; for God took him. Genesis 5, verse 24." (Even now I remember it.) That silver Scrambler with red-orange bucket seats whirring to and fro, like a big old-fashioned eggbeater, David and myself standing behind two girls both with braces and long blond hair. Smell of oily gears burning inside the clown-faced machinery, and hot black asphalt smelling like burned-up licorice. David brushing up against my leg, and David shielding sun out of his eyes.

"Troy," says David.

"What?"

"We gonna ride every ride?"

"Sure."

"Every one?"

"Yes sir."

"Good."

"Yeah, we'll have fun. You won't know what hit you."

We are speaking in fake-fun voices. We are boys from another galaxy, too pleased to be in this dumpy place, too gosh-darn happy waiting in line for the Scrambler. David and I look so out of place, like orphans with new haircuts, like runaways. When I pick him up from the ground, it surprises him. His legs dangle into my thighs. I do it out of the urge to let him know how much this whole thing means to me, being here with him today. I pick him up and drop him back down, a gesture to show him I am older, I am in charge, but I will protect him too. Also I do it to feel him, to smell his sweat and his sweetness against me.

Back down, he wobbles a little. He looks up.

"Why'd you do that for?"

"Had to," I say.

He doesn't say anything else.

We ride the Scrambler. The Tilt-A-Whirl. The Eskimo Train. The Tarantula. The rackety rollercoaster they call the Gunshot at High Noon. We laugh and laugh and touch and get to feeling amazingly good. On the Tilt-A-Whirl, we are in little cauldrons spinning round and round and I slide my hand up close to his little butt and tickle him there, while we jerk and spin. He lets my hand stay there, up close, while we spin. He is giving me the okay. His face is pure happiness.

We see Mom and his mom and dad by the carousel at the end of the midway, a long while later. I wonder now, of course, what they were thinking. Why did a sixteen-year-old want to be around a six-year-old so much? Why were they dressed so much alike? My mom was thinking this, I am sure. But David's parents? His dad was eating a big long coney-dog, his mom sipping a Coke, sitting on a bench, way across from one another. Earlier, in the car, they had gotten into a fight. Paul had used their credit card at Sears to buy one of his buddies a new golf club for his birthday, and when they were fighting, Irene was tight-lipped and embarrassed, almost laughing, but Paul, driving, went red in the face, furious.

"I can goddam use that goddam card for what I please," David's dad said. David's mom looked back at Mom and David and me, laughing kind of.

"Whatever, Paul," she said.

He yelled, "I will buy anything I see fit!"

The car accelerated. Irene was still looking at us, upset but trying to get out of the fight to go back to ignoring him.

"Okay," she said.

Now David stands there in front of the bench they are sitting on.

"Having fun, kiddo?" his mom asks.

He nods his head and smiles.

"Wanna go swimming?"

He shakes his head no.

My mom steps out of the Magic Pony bathrooms. She comes over to me, silent, messes with my hair out of love. She looks tired and sad, and I face her in the grim, humid sunlight.

She's sleepy, her auburn hair damp and mashed down. Suddenly I can tell she doesn't know what to do about me. I think she knows how much I love him. I wonder if she saw me look at him in a certain way, or if she can smell it when she washes my dirty clothes. She closes her eyes and opens them slowly.

"Let's let them have some family time," she whispers.

"Okay," I say, my gut tightening.

"Let's go have us some supper."

She walks away, and I follow behind her. David is sitting between his mom and dad but he doesn't want to. His dad is giving him part of the messy coney-dog. It is disgusting. They are faking it. His mom is tying his left sneaker for him. I wish right then that I had the powers of a warlock, to make them back away from him, to make David enter into me like a puff of smoke, David entering into me through my mouth and nose, into my lungs, heart, brain.

My mom and myself go get elephant ears and lemonade and then sloppy joes. I feel sick as we walk down past the dart games, the throw-the-ball-in-the-fishbowl game, the haunted house. AIR CONDITIONED is written in blue ice-cube lettering above the doors to the haunted house. Frankenstein is painted with his arms stuck out, chasing after a big-chested woman in a polka-dot dress, Count Dracula about to sink his teeth into the neck of a big-chested blonde in a nightgown, the Mummy juggling knives on a nearby hill covered in tombstones.

"Let's go in here," says Mom.

Without David, this whole amusement park takes on a lonely desperation. We sit in a little cart on tracks outside the haunted house. Other people join us in other carts. I want to kill my mother for a second, to strangle her for separating me from him. She looks sour in the face, like she wants me to die, and I know what she thinks, but so what? So what?

Inside the haunted house, Day-Glo mummies, windblown zombies, a Dracula doll flying out of a casket on a string. All of it smells mildewy, and nobody gets scared. Then the carts stop as we are sliding up to the second-story part. We're stuck at a diagonal, our heads tilting back toward the floor. A rubber vampire bat is staring at me. The black lights go out and the white emergency ones kick on. In that naked light, the walls are just spray-painted plastic backdrops, and if you look up the ceiling is a bunch of rafters and string and plastic and staples and nails and Christmas lights. People mumble in the other carts, but Mom and I don't say anything for about five minutes.

Mom eventually says, "I hope they get this thing going." She looks at me, laughing at our situation here. Then her face goes completely serious. "They needed family time. We did too," she whispers, out of the blue.

I nod my head, cannot look at her anymore, frustration bubbling up into my fingers and toes. I picture him with his mom and dad having a good time. I imagine myself taking him away from them, becoming his mom and dad and boyfriend all combined, and the imagined sweetness of it gives me such sorrow and such joy mixed: sorrow because I know it won't happen, joy that it *can* happen a little at a time in the garage.

It is like an unwritten rule on these things, if they stop you remain in your seat or Nazis come out and shoot you. We are silent still. I want to put my head on Mom's lap and to sleep and wake up in another town with her in a magic transfer. Almost like being in here stuck with her allows me to see a David-less existence. This is what is between me and me-and-David: the diagonal slant, this musty, over-lit stall, this rubber bat smiling at me like the retarded kid I sat next to sometimes on the school bus because nobody else would.

A skinny teenaged boy jumps off and walks away, like nothing. People start talking mutiny. Nobody else moves, though. Mom pushes in on her auburn hair, then gets into her purse and gives me some gum.

"Gosh," Mom says. She's sweating. "Air shut off too."

When it starts going again, about twenty minutes or so later, we chug on and out. It's gotten dark outside, a little hotter. The whole place is lit up with neon and naked bulbs, the water on the brown beach lapping slowly in, stagnant-smelling. Mom and I get out of our cart, and people start looking for other people to complain to about the malfunction.

We go over and sit down on a bench. I'm nervous, scan for David in the crowd. All the neon-lit midway rides remind me of him. (They still do, especially that Tarantula one, black aluminum with yellow and white neon piping, wire-mesh baskets with people in them, Dave and me at the top, like two babies caught in a dryer tub, spinning round and round.)

Mom looks at me with her sour, sorrowful eyes again, as if she just can't get it out of her darn mind.

"Let's try to leave him alone, Troy," she says.

"Who?"

"I think you know."

I hear a deep fryer hissing, kids laughing. "No, I don't," I say.

"Yes, you do," she says. She won't look at me. I look up at the rides. I wonder what taking psychedelic drugs would be like, or what dying would be like, something close to this damp heat, this sleepy shame, the old lady's hand suddenly on my shoulder, this lady who loves me. I shrug her off, walk away, see David with his mom and dad on the nighttime beach, as though they have landed there after a shipwreck. David sees me, runs to the fence. He tells me he has to go to the bathroom.

Fireworks shoot off up in the night sky. Big bad ones exploding in blue and green and yellow, sparks falling down. David's face looks like as if it has been smeared with yellow jam in the light of the fireworks. Not smiling, he says again, "I got to pee."

He is holding himself there.

I yell at his parents, his dad sitting on a bench, his mom smoking at the edge of the water, far off.

"I'm taking David to the restroom," I say, using my good Bible-studying boy smile.

His dad smiles back and yells over, "Where you and Carolyn been?"

"Stuck in the haunted house. She's coming on over," I say.

"Stuck how?" David's dad comes toward us on the sand, looking concerned. David walks around to the gate. "This place is just a pit," Mr. Brewer says, totally outraged.

"Yeah," I say. Then I want to ask him what isn't? What isn't a pit in your life, Mr. Brewer? Life is a pit, except when I am with your little boy, except when I am thinking of him, then life is no longer a pit at all.

David and myself go over to the Magic Pony toilets. They are filled up. Somebody has placed some Port-O-Lets beside them, so we go into one, this smelly blue plastic toilet, the size of a phone booth. There's no light. As he unzips, I am overcome. I grab him slowly and tenderly, but somehow quickly too. I try to help him with his zipper. Lust takes over, though. I get grabby and mean. In response to my mom's talking, in response to the gray, humid day here at Indiana Beach and all the bad food and all the rides and the haunted house. I *need* to do this with him. I deserve it. I realize, in the Port-O-Let, that I just want him and nothing else, not even my own life.

This sudden exposure of my true self makes little David cry. I sit on the dirty toilet and pull him back to me, hold on to his little wiener. I can't stop. You know that. There's an ooze to it all now, a toxicity. Maybe I need to be shot in the head. Right there, execution-style. Love is at the bottom of all executions anyway.

Love that makes you lock the Port-O-Let door and hold on to him tight, white, scared, and wet with pee, whispering, David whispering, "Let me go. Let me go."

He squirms, but stops. I turn him around and tongue-kiss him. Hear Indiana Beach's sounds through the plastic walls. Whoosh of rides, screams, deep-fry hisses, music, miniature racing cars. Smells of pee and shit and food and water. I tongue-kiss him and then I want to fuck him. I put my finger close to his butt-hole. Tickle him there. Feel around his little hole. He does not want anything to do with that. I have never gone this far before. It's always kissing and touching and watching. I have never touched him there, all the way, before. Never have I been inside him in that way.

"Let me go." He keeps squirming.

I want to sacrifice him like that all of a sudden. It is a shock to me too. Want to bury it up inside him like an animal. Once I want to do that, "fuck" him, though, I imagine him crying out, and what he is, my David, going away. Once I "fuck" him in the butt. I don't hear and see the word *fuck* in my sixteen-year-old brain. I don't know if I have a word for it then, I just know the image of it, the pain it would cause. He is too little, and I know once I do that it would all be over. He'd bleed up there. Evidence they might see. Bloodstains in his underwear, a red starburst. I would hurt him physically with my love, but hurting him might make it better, I'm thinking: might give me the chance to bring him back from the hurt, to massage the hurt I had caused away.

I let him go, though. I'm too chicken, and maybe I love him too much to actually do it, or I'm just holding off for a better place, for in my dreams I have "fucked" David on a silver-sheeted bed somewhere in a drippy, flowery Paris, France, saw him want it in my dream, saw him laugh joyously and seduc-tively as I did it, laugh and laugh, and it fit, *I* fit, into him per-fectly.

David stands there in the Port-O-Let, looking at me as if I am a stranger.

We leave soon after. We go out and get back into the

Impala. Mom falls asleep, tired of keeping me away from David, tired of always losing that fight.

David and myself watch headlights in silence.

David's mom whispers to his dad up front, "What a lovely journey."

David's dad goes, "Just please shut the hell up."

12
TROY

"Just please shut the hell up," Doris says, just a joke. You know Doris. Always joking. We are standing outside a Day-Glo–painted trailer that has a funky, stylish sign on it: BE A STAR!!!

We have ridden rides for two hours. Every ride. Even the rollercoaster, where when we got on there were paramedics helping a little boy with a bloody nose, and Lyle looks at me and says, "Don't worry." All serious, he was not going to let anything hurt little old me. Doris had to sit all by herself, as she was too damn big for the two-seaters. Still, she screamed like a little girl. I screamed like a little girl too. Lyle and myself rode together, his bony knees coming up toward his chin, and as we went up the coaster's biggest ramp he turned to me and offered me his hand to hold, and I took it, hoping Doris wouldn't see.

After riding some other rides, we ate the same crap Mom and I did at Indiana Beach years before, watched a country-music show with some bearded, middle-aged fat guy pretending to be Waylon Jennings, singing along to a tape.

The whole time, Doris and Lyle kept mentioning how much fun, how much fun.

Now Lyle wants to go into this trailer where you can record yourself singing the hits of yesterday and today. He wants all three of us to go. The trailer is right next to the Tarantula ride toward the back of the midway here, and it zooms dangerously, big black tentacles with baskets at the end. I stare at the neon piping on each tentacle, swirling like what you see when you close your eyes and rub.

"You can sing, Doris," Lyle says again.

"I told you to shut the fuck up," Doris says, but she is playful, she wants to record, to become a Muncie Free Fair Superstar. I just stand there, all blurry from confronting the Tarantula. It is my new god, something to pray to, an idol. It whirs up into the air, and the people riding it scream and laugh, then it plummets back down to earth, as if it is going to hit concrete in a tragedy of epic proportions.

"She can sing," Lyle says, turning toward me. "Can you?" He grins, trying to seduce me by acting cute.

I nod my head. I used to, when I went to church, sing in the choir. Sing in a high-pitched, fake-sweet voice.

Over the PA system hooked up outside the trailer, a man's deep-pitched voice is singing an off-tune rendition of "Butterfly Kisses," with a scratchy orchestra backing him up.

"It's fifty bucks, Lyle," says Doris.

Lyle pulls his wallet out, flashes his Visa, smiling. "Everywhere you want to be."

Doris laughs and laughs. Such fun kids. We go on in. A teenaged girl with red hair gives us a list of songs we can do, and we finally choose "The Flame" by Cheap Trick.

"They totally rock," Lyle says, grinning. "I used to have all their albums, when I was in high school."

The trailer's interior is paneled in dark red Formica with a burnt-orange linoleum floor and aqua and lime-green chairs, like a really cheap MTV set, pictures on the walls of fake gold records and recording stars xeroxed and colored in with markers. We fill out the necessary paperwork have to come up with a name for our group, as they laser-print out a cover for the cassette they give you. Of course, Doris writes "Three's Company." She laughs. I laugh, so does Lyle. There's something so wrong with this that I like it suddenly. I am being led through, as though I am nothing, and these two are everything. I am completing their pervertedness by being number three.

Lyle pays with his card. We go back to the "studio" at the end of the trailer. We surround a music stand with the lyrics of "The Flame" displayed on it. Headphones dangle from the stand, and we put them on, the AC purring, the smell of old hair and mildew and their colognes, me in the middle, the microphone in front of us, like one of those in the "We Are the World" video. We get two practice sessions, and we start right off. Coming through the headphones is the actual song done by Cheap Trick. We try to sing along with the guy who is singing. The music starts getting to me, filling me up.

This Cheap Trick song is not that bad actually, almost a country ballad, lush and bittersweet, and when I sing along with the guy's voice I don't hear Lyle and Doris. Then the guy's voice fades, and I just hear myself. I start belting out the slightly cheesy lyrics, as if suddenly there is no tomorrow, only today: today and the words that are in my head.

> *Wherever you go I'll be with you*
> *Whatever you want I'll give it to you*
> *Whenever you need someone*
> *To lay your heart and head upon*
> *Remember after the fire, after all the rain*
> *I will be the flaaaaaaaaame*
> *I will be the flame.*

We do our final taping, sounding pretty good, at least at that moment. Of course, as I sing, I think of David. Imagine a video with images of him splashing across the screen as I sing into a microphone with true feeling. Dressed up classy like

Barry Manilow or Elton John or Sting. Sentimental, serious, artistic. Maybe seated at a grand piano. See David running to me. See David eating a sandwich. See David riding his bike. Kissing me in bed. Saying good-bye. Waving. Disappearing. But always coming back again.

Lyle looks like a gospel star as he sings, some hyperventilating evangelical superstar. He opens his eyes to wink at me, to wink at Doris every once in a while. Doris keeps fucking up and laughing, but then they can edit out mistakes.

After we finish, we go out to the MTV room to listen to what we have done. The red-haired girl sits us down in here and then walks out without saying anything else, tired from ugly people like us, dumb-asses who think they can sing, adults acting like goddam shameless kids (which if you think about it is a pretty good definition of what a pervert is). After she turns back, we can hear our singing loud through speakers. For a second, I'm thinking we aren't bad. Then I notice Lyle listening. He has a face of ecstasy, his half-rotten teeth showing, Doris sitting beside him, that huge chunk of cleavage, that hair: Who am I to judge?

I listen, and the beauty of the song, if there ever was any in it, is drained off, like grease from meat onto a paper towel. There is no innocence, only their slightly sickening joy at hearing themselves sing the Cheap Trick song. It seems that unless people are almost dead and old and decrepit, I cannot tolerate them anymore. Old and half-dead, or six and completely new. I mean nude. Completely nude. Freudian slip.

Lyle smiles great big, lifting his eyebrows up.

"Pretty good," he goes, the song finishing.

"Yeah," I say.

The fluorescent light in here, the Day-Glo pukey colors, the sweaty odor outside from the fair, Lyle's sad ecstasy, the Tarantula ride, this and that—it all comes into me like smoke being blown into my mouth, shotgun-style. I always go back to

David. No matter what. Go back to that moment in time, as living within the present is like tasting an undercooked egg every day of your life, like spraining your ankle and losing your voice every day of your stinking life, like sewing on a fucking button, etcetera. Then I make out the two of us, David and myself, in a bottle, formaldehyde-soaked fetuses in a science laboratory. I envision David as the perfect fetus. Fish-faced alien against the wallpaper of a womb. Picture those webby hands reaching out, like the hands know more than the brain. Fetal eyes, empty spoons, black holes.

We have a cassette tape with a laser-printed label: *"The Flame" by Three's Company*. In the jeep, Lyle plays it over and over. "The Flame" becomes my own personal torture. "The Flame" gives me heartburn, but also it has become, to us in the jeep, a goddam national anthem.

Doris turns around. "Your place or ours?"

"Mine."

I smile. I am detached but also understand what she means. Understand her. Understand what we will be doing. Understand the whole fucking schematic of the thing. Like I understood my mom's face the last time I saw David.

My boy and myself take a bath together. My boy and me have lots of bubbles. In that, I aim to "fuck" him. "Penetrate" has become the word.

How I helped him out of his clothes. How I told him before that outside in the garage, smelling his hair, "You stinky, honey," in a clown's baby-talking voice.

He agreed. He was so lost. He agreed he stinkied.

How we come into my house, never having done a bath together. Seems like we would have, but no. The move into the bathroom. Mom's rose-and-daisy wallpaper. Out with Shar, who likes to pretend the bathtub is her secret hideout, behind the pink plastic shower curtain.

David naked. You know what I am saying. And the Mr.

Bubbles, a pink box with a silver spout attached, Mr. Bubbles a see-through soap bubble on the box with a face smiling like a benevolent God.

And me singing that Beatles song, "Mother Nature's Son," as I don't think "The Flame" had even been recorded at that time.

And me, myself, and I not locking the door because Mom was working a double but then just when I get into the luke-warm suds with him, into that new luxury I have found with him, thinking of letting him slowly feel me go up into him there, his back to me, his little spine shining out from that white Mr. Bubbles foam. I find his hole in the bubbles and he begins to feel the total terror of it, the fear you get when it happens.

That's when the door opens, hangers on the hook clanging, the doorknob turning: me and Mr. Bubbles and my best friend David, interrupted by fate or what have you.

(Lyle and Doris are gone now, and I guess I could show you what we did, but will not, as it does not really matter, but Lyle and myself did it while Doris watched, playing with her bad self, and some things, believe me, are not fit to print, so I will now go on to explain to you how I tried to commit suicide.)

That night, Mom was going to make us a yellow cake with chocolate frosting. She bought all the stuff to make it on her way home, as she had got off early from work. (She told me all this later on, while I waited to be discharged from the psych unit.)

Mom came home, put the grocery sack down in the kitchen first off. Put it down, and heard the water running in the bathroom. Shar kept barking. Sometimes Mom would buy cake mix to make herself feel better. That sounds pretty stupid, but often cake mix could do the trick, cake mix with frosting, or some of those coconut candies from the Dollar General Store. She was a beautifully simple (not simpleminded) woman.

The water kept on running in the bathroom, though. Mom got scared right off, as I normally did not take baths. Just showers. Louie, my dad, took baths. Like a cowboy in a western, every Saturday night whether he needed to or not, Louie would joke, and maybe it really was Louie, my mother thought that night, and she got scared. Louie's ghost taking a bath.

Mom stirred the yellow batter good with a wood spoon. Her mixer was out. Stirred, listened to the water, stirred, listened. It cut off. She heard me.

Troy never takes baths, she thought. Never.

Then Mom heard another voice, a little voice, and water splashing. She poured batter into a greased and flowered cake pan and shoved it into the oven, made her frosting according to the box, which was pretty hard as the directions were to use a whipper. Shar came in then and Mom picked her up, kissed her head, put her back down, worried. She went on back to investigate the bathroom.

There I am. I can see it through my mom's eyes. In a goddam bubble bath, David and myself. When I see her face, flabby and so pale, I feel the whole universe come to a halt.

"You get out of that goddam bathtub right now," Mom says, her face blank and angry with awe. She would not ever recover her other facial expressions. She was still in her Holiday Inn Buffet uniform.

I was a skinny teenager, bubbles of foam going down my shiny white skin, my privates, you know, excited. Caught by her finally, I was relieved, shocked, and terrified, but then numb from knowing I was not going to be allowed to do it anymore. It felt as though all of me was just inside her eyes, merging with her optic nerve, or maybe her soul.

David stood and ran to her, crying.

"Let's dry you off," Mom whispered.

I stood there, dripping, frozen. Mom got David toweled off, dressed as best she could. Combed his hair. His face was empty like the inside part of a mask.

Out in the living room, her cake smelled so warm and clean. Shar was chasing her tail, trying to be funny, by the couch. David had stopped crying all the way now. Mom sat on the couch and tied his shoes for him. I watched her do this. When she was finished, she looked up. I was standing in my underwear in front of her, still wet and sudsy, the underpants I had put on wet too.

"He can't go," I whispered, caught and stupid. I wanted him back with me as soon as she tied his shoes.

Mom laughed sarcastically, her auburn hair matted with sweat. She had just had it. David stood there, looking around the room.

"Yes, he is going right now, Troy!" Mom yelled very loud.

I said, "I love him!" I guess it was the only defense I had.

Then I started to cry.

"I love him!" It was a declaration I suddenly wanted the whole neighborhood to hear.

"No, you do not." Mom was staying on the couch, holding David's hand. But then she stood up and jerked David toward her. "Get in there, and you dry yourself off, buddy, and you just dry off!"

I sobbed. David started to, too.

"Now, don't you go doing like him," Mom said to David, crazy with all this, in her singsong momma's voice.

"No!" I yelled, going toward them.

She knocked me down. Her strength at that point was amazing. It felt like I'd been pushed down by a prison guard.

They left then, with me on the floor. I got up a few minutes after they were gone, and I took the damn cake out of the oven.

Maybe it was my first moment of apology, or maybe my last. I know I got some dish towels out of a drawer, still in my soggy underwear, dripping almost-gone suds, opened the oven door.

I took the cake out, put it on a plate, shaking it out very slowly so that its whole oblong body came out in one piece. This was very important to me. I was without the words to say, or scream, anything, and I stopped crying. Quickly I went out to our garage after doing the cake, still in my underwear, went to the table where earlier David and myself were playing school, got magic markers and a piece of paper, drew a flower with a peace sign at the center, and multicolored petals, a green stem with two leaves coming out of a red red heart. Beneath that I carefully wrote "DAVID + TROY."

I folded it and Scotch-taped it to one of the painted-on windows. As I did that, I wondered if he would find it. Wondered if he cared. Because I was going to do what I had told him I would now. Right now.

I was scared shitless. A scared-shitless, born-again Christian molester just caught by his mother. Still I was in love, though. Still.

I walk back into our house, and when I pass the perfect cake and smell it like the perfect smell of fabric softener from a dryer vent or the clean sweat that comes from running a long time, I feel this utter exhaustion that almost pleases me. A sleepiness from the shame, sure, but also from recognizing that I will keep my word for once. I think of God then, who isn't the God I thought He was, just a passing thing, like a wart that goes away, or a mole changing color; God is not God, and then I know that I am now through the phase of pretending not to know what's right and what's wrong.

Now I know exactly who to blame, and it is not even God, or even David.

Of course it is me.

And that makes this very religious, as, slowly as Joan of Arc,

I go tragically past Shar licking her butt on a living room chair, past Mom's lavender-dream sofa, into the small hall, into the bathroom. John 3:16 pops into my skull. The one about for God so loved the world he gave his only begotten Son, and as I search for good razors after closing the door, that stuff goes through my brain like rain, each tiny word a separate drop, each drop made up of a thousand religious molecules.

When I cut the wrist of the left arm it hurts like a paper cut, and I bleed all over the place. Float down, animated by Walt Disney. The other wrist I do, nervous as a cat. The sound of a pillow rubbing against a bed, that's the sound of this shitty razor going through soft skin. Blood doesn't pour. It sort of trickles. I like it even though it hurts. I don't like the hurt, but I like the change in myself.

Calgon take me away: blood filling the tub, already filled with Mr. Bubbles and possibly David's pee. I let my wrists sink to the bottom like fish with sliced throats, feel the bathtub water go into my cuts, feel my death-angel come over and laugh at what I tried to do, which is not enough. Never enough.

After finding me, Mom did not take me to a place in Anderson, as she did not want any of this coming out. She checked me into a Muncie hospital, down the interstate. I got put into the psych unit right away. Later Mom would tell me, "Your wrists, like I figured, were just fine. You used one of them old razors I shaved my legs with."

The doctors kept asking me why, and I never told them a thing. That one doctor even, the nice one who looked like Tony Orlando, even him. The psych unit was on the third floor east, and you had to go to a secret elevator to get to it, say your name in the P.A. after pressing the 3E button.

Mom visited me every other day in there, brought me

sweets and books and magazines, even my Holy Bible. As Mom and Louie had been renting the house month-to-month because Louie had been thinking of retiring anyways, selling the station and going to Florida, she moved us out pretty easily, after getting a place in Muncie. One, two, three. I mean Mom did all of this while I was still in the hospital, while she was still working a full-time job, and she did it all probably with close to two hours' sleep a day.

Soon my hospital bills would pile up. Soon I would get out and have to start in a new school, but that was okay. I was going to become a new person, little by little.

Right now I was sitting in the psych unit, close to being let out. Mom came in with a head scarf on, mint-green polyester skirt, a floral blouse. Right before my very eyes there she is, thin and scary, but smiling, holding a fruitcake pan full of fresh-baked cookies. I am sitting on an orange vinyl chair in that stink-pit dayroom with beige grease-streaked walls and posters of kittens. Other, of course, crazies in pajamas, old ladies and young, teenaged boys and baldheaded ex-businessmen, all of them were around. Only Mom's eyes were focused on me. I was coming back to myself. I was getting a philosophy going. Smiling too, like her, in my pair of pajama bottoms and a fresh white T-shirt, just a little bit of toothpaste spit on it. I was on major tranquilizers.

Mom sat down beside me, gave me the pan of oatmeal cookies. "Here," she said, still smiling.

"Mom," I said, making that word last too long, turning it into a hum. I looked in at the cookies after taking the lid off. These weren't from a box. These she had made from scratch in the tiny kitchen in the new apartment she'd found us in Muncie. I was overjoyed, I guess. Full of pain, full of gratitude—that kind of joy.

"Mom," I said again.

"What?" my mother said.

The room smelled of bad breath and Right Guard. Nurses monitored everyone from their station. Mom looked at me as I tried to come up with something to say. She got nervous and said, "No matter what, you are still my son." Her lips closed tight, but then opened up again. "Me and Louie's," she added. "You don't know how long we waited, Troy, how many times we were promised, and finally we just had to make do."

"I—" I started to say.

"What?"

I bent toward her like an old man.

"I don't love him anymore," I whispered. That was the biggest lie I have ever told, but at least I wanted it to be the truth.

"Shhhhh," said Mom.

I started crying, but stopped. Something must've hit me in the head then that this was an opportunity to get all of this closed up, nice and neat. Then we, my mother and myself, could just go on. Which is exactly what we did.

"I'm ready to forgive you," Mom said, in a whisper. "Just don't get upset no more. And don't do it no more." Then she sat up straight and stared at me. She said, "Now let's just get on with life. Okay? I can't take no more of this foolishness. Do you understand?"

I smiled right then. I did. I understood. My eyes were filled with tears. I understood!

"I can't love anyone," I whispered, but it was not pessimistic. It was as if it had just come to me, this brilliant idea.

"I cannot love anyone," I said louder.

Mom looked at me with compassion, with her mother's love that had been worn out but still was there for me.

"Even me?" she laughed, punching my shoulder in a joking way.

I laughed too, but it was choked. I had a cookie. I swallowed the thing whole.

I don't know how I kept my mouth shut with those crafty Muncie, Indiana, psychiatric professionals. Just the mummification of David, I guess. Each word I did not say preserved his little ass. What I live on now is that glorification that he did not talk, and I did not talk. Telling would have turned it into something else altogether, would have bent it toward a change. All of it has stayed with me as is, and to find that preserved, to find that now, is why I am still alive.

Is why I can wake up to go to work at Sunnyhaven to exchange my time and labor for six-fifty an hour, to do what I must, because David let me have him back then, and all the rest of my life has been re-creating those moments, retelling the same 1972 story like a videocassette I am never taking back to the rental place. Constantly watching, constantly craving to watch.

Constantly feeling that feeling, the one that makes you want to live on even though you just fucking know you aren't really alive anymore.

That's me, and tomorrow will be that, the next day too. Poor, poor, pitiful little me.

Find pleasures in the little things, some fortune cookie once said. What was inside that cookie on a tiny piece of paper happens to be the complete and unedited story of my life.

PART FOUR

13

TARA

Saturday night, Dave and I go over to the hospital to see Paul. The smiley-faced social worker happens to be there.

"Hey! You two! I am so glad I caught you," the guy says. It looks to me like he gets his hair bleached.

Dave's dad is asleep then. We have not gone in yet, just to the door. He's been sleeping the whole time, skinny as a rail, covered up, lots of equipment. I hate seeing what he's been put through to stay alive.

This social worker comes up to us, saying in his prissy voice, "Can you come with me to my office for a few minutes? I was gonna call you, but now you're here. I spoke to Dr. Calusin-kinghom, just last night, about Paul . . ."

He keeps smiling in that fake hospital way. We really don't have any choice, so we follow him to his office in the back, a little room the size of a walk-in closet. "Um," he says, sitting down behind his desk, rolling up his sleeves. "I'm not normally here on Saturday nights, but I got caught up in something." He keeps flashing that smile, nervous but trying to stay gentle.

Dave is very quiet, not looking up from the floor. He gets totally quiet doing stuff like this, never wants to have to take things serious. Maybe he doesn't know how to. He's all for going out to eat and having a birthday party and this and that. When it comes right down to it, he avoids most anything of a serious nature.

But then Dave does look up, and he says, "So what's going on?" I sit close to him. Paul keeps going through my head. Paul sleeping with his mouth wide open. Paul standing outside his trailer, afraid to go in.

"The doctor thinks it might be time for us to think about care options once Paul leaves the hospital."

"Is he getting that much better?" Dave asks. "Because the way Dr. CK has told us is that it don't look good?" Dave looks back down at the floor.

"No," the social worker says. "Um. Dr. Calusinkinghom is going to give you the details. God. The situation is getting worse."

Looking the guy right in the eyes, I say, "We'll let the doctor tell us."

"I know that, but what you might want to do real soon is go over to the Department of Welfare in your county, okay? You live in Anderson, right?"

Both of us nod.

"Go to the Madison County Department of Welfare and fill out the application for Medicaid. Okay?"

"What?" Dave asks.

"I think once he gets out of here your dad will be moving into a nursing home. Now, um, his insurance through his work won't pay for anything home-based, except for home health aides, and he is going to need a lot more than that. Lots more. So get him on Medicaid, and he can move into a nursing home."

Dave says, "The cancer ain't regressing?"

I touch Dave's arm, but he pulls it away.

"I'll let the doctor tell you all that. He wants to meet with you on Monday." The social worker stands up from his little chair, crosses away from the desk and leans back on it, looking at both of us. His prissy, professional smile is now gone, replaced by a dumb, hopeless frown. I appreciate that, though, this moment of his being real to us.

"Just tell me now," Dave says.

"Tell us," I say, taking up for Dave.

"Well, it's not regressing, according to Dr. Calusinkinghom, and it's spread. He'll give you details. He just told me that probably the best after-care will be at a nursing home or maybe even a hospice. Both types of facilities have nurses on-staff twenty-four-seven. He'll need that. Now, I am going at this like your father does not have a lot of resources, am I correct?"

Dave mumbles his little yes.

"Good. Because it's gonna be majorly difficult, but I've seen people in worse situations pull on through."

That final pep talk makes me want to puke. But we don't get mad. We let him finish.

"We're looking at maybe next Thursday as his discharge. Hopefully into a nursing home around your area. Now, sometimes there aren't any beds in local nursing homes, but I'm going to make some calls and get one as close to you as humanly possible."

Again that smile. He shakes hands with Dave, but I am already walking off. I hear him in the background giving Dave the address of the welfare office in Anderson.

We've never gone to welfare before.

Dave walks up to me, lost and his mouth half-open. I try to be close to him. Try to be his strength. But it feels like he wants to be left alone. This dad thing has sent him into a major depression, and even though he took the day off yesterday, you can tell he still won't be able to be his normal self. He has always been a sensitive guy, sure, but also he's always had a good sense of humor. Practical jokes make him crack up, I mean crack up. We used to watch *America's Funniest Home Videos,* and just both of us would die. I know it's stupid as hell, but somebody falling on ice or a baby falling into its birthday cake—that's our kind of stupid sense of humor. Three Stooges and Saturday-morning cartoons, you know, the suave skunk chasing the scared cat. Dave used to sometimes imitate that skunk's French accent. I mean I'd be laughing my ass off and getting turned on too.

Now, as we approach his dad's room at the back past the nurse's station, he tells me he doesn't want me to go in with him. All this time I thought I was needed, and for a second I want to lash out at him.

"What?" I say.

His face, you need to see it: it's got fatter in the last few weeks, like he is growing within it, growing out, a double chin, a bigger forehead. But his body is losing weight, funny enough. His hair is going. He's handsome still. He's cute, but the weight change makes him look wounded and used up.

"You can go with me, but we won't say nothing about this. I'll tell him later sometime."

I don't say anything. Then as we go in, Paul's still sleeping anyways. He looks like what I said, but more innocent than I remember. Like he is about to float up out of himself. Dave stands, and I sit. We watch him. I look at Dave, in his golfing outfit.

I whisper, "You can tell him tomorrow."

"I guess."

"You don't want me to come and help you?"

"No," he says. Then he starts crying. The tears fall out of his eyes, but he doesn't seem to want me to notice. He doesn't make a sound.

"No. I need to be a man about this."

His dad won't wake up, and we don't want him waking up on us, really. It might be too scary to see his eyes open. To hear how weak his voice is.

Finally we just go home.

. . .

I remember at our wedding reception his dad got so damn blitzed it was embarrassing for everybody. Dave's mom had her new husband there, and Dave's dad came stag of course, and he got blitzed on wine. His dad in a sky-blue tuxedo. A funny sweet drunk, he came over and asked me for a dance.

"I don't know," I said, surrounded by all the presents we raked in. Boxes of Fry-Daddies and towels and even somebody got us a sex book as a joke. Big old encyclopedia of sex. Makes you wonder what happens to all that stuff in your daily living. I don't have a Fry-Daddy or any good towels or plates left to speak of.

Dave was over by the front doors. He was with his mom and her husband as they were leaving. I looked at Dave's dad's big face. Short guy, big head. Bald. Red from being drunk.

"You don't know?"

He laughed and got into my face. His breath just reeked.

"I promise," he said. "I promise I won't embarrass you, darling."

I got up, hypnotized suddenly. I could not disappoint my new in-law, now could I? Our reception was in what used to be this Pizza Hut, but they'd turned it into a rental party hall, over by the high school. Silver and blue balloons, and all our friends. Not too many left now, close to the end where we would have the traditional throwing of the rice. There was a DJ from the lite-rock station one of my girlfriends was dating at that time. Dave's dad drug me over there. Me in that damn dress Mom picked out for me, not letting me have a say-so, some big dumpy ornate thing. Like I was a big beautiful virgin queen (not).

The DJ, this middle-aged guy with a severe chin like Jay Leno and an eye patch and long, curly hairstyle, was behind the turntables and tape decks he'd set up with a banner of WLNK LITE-ROCK 97.5, THE LINK.

"You got any Eddie Arnold?" David's dad asked, serious as a heart attack.

"No," the DJ said, smiling.

"Huh," Paul said. He was just dripping the sweat. "How's about Patsy Cline?"

"I guess so, yeah, here, I think I do." The DJ stooped down to a milk crate of records he'd brought. "Yeah. Got her greatest hits here. Yeah."

Paul was all smiles. He had dentures. He had led a hard life of drinking and carousing, and, God, did he look it. Cleaned up, he wasn't bad. I thought if Dave turned out like this when he was fifty, it might be okay. Potbellied and drunk, but mostly friendly—too friendly, really—and sweet and kinda pathetic. These were qualities that drew me to Dave.

I remember: that song still hangs out in my head like birds inside a picnic shelter. Whenever I come across it, like one time when me and Tammy, a friend of mine, rented *Sweet Dreams* with Jessica Lange back when Dave was working nights, before Brit was born, that movie about Patsy Cline, and Jessica Lange was singing along with "Crazy," I got goosebumps, the *oooo-ooooo* background voices and the tinkling piano keys, Patsy Cline's voice on the edge of crying, but she isn't taking any shit either. Whenever I hear that song, I get goose pimples because you know what?

Even though Paul Brewer was drunk as a skunk, he danced *right*. I mean this man held me in his arms—danced me around. The song was like a religious song. Paul's face as he danced was like he was trying to get us both somewhere. There was joy, pure and true, in his face.

I hope that doesn't sound stupid. Now that he is asleep, a dying man with cancer. But even in his sleeping face you can see that he liked to be alive. Paul liked, he loved, the taste of all the booze that got him here, and all the you-know-what-else he'd done, whatever: all the sin he had committed. That was him and the way he lived, the way he wanted to live, and he can't get out of that now anyway.

I remember too that night at the reception Dave was watching us. "Crazy" played again, as Paul screamed he needed to hear it one more time, chugging from his big tumbler of white wine.

"Paul Brewer," I said, a blushing bride, "you are one crazy son of a bitch."

Dave didn't like me cussing, but Paul laughed like a hyena. This made Dave laugh, and after saying good-bye to his mom and her husband, Dave looked happy. Just me and Dave and Paul and the DJ and a few others were left. That song come back on, like I said, in the ex–Pizza Hut. Magic time, right? Dave come over and asked to dance with me, but Paul said no, no, no.

He took Dave in his arms and they danced. Both of them laughing. Laughing and laughing, me standing off at the side, laughing too. They danced awkward as all hell, but still it was nice to witness it. Afterwards, Dave came up to me and said, "Boy is he blitzed," and then I looked and saw old Paul just land quietly onto the floor. He laid there with his legs spread like a toddler, looking up at the ceiling and yelling now that the music was gone, still yelling the words: *I'm crazy for trying and crazy for crying and I'm crazy for loving you.*

I drop Dave off at the house. I gotta go get Brit. He doesn't want to see Mom, so I agree to let him off. Right before I pull in, I get a good look of his face, the same face he had on when he was standing there with his mom in the parking garage the night of his dad's surgery. His cold fish of a mother wanting to get the hell out of Dodge, and he stood beside her trying not to cry. I wondered why she even came. It was like he was this little kid all over again with her. It pissed me off. She just starts her

Accord and bye-bye. After she took off, Dave turns to me like I am supposed to help. I was supposed to make it all better somehow. I don't have that kind of power, I wanted to say.

She left, not knowing if Paul was going to live or die! I wanted to like say something smart-assed about her, something hurtful, but I kept my mouth shut. A few days later he got a card in the mail. A card meant for a kid, a puppy dog with a thermometer in its mouth on the front. *Son, I Hope You Feel Better Soon* in curlicue writing, and inside she wrote the simplest message she could: "David, I am so sorry. Love, Your Mom."

Dave took the card and read it, his face not changing except the jaw muscles going tight. He gave the card to me in the kitchen, not saying anything. I put it in a drawer somewhere after looking at it. I just couldn't throw the thing away.

Now I leave the car running and watch Dave go into our little white house in the headlights, his head tilted down. Lights click on in the front windows. I get a creepy feeling like I should go in to see if he's okay, but I pull out.

Mom is in her big maroon nightgown, watching a movie she rented with Jane Seymour. *Dr. Quinn, Medicine Slut,* I kid her all the time. In the movie, Jane Seymour is traveling back and forth in time with Christopher Reeve.

"He was so handsome," Mom says, on her big flowery couch.

"He's still living, Mom."

"Yeah, but his neck broke."

"That doesn't mean he's ugly," I say.

Mom just shakes her head. "You are always wanting to argue, aren't you?"

I just let it go.

"Britty's sleeping too good," Mom says after coming back from checking on her. She got her a baby crib special for her apartment here. "Why don't you just let her stay all night, Tara?"

I'm afraid I'm letting her stay all night too much over here,

afraid she won't know me if I keep doing that. Mom clicks the
TV off.

"So how is he?"

"Pretty bad," I say.

Mom goes over to her sewing machine, the big one she
bought last year, space-age thing she can do like fifteen thousand kinds of stitches on. She pulls from the cupboard underneath a pack of cigarettes, ashtray, and gold lighter.

"Mom," I say. She told me the other day she was quitting,
but still I'm just glad she has some.

"I've been so nervous about old Paul and just—well, I don't
know. I know I said I was gonna quit, but I'm nervous in general. I know it is a big sin and I'll die of emphysema or whatever, but I just needed some. My emotional crutch."

She laughs loud. I love her right then as she gives me one,
and we go out on her little patio-type porch, sitting on the
swing she had put up last summer. The apartment manager
was against it, but she did it anyways. Her complex overlooks
this cornfield right behind a line of fast-food joints, and the
light from the fast-food places gives the cornstalks a back-glow.

Mom smokes like it's her version of sex, and I probably do
too.

"He's dying," I say.

"That's hereditary, you know," Mom says.

"What?"

"Cancer."

"So?"

"So Dave needs to be careful. Get examined."

I laugh, hurt. Her saying crap like that when all I want to do
is forget about cancer and forget about death.

"Mom, shut up."

"What?"

But I just sit back and watch the corn. Smelling Mom's and
my smoke. Listening for Brit.

Mom doesn't say anything else. I go ahead and let Brit stay all night.

Back at our house, Dave is asleep on the La-Z-Boy, reclining all the way back. In the dark he looks like a man thrown from a car, out onto the road. Spread out, comatose. On the screen are Brit and me sitting and playing patty-cake. I wish I would have brought Brit home with me. Sometimes she sleeps with us, I know that's bad, one of us could roll over on her and kill her, but I'll go get her some mornings, and Dave gets this grin on his face, you'd have to see it, just like *Look what me and you did. Look,* his face says.

I look at her daddy's face now. Suddenly his eyes are open, which scares the crap out of me. "Are you sick?" I say, my first impulse.

"No," he says. His expression is all pouty-looking and red-pink, almost like a picture of a bad little boy in a story book. The love I feel for Dave right then isn't the deep kind you have for a husband, or even a boyfriend. It's the love you have for dying animals or far-off starving children.

"You are always watching this," I say, laughing.

He still doesn't look right, but he puts a grin on. "Do you know how much I love you and her?" he whispers.

"No," I say, stunned, not because he said that but because his voice is so weak and different.

"Well, I do," he says. He sits up, goes over and turns off the video. He comes back and kisses me. The kiss is like stale bread, dry and cold, but you can tell he wanted it to be something beautiful. Maybe that's what counts, after you've been with somebody so long.

"You smoking?" he says, pulling away.

"Yeah," I say.

"Don't do that," he whispers.

Dave goes and sits back down. I look at him, and I don't know what to say, but finally I go: "We both love you too."

He closes his eyes back, like he wants to play possum, or he wants to really go to sleep. "I hope so," he says, keeping his eyes shut.

I stand there, looking at him, until finally I just go and get ready for bed.

14

PAUL

Irene, my ex, came in the night before my surgery. She did not hug me or nothing. She had short hair, wore pants. A fancy elegant wristwatch.

"Look who's here," I said. "You and Jerry doing okay?" Inside myself, I did not want to be jealous. Hell, I'm sick as a dog, don't have time to be jealous, but still I felt like that.

Irene just smiles in her way. "We're all right." Smiles like she is supposed to. A funeral smile. I get mad, but hold it in. Embarrassed too that I might have a stink from being so sick.

"Yeah," I said, for no reason.

I mean you live with a person for close to twenty years . . . Mostly I remember the boring times which turn into the good times just from nostalgia. Me and her sitting around when Dave was a year old after he got put to bed when we were living in that apartment before moving to School Street, her flipping through a magazine or sewing in her housecoat and me drinking a beer in my sock feet. Then another beer, and she clicks on the radio to some news or country music because we didn't have a working TV. Maybe that was our problem—we never talked, we just sat there. Then again that silence we had going wasn't mean-spirited, just the comfortable decline of a long-assed day.

"So," I says, trying to sit up in the hospital bed to see her. Irene was way over on the other side of the room.

She laughed. No reason. Nervous.

"I guess you came to pay your last respects. To a dying man," I said.

She looked mad all of a sudden, and I was glad at least I could get a flicker out of her.

"You're not going to die, Paul," she said, smiling.

Really, what did I do that was so bad to her? I never laid a hand on her.

"I got a good chance," I said.

Irene came close to me and, in a whisper that was a little too loud, said, "Sounds like you want to."

She was looking straight into me. My face got cold, and I wanted to apologize to her. I licked my mouth.

"I don't want to," I said, so serious it accidentally went into an imitation of her loud whisper. "I don't want to lie to myself no more," I say, and it comes out embarrassing, like those kinds of things do. I imagined her forgiving me, although she did not say nothing.

Forgiving me for what? I'm thinking now. I get mad in my head, as mad as I can still get. I close my eyes and she is standing by the door, her face lost in fluorescence.

What are you forgiving, Irene? I imagine myself standing up from the bed and looking into her eyes, wanting an answer, all my goddam hospital equipment dangling out of my skin like sucking snakes.

"Forgive me for what?"

But Irene only says, suddenly her expression wild, suddenly her eyes wide open, suddenly her hands into fists, she says, "Ask Dave that question. Ask him!"

It's just a dream, I guess. I'm dreaming too much. She left hours ago. Days ago.

I roll on over into another dream. This next one is about my stomach which got took away. Took away and placed in somebody else's belly, a little kid's. It's on the news. In the dream I did the stomach operation as a volunteer to save this little kid's life. The kid's mom and dad were just really handsome people and the mayor gives me a great big key to the city, and all that. I'm a total hero. I can watch the surgery in the operation room, standing next to the surgeon. I don't got no mask on or nothing and I'm in my hospital skivvies, but still I stand by and watch as my stomach comes into the operation room in one of them coolers, iced and all. Opens up. My stomach is red and it is a baby. Are you kidding? My stomach is a baby. It has its own face and everything. It ain't screaming. It has its eyes closed. I get scared, as I see them open up this blond-headed boy to put my baby-stomach into him. Scared as hell. Want this whole thing stopped.

"That ain't my stomach," I tell one of the operation nurses.

"Yes it is, sir," she goes.

One of the operating surgeons says for me to be quiet, or I might have to be removed. It's my goddam stomach and I'd know my goddam stomach, I think in the dream. That ain't my goddam stomach!

"That there is a baby," I say.

They escort me out, putting me in a straitjacket right away. The kid gets the stomach put in and dies. At least that's what I think.

I'm carted off to another part of the hospital. It's ice-cold here and full of filing cabinets. I sit on this stool and feel dumb as hell. Like I made a goof of myself. On the floor is little drops of blood, and I notice from where they took my stomach out I'm goddam bleeding. Blood dripping out from under the straitjacket.

"Dave."

He is standing above me as I wake up. He has on a suit like an undertaker.

"Dad," Dave says.

I open my eyes wider.

"They say you might get released next week," Dave says.

"What time is it?"

"Huh?" Dave bends down closer so he can hear me. Then he laughs. "Oh. About eight on Sunday morning. I come over before I drove the church bus 'cause I can't come over this afternoon."

"Why not?"

"Got too much to do. My lawn is overgrown, Dad. I'm gonna try to give that old Escort a tune-up."

I straighten myself a little, automatic rush of real bad pain. My dream, my nightmare I had about my stomach, is still with me. I see the nurse's face in the dream, blurry but female-mustached.

"I get to go home," I say.

"Well, I'm not too sure about *that*, Dad. They say you'll probably go to a nursing home for a ninety-day convalescent stay. You can get your chemo and they can watch how your G-tube and colostomy thing is doing."

Dave is smiling. Smiling like he don't know what else to do but smile. That's the smile of someone who knows things.

"Nursing home?" I say. Pain still there. I see the nursing home in my head like a haunted house, or a ghost ship.

But I smile back at him. "Can't I just go on home?"

Dave's smile goes away. "The social worker here at the hospital told us that it might be better for a little while for you to go to the nursing-home place, so that there will be nurses around all the time just in case."

I want to make a run for it, but there ain't no way, so I try to get rational inside my own head. All along, since I started puking and shitting like I did way back last year, since I started feeling that pain, that rotten fucked-up pain, I'd been dismissing it, and *that* seemed rational. I'd down my Pepto, or take Rolaids, or get drunk or whatever, but now it was all over. No "rational" left. The jig was up, people. I was in Indianapolis, home of the 500. I was a dead little man. A nobody, if you really cut to the chase.

Dave goes and gets a chair and sits down. "You'll need to go on Medicaid." He isn't crying. I wish he was, then I could feel sorry for him. Right now, it's like it's his fault. I remember right then how I used to beat his butt for the silliest things. Beat his butt with a switch like my dad did me, beat Dave's butt for what? For getting money out of his mom's purse, for not washing the car, for watching too much TV. And now I am blaming him for my stomach cancer, ain't I? Want to beat his butt for that. But I know it ain't. His fault. Don't take the head off the messenger.

"Medicaid?" I manage to keep the conversation going. Can't swallow for a second.

"Yeah," he says without turning around. He starts talking about my healing process or whatever but I can't hear it no more. In fact, his words go away. I get a picture of David as the son I used to have when he was a kid.

Quiet, quiet kid, would rather color than go outside most of the time. I used to not like him as much as I do now, even though he is giving me this shit I don't want to hear. Used to belt him good too—not just switch him. Used to cuss at him. Used to joke with him too hard. You have to be gentle sometimes. Now he is going to have the pleasure of putting his old man into a nursing home.

Dave says, "Dad?"

I look up. "What?"

"Nothing's written down in stone."

"I ain't going to no goddam nursing home."

Dave just looks at me like he's shocked. "Don't, then. Fine. I'm going," he says.

"I guess you are," I say.

But then he bends down to me. He kisses my forehead, and

my feelings are hurt by that, the deep hurt I can only feel here.
I love the kid. You got to love him. Got to love a loser like him.

He stands there, not moving at all. Before he leaves, I fall
back to sleep. Him looking at me helps me to go to sleep.
Thank you, son.

Remember, Dave, the trip me and you and your mother took
when you was eleven? Remember? It was the summer of 1977.
We went to the Great Smoky Mountains. That's what we did.
Camped out, used this camper a friend of mine had. Remember, Dave?

(He's gone.)

You were a skinny little son of a bitch. Your mom was
skinny too. I had a little bit of a belly (not no more!). From
drinking. So we set up on this mountaintop to camp in this
ancient camper, and your mom is laughing at me 'cause I don't
know how to hook up the goddam propane.

"Laugh, you laugh all the fucking time, don't you?" I say.
But I'm jolly. I'm on vacation and I'm good and drunk. I'm an
easy guy to get along with.

You are as quiet as always, just a quiet little guy. You got on
cutoffs and a T-shirt, your hair buzzed. You are so pale. Need
some sun. Your mom is pale too, working all the time. That
woman loves work, don't she? Or maybe she's just trying to get
away from me.

She's got her hair curly-permed, and she has on a halter top
and shorts. Looks pretty damn good. This old camper is a Winnebago masterpiece. It's a piece of shit really, but, hey, it got us
here. We are near some evergreens and there's this pissy sweet
smell. It's close to sundown and I'm trying to hook up the goddam propane we bought at the bottom of the mountain so's
your mom and me can make steaks and fried taters and corn on
the cob plus there's an apple pie I bought at the grocery store

too and there's fresh whole milk in that Winnebago fridge. The ground is all orange nettles. There is a clean mountain chill. Clouds up here. Clouds just smear across your face like sheets drying on the line when I was a kid and I would go through the sheets on the line face-first, running back and forth while they was still wet to feel the cold wet sheet slapping softly into my forehead, eyes, lips.

Driving that damn Winnebago up the mountain, now that was scary as hell, Dave, the thing's worn-out transmission grinded all the way.

Dave, you were back there at that little dinette table, coloring. Eleven and coloring. I kid you not. You were coloring, and I saw you in the rearview mirror and I remember I loved you right then, like a news flash. Seeing you in the rearview mirror as it shook from the grinding gears, I loved you and I loved your mom.

If you want the Honest to God Truth, Dave:

I loved all of us.

The mountain air cleared my head. Cleared it right up.

Never did get the propane lit. Instead we used this electrical skillet your mom brought, hooked it up to the battery. Damn, that stuff was tasty. Your mom laughed all the way through and I remember now how much I loved her laugh, even though most of the time it pissed the hell outta me 'cause she was laughing at my stupid ass.

Me and you walked in the mountains up a trail, that next day. We went hiking up to the top of the Appalachian Trail. Heaved it up there, me and you. Looked like heaven. Up these rock faces and ugly, grass-covered mounds, up toward the sun, where the clouds just kind of lingered. Me and you, son, on the big green rock, clouds and sun on top of us. That view of nothing but trees and big humps, like animals from the prehistoric era, but mountains, everywhere, mountains, and you stood there, hand shielding your eyes.

"Where's Mom down there?" I said. "Can you point her out, hoss?"

You pointed down to where we could barely see that Winnebago. But yes it was her, we knew, the two of us.

I love God. God and the mountains. Dave, I don't want to get all fucking gushy at the end, 'cause I'm scared, 'cause I'm a damn dying man scared of dying and I'm telling you I love you so I won't burn in hell.

No. That ain't fair. I don't want you thinking the only reason I'm talking is 'cause I'm scared, Dave. No.

But, Dave, them clouds, Dave, wet like whales, see-through albino whales from some other place we never heard of, whales in the air, coming right into us, nineteen hundred and seventy and seven.

15

DAVE

Sunday, I picked Nathan up for the first time on the church bus. He was waiting behind the screen door. His mom had her waitressing outfit on behind him, and she had that puffy face of night work, like she had just got off. Nathan came out in a white shirt and red clip-on necktie for little boys and a pair of shiny new blue denims and tennis shoes. His mom reached around and opened the door. He came out slowly, but then he started running to the bus.

"How's it going there, Bud?" I said, opening the door.

For a sec, he stood at the bottom of the green stairwell up to the bus proper. I felt breathless, like this was another one of those moments which I will savor later. His mom shuts the door behind the screen, goes back in, Nathan at the bottom of the stairs, framed in the bus doorway. Pale with black hair, big eyes, he is looking up like he is going to walk up a ladder to me.

I have automatically forgot visiting my dad in the hospital. How dead he looked. Automatically forgotten. Over and out.

Nathan steps on and walks up and then plops down in the front seat on the right side of the bus.

"Yeah, there you go. Sit up front. There you are." I laugh.

We go on and pick up the redheaded twins, some old ladies

at a retirement community who don't have rides, and the three brothers who have the same haircuts and almost the same clothes but are three years apart each, coming out of a trailer. The whole time I keep my eyes on Nathan as he stares out the window, like this is some total new experience, a spaceship to Neptune. I wonder what made him want to come. But then I knew it was me, and I was flattered totally, and although I did not make a whole lot of conversation with him on the bus, I did look at him a lot, keeping my eyes on the road of course, but also I looked at him in the seat, and he would smile, noticing. Lick his lips and smile, but it was not the smile I wanted. This was a scared smile, a smile that he had made a mistake.

I wondered if it was his mom who pushed him to come. She seemed like she had wanted him to, had talked about being saved when she was a little girl, and then as I drove I think how she probably thinks that going to church will change things for him, turning him into a nicer boy. Someone she can be proud of.

We arrive at church, and I make it so Nathan is the last one off.

Nathan stands beside me, me holding him back while the others get off. I hold him by the shoulders, still sitting in the driver's seat, and people pass on by, the old ladies smiling as I hold on to him like he happens to be my property. I feel like they are okay with me and the boy, and this makes my heart open up like finally I have what I want (even though I know they just are seeing me as the kindly bus driver taking the new kid under his wing), but still I think they want me and Nathan together. They need us to be together, I think. I know I am reading into their faces, but still I have the proof that instant inside my head, and this is all I need.

I breathe down onto the top of his head. He must feel my hot breath. He don't move as the people pass us on by and go into the little white church at the end of the sidewalk. His hair smells of apple shampoo. He smells like a baby eating applesauce, getting it all over him.

I stand up and say, "Well, let me show you around, Bud."

"Okay," he says.

I hold his hand and walk down the stairs of the bus up to the church. I'll come back once I get him settled and park the big bus. I can see the church through his eyes then, how big and pretty and clean it must look to a little white-trash kid living in lower-income town houses. I felt him kind of cling. Mrs. Lewis, the pastor's small wife with high hair coiled up like some kind of beautiful hair-cathedral, comes over when we first come in.

"Dave, you got you a little adopted son there, don't you? Brit's going to be jealous," she said, laughing, her earrings dangling.

I laughed, feeling special with him.

"Yep. This is Nathan."

Nathan was right next to my leg, and he seemed, at least his face did, impressed how people seemed to look up to me here, like I was somebody people respected.

Mrs. Lewis bent down. Her face was pockmarked and covered with orange makeup. Her lips were glossy red.

"Welcome to Norris Road Baptist Church, Mr. Nathan."

She did a salute and walked off, laughing.

"That was the preacher's wife. Nice lady. Come on, Bud," I said in a low voice.

We walked down the hall off the foyer. It was dark here as no one had turned on lights because nobody was using the coatracks in the summer. At the coatracks in a dark place, by a water fountain, scared to do it but having to, I picked him up and I could feel him shaking and I kissed his cheek with a wet kiss, then wiped it off.

"I had to do that," I whispered. I had to, even here. My

teeth felt like they were buzzing inside my mouth, and my eyes were throbbing. But also I felt a little peace coming out, as I was doing this thing in church. Almost like it was supposed to happen in this way.

We made it to the back part, where Mrs. Maloney, a short woman with curly hair, was handing out little books to five other kids in this paneled room with blue carpet, folding chairs, and toys on the floor.

"Mrs. Maloney. This is Nathan, and he's new," I said.

He still clung to me, but Mrs. Maloney came over and took his hand.

"Always happy to have new gentlemen join," she said, her voice sounding like Miss Piggy's.

I stood in the doorway, and Nathan looked up at me. I smiled and I winked, and as soon as I left I knew he would be scared. Scared that he would not see me again, but then he would sit down at a folding chair, almost on the verge of tears he would sit down and then he would remember that it was me who drove the bus. He would be very glad then, because he would get it that I, me, I was his only way home.

I went out and parked the bus in the slot at the back of the gravel lot and sat there in my seat, shielded by heavy tree limbs hanging down in need of trimming. I smoked a cigarette in the church parking lot, seeing Dad in my head. Dad was going to die, and here I was more enraptured with my boy than with his death, terrified of myself, not of Dad dying, terrified of what I was gonna do next with this boy. I wondered to myself if the boy and my dad had anything to do with the other. I got this triangle in my head, this trinity, of me and Dad and the boy, connected by a strange dotted line, like the yellow passing line on highways, glowing. The three of us were somehow linked in the triangle-trinity of our minds: the Father and the Son and the Holy Ghost. Which one was which? I did not care if my dad died then, if the truth be known. I did and I did not. It was like I did not know him anyways. But I really did not know the boy either. The difference was that I needed to know the boy, and I needed not to know my dad.

But then I smoked and the sun was coming in all the cruddy windows of the bus, and I thought I would buy some Windex today and just like do all the passenger-seat windows on the bus, get a stepladder and do that outside and then come in and do the inside. Sunlight was glowing in the bus right now. I felt like I was more at home here, right now, than anywhere else.

I put the cigarette out with my fingertips after licking each tip. I walked out and shut the doors behind me. When I got back inside, there was singing going on already, beautiful singing. When churchgoers who can't sing get combined with the ones who can, you end up with this beautiful ragtag chorus going, and all voices when they combine sound complete, like the voices know one another in another way outside of human beings. This is what I heard. My heart was filled with a joy, which is the joy of knowing where I was, combined with knowing what the rest of the day held: me and Nathan, together somehow.

I walked on into the auditorium, smiling.

At the end of Sunday school, Mrs. Maloney made all six kids in her class hold hands and walk chainlike together into the auditorium where us adults and some of the teens already were gathered together after our Sunday-morning Bible study. As soon as they entered, I spotted Nathan among them, holding the hands of a girl and another little boy, but him glowing for me of course. The red carpet and dark pews, the organ and piano (nobody playing the piano because our pianist had passed on a month ago and no one else had replaced her), the silvery pulpit, the big painting behind the baptismal pool of a sky and trees, like a movie set. Nathan the central figure in the movie. Everything else grayed out. Just him and background.

I was sitting up front with Tara's mom, who had Brittany with her. Now, normally Brit would be in the nursery, but there was no other babies today, so Tara's mom decided just to see if Brit could tolerate regular church. She was doing pretty good. Tara, of course, was working.

I turn and get a better view of Nathan, and then I motion for him to come on over to us. He recognizes me and waves and breaks off from the other five. Stands next to me and Tara's mom, who has on sickly-sweet perfume and an elaborate dress made out of some fabric that shines.

Tara's mom goes now, "This must be that little boy, that little Nathan. Mrs. Lewis was talking about you. You are a cutie."

Me smiling, Nathan smiling. He was going to my little Christian Boy. All sweet and nice, you can tell, give his life over to Christ and to me. I liked me and Jesus Christ being on the same team together and choosing Nathan to join us.

Tara's mom lifted Brittany up so's he could walk and sit next to me. He did. Close. Clinging again.

When Reverend Lewis came up to the podium, everyone went quiet. There was this feeling like everybody had suddenly lost the ability to speak, and Reverend Lewis talked breathy into the microphone, telling people to bow their heads. Me and Nathan and Brittany and Tara's mom with her dyed red hair are a family. Brittany cried a little now, getting fussy. Pastor Lewis prays. I realize I'm not sposed to be having my eyes open, but then I see Nathan ain't got his closed either, and this turns out to be our little conspiracy. It is a sweet closeness mixed in with the pastor's praying through old speakers, me staring at Nathan, him staring back. My eyes feel glassy then, like I could pop them out and swallow them in a magic trick where my eyes would be made to come out from behind Nathan's ears after I swallowed them. I look good into Nathan eyes as Pastor Lewis prays. See something like what I have in my eyes in his: me inside his eyes vibrating maybe, but not, and then I feel like God was in there too. In Nathan's half-grown eyes.

Brittany starts crying big-time then.

"Shush," Tara's mom says. But Brittany keeps on and she has to take her in the back.

Pastor Lewis stops, then Alan Winston, who looks a little like a fairy—but that's okay, he has two girls and a beautiful wife—he stands up and leads the singing. People start the good and the bad mixing, and that chorus happens again, like the wounded and the healed are combining into a version of holiness. I lift Nathan up onto the pew, so that he is almost tall as me. He doesn't want to sing, and that's okay, little thing. But I sing, loud and proud, right next to him, holding up the red hymnal so we both can see the words of the songs. My voice comes out low-pitched, like I am trying to be a real man.

After two more songs, Pastor Lewis preached. It was about the Second Coming. He was on that big-time. Jesus coming like a thief in the night, you know. When he preaches about this I always take it seriously, scribble down notes in my Bible for later study although I don't have time to study nothing now that I'm so interested in Nathan and Dad's at death's door, but still I write down words in the margins of my old Bible, write down RAPTURE and MILLENNIUM and ANTICHRIST.

Times are ending, says Pastor Lewis.

"The millennium is almost here, folks. Look around you. At your government, at your neighbors, at your family, at your TV. End of the world, folks. This world. This ugly world. When I think of all the terrorist acts not only in the rest of the world, but right here in the United States, I am immediately reminded by the Lord of the verse in Genesis 6, verse 13. Let's turn in our Bibles to there right now."

Pastor Lewis is giving us time to turn in our Bibles, and we do. He finds his place and looks up. "'And God said unto

Noah . . . the Earth is filled with violence.' Well, the implication is beyond clear, folks. The same things that were happening before the great flood are happening now. The Bible says that this violence precedes the end of the world when Jesus will return to carry up His believers to Heaven. Jesus is seeing this, friends. Jesus is not blind. He is not stupid. He knows it's time."

Pastor Lewis grins and sweats. He knows he's right, and we all of us know he's right. Nathan sits next to me close, curled up against me almost, sleepy but listening. I love him better here in the middle of things.

"And, oh, when he comessss." Pastor Lewis stretches the *s* at the end, scopes out the audience, smiles like he is so happy that he belongs in a loony bin, but not the loony bin here on earth. "Oh Glory! When he comes I know I'm gonna be up there. What about you?" He whispers that last part, pointing out, squinting his eyes.

Nathan looks up at me, like the pastor was talking directly to him. I don't smile back 'cause I want him to know how this is serious business. This ain't kid stuff, Bud. I nod and look up at the pastor. I say "Amen," loud. Look back down at him. He smiles then. Then I smile. He seems to love me at this point, at least this is my interpretation. I mean I was driving the bus, I had given him money, had chased him, pursued him, walked him into Sunday School, came into his house and found him: maybe he loved me then because I was all there was to him and because I seemed to look at him like he was nothing but my own beautiful star.

Pastor Lewis wraps up by inviting sinners or "lost" people to come up to the front to be saved. Organ music by Miss Lily Randoll in the background, funeral music. Preacher Lewis is still sweating bad, his face a little crazy as he pleads for the lost to be born again, and after he puts out his call three more times, Nathan stands up, and I cannot tell you how good that feels, to know he has done this of his own calling.

Nathan is the only one going up. Walking down that red carpet.

Pastor smiles, there are polite laughs from the audience, people in the audience thinking, *Oh, how cute, this little boy wants to be saved.*

Then Pastor Lewis is looking at me. He motions for me to come on up. Like since it was me who found the boy, I could have the privilege of witnessing to him. I go up because I have to, because I need to, because I am being called to service.

I take Nathan's hand at the front, before everyone. I take Nathan to that little room beside the baptismal tank, the little room smelling of chlorine, the organ sounds vibrating the shaky door handle. Two folding chairs set up for the purpose of witnessing in here, a cement floor, naked wood walls, boxes of old tracts and folded buffet tables. I feel light-headed and yet purposeful.

I can hear Pastor Lewis praying out there now. Asking for others to come up and be saved.

I hold both of Nathan's hands. "I love you," I whisper, overcome.

Nathan nods. We sit down, me still holding his hands.

"I want you to open up your heart, Bud." I lick my lips. His hands are soft and small as ripe leaves just pulled from a tree limb.

"Jesus wants in."

People would think how sick. How sick, what this pervert is doing in a House of God. But right then I was pure. Pure as the blood of Christ. It doesn't matter now what I say, but still the beauty of the moment is in my head, the purity of it. The pureness is what saved *me* too.

I read from my Bible. John 3:16. Romans 6:23. We have been trained on witnessing in our Bible class, witnessing to adults and witnessing to kids. I stop after the second verse and this is when I start to lick his small fingers, placing my Bible to the floor. I don't think about it. I raise his fingers to my mouth after putting my Bible down. People are out there singing a hymn and the organ is going, and I have his fingers in my mouth. They taste like uncooked dough and taste too kind of coppery with little-kid germs.

I spit each finger out slowly. I feel myself depart, my soul shrivel up into a small button that has fallen off somebody's shirt and gets kicked under the couch. But in the smallness is where I will exist, I think: small as a button under the couch. As a grain of rice in a cabinet, one grain, hiding and small and hard.

Nathan wipes his hand on his jeans.

Funny how he did not scream, how he wiped his fingers off on his pants and just sat there. We get up and walk back out, me whispering, "You are born again, Bud."

The view of the auditorium from the front is mighty scary. People are all staring at us with benevolent smiles and eyes. Me and Nathan and Reverend Lewis.

Reverend Lewis says, "What is this child's name, Brother Brewer?"

I answer, "Nathan Marcum."

"Nathan," Pastor Lewis says in his ceremonial-type way, looking at Nathan, who is sliding the hand I had in my mouth against his pants.

People continue grinning and smiling and staring.

"Nathan, did Dave here just witness to you? Are you saved, Nathan?"

I stood there scared and shaky but having to put on how gleaming-proud I was, which part of me was, the pride of a suitor bringing his fiancée to his parents' house after a long struggle. Look who I found to spend the rest of my life with, he says. A bachelor finally finding his perfect match.

"Nathan?" Pastor Lewis repeats. He stops smiling as his gold teeth disappear.

Nathan is looking up to me. I nod my head.

"Yes," Nathan says. "I got saved."

Everyone says Amen. Everyone loves me like they love an old relative. They love Nathan like a newborn son.

I make sure again Nathan is the last one off the bus, when we go home. It is so sunny and pretty out here, in the middle of the flat country. Way out. You remember where, to that old house. At first I kind of thought we were lost, but then I recognized some old fencing, a billboard for motor oil, and then I recognize exactly which way to go toward where that abandoned burned-out house is.

Nathan is in the front seat. He looks in the rearview. He doesn't say a word. It feels like I am going ninety miles an hour, but it's just forty. Nathan stands up, like he wants to get off.

"Sit down, Bud," I say, angry a little. "You don't want to fall, now."

He sits down automatic.

I drive past cornfields and other old houses to get to my place. The sun, the blades of corn, the other anonymous houses, the wire fence, the gravel and then grass, all this has meaning to me and Nathan because we are seeing it on the day he was born again. I want to let him know this, so that he can save mental pictures of this day, but then I feel like he won't get it anyway.

Today is the day you were washed in the blood of the lamb, I want to say, but then I am pulling up the long drive to the house nobody owns anymore.

When we get to the end of the drive, I am very quiet. Can't speak. I turn off the bus. There is our burned-out house. Two stories high, with singed, cracked-open windows, surrounded in tall weeds in front, a forest of stink-trees in back, the corn on all sides, the interstate churning past about a quarter-mile off.

I get up and grunt. Turn around. Smile. "You wanna see a haunted house?"

I feel changed from the church-Dave, but then not. Still holy inside and pure. But then I have this fun-crazy feeling going off, like I am a kidder behind my serious ways, there is meanness to me, a kiddingness turning to meanness in a split second. A meanness that I wouldn't want anyone to see, but who I am kidding with.

Nathan picks up on it. The feeling in the air around me. He smells the meanness, it's almost like mischief, what I am thinking and feeling, like I have conquered myself and am crawling out of the mess mean and sweet and a little ugly.

Nathan runs to the back of the bus because he sees that face on me. The kidder face. But then again it is not meanness. No. It is want. The wanting of him. He gets that. It seems like maybe I have hid it all this time from him, like I have been lying, and I want to tell him I have, as a confession, so that he knows his fear is not made up. Because I do understand why he is so scared.

Troy had that face, of course.

"Don't get scared, honey," I say. My breathing is hot inside my throat.

Nathan nods his head and walks backwards. His fear does not scare me. It is a part of what I feel too, I want to tell him, something we will both need to get over, if this relationship is going to work.

I walk toward him. Smiling, trying to get that one smile back, the one from the pool, the twenty-dollar-bill smile. But we are here in the middle of nowhere, and I don't got to hide no more. I know this, but still the decent aspect of me wants me to hide. But what is "decent" out here?

"We don't got to go. Come here. You don't got to see the haunted house today, honey. Oh, come here." My voice is like slow singing. I can hear it from outside my own head. Nathan stares at me, not wanting to cry. I love him with such tenderness then that he has to walk back to me, and he does. I grab him and sit down on a seat, Nathan on my lap. I kiss his head over and over, like I'm happy we are not going to the haunted house today. And I am. Happy we aren't. I rock him like my baby on the church bus. My thing swells up. But he doesn't move away, probably figuring whatever it is that is swelling up will go away soon.

"We don't have to go in there, honey," I keep saying, kissing, saying, kissing, saying.

Finally I put him onto the other seat, across the aisle. He stands up. We all know what is wrong with me. I stand up sixty or seventy times slower than normal, it seems like. I pull off my shirt, unbuckle my pants, am about to take my pants off when he looks me in the eyes and I have to stop the stripping because his eyes contain the secret of who I am, his eyes tell me to stop.

"You don't love me, do you?" I ask. "Do you?" My voice is raised.

Nathan nods his head. He loves me, he loves me. But it doesn't matter. I can't do nothing, thank God. Today is a done deal! I slide my shirt back on. I tuck it back in. I go up to the front and sit down in front of the big steering wheel.

I turn back around for a sec, to see him, then reposition myself.

"Let's get you home," I whisper with my back to him.

16

TARA

In the parking lot of the welfare place, I get this feeling he's not coming. At the last minute, he is abandoning his dad. I am standing out there in that nasty heat, outside the car. I did not want to run the AC, afraid this car, the Grand Prix, the good car, would break down, so I am in my damn Bob Evans outfit, outside the welfare, trying to stay cool. Just gray siding and black-tinted windows, scorched grass and sidewalk, about as big as a midsized bank. People walk in and out, going in disappointed and pale and coming out frustrated, red in the face.

I wait. Appointment is for three. I had to ask Miss Snot (Molly, the day manager) to be off. I said, "We got an appointment with Dave's dad's insurance people." Like Dave's dad has any "people."

In that last meeting with Dr. CK, I wanted to say, "What if we were to take him home with us?"

I stopped myself before saying it, though. There is Brit to think of, my job. Plus Dave. I don't think Dave wants that.

The social worker said, "I'll look to find an open bed. It won't be easy, but we'll find a place as near to you as possible." He was smiling and acting all caring in front of the doctor.

The doctor just nodded his head, Dave quiet. I couldn't say anything either. I was tired of meetings.

It is now three-twelve. There is a baseball field across the way, and a water spigot. I'm almost tempted to go over and get me a drink and then just leave. I picture old Dave's face if I wasn't here when he shows, Dave's wounded expression. Then I start getting scared that he is losing it all the way, like he has turned into a zombie over his dad. He can still kiss me good-bye of a morning. But then it's like that's all he is: a kiss good-bye. And then I think I'm a zombie too.

Finally, Dave pulls up in the Escort. It is making a funny noise and smoking. He parks, and I stand there, trying not to be mad. He gets out looking stunned and angry, like he has spent the whole time in the car talking to himself. He walks over.

"Sorry. Damn thing kept stalling," he says. There is booze on the man's breath.

We walk in. Bullet-proof glass guards the front desk. Behind the glass, a frosted-haired old-lady receptionist ignores us. Dave coughs, but still she flips through papers at the front counter.

I go, "Miss. We got an appointment for three with a Mrs. Hazelton. For Medicaid."

Slowly the old bitch looks up. Her makeup job is like she did when she was young and she hasn't accommodated for the aging process, so it's all caky and filling in wrinkles like spackle, and her eyes, sagging, have these big false 1961 eyelashes.

This lady at welfare says, "You filled out a 7100?"

"A what?" I go, Dave behind me biting his index fingernail. I can see his reflection in the bullet-proof glass. Him with his Garth Brooks face, not as handsome, of course, but Dave on his good days has Garth's shiny skin and his handsome-good-old-boy eyes, gnawing at that nail.

"7100," says the receptionist.

I laugh like I am lost.

"Nope," I say.

She exhales a great big sigh. "Let me get you one. Hazelton's running like a half hour behind anyway. Hold on."

She goes to a filing cabinet back there.

"Quit biting your nails, honey. You'll make yourself bleed," I say, laughing.

"Shut up," he goes.

I turn around. He has a monster-drunk face suddenly. Like someone caught in the act and very mad about it. He has his jaws clenched tight, his eyes almost bulging, and he is about to explode. He does not want to hurt me, though—more like he wants to eat his own hand, finger by finger.

"Okay, I know you are upset," I say, low. A big hate opens up inside my head, an explosion that dies almost as soon as it goes off, but it still leaves heat. "But you tell me to shut up again, buddy, and I am out that door over there. You got that?"

"I'm sorry," he whispers.

"Okay," I say, and see his face in the reflection again. This time it is monkeylike, stupid and sad. He has let it all go out of him suddenly, and that's even scarier than him holding it all in, because then you are wondering where did all that hatefulness go?

The old lady comes back with her serious eyeglasses on her nose, with a clipboard and papers on it. She slides it through the little portal in the bulletproof glass.

"Here. Fill it out," she says, taking her glasses off. I'd like to tell her to shove them things. I stop myself. I turn with the papers. Dave's dad has got no assets. He sunk all his money into the trailer. Plus the company he worked for screwed up his 401K. He took early retirement before they laid him off.

Dave and me fill out the forms in the cement-block-walled waiting room. That hospital social worker said there weren't any "open beds" in Anderson. He is looking in Pendleton, Muncie, Alexandria, even Indianapolis. He said by the time we got Paul's dad "Medicaid-eligible," there may be an opening close or closer.

I fill in each blank, asking Dave through clenched teeth

when I don't know something, but he's too inside himself to notice. Dave tells me slowly, like he is about to drop off.

"Does your dad have an IRA? What is his social security number? How much is his monthly gross income? Do you got his checking account number, Dave?"

Dave already has a lot of the information. The social worker helped him last night, thank God. Dave and me have finished it all right when the caseworker calls Paul's name. We get up and go back like it is somebody's execution. For a second I feel that stupid urge to giggle, giggle at these gray cubicles back here and all the pale fat people pushing papers and pressing keyboard buttons and all the poor people sitting before their desks with faces that kids have when they go to the toy store with their parents, like, What can I get? What can I get?

But I don't laugh, at all.

The Hazelton lady is small and brittle-boned. Her hair is in a crimped perm, brown like a German shepherd, and her face is just everybody's face here, pinched-in and numb-looking. Dave sits before her, and I sit next to Dave.

"You did the 7100 right?" Mrs. Hazelton says, sitting by her nasty old computer with sweat stains on it.

"Yes," Dave says.

I have decided just to let him carry on.

"Can I see it?" she says. She chews on her gum.

He gives it to her, apologizing for him still holding on to it. "I just feel dumb as heck," he says.

Mrs. Hazelton doesn't say a single thing. She starts typing stuff in, asking us questions every once in a while, being skeptical, like, "He has nothing?" Dave pulls out the stuff the social worker told him to bring. She takes it and copies it. I get hypnotized by the ceiling. It's not covered. They must be working on the air-conditioner ducts and stuff, so the ceiling's pipes and wires are all exposed, multicolored wires like the guts inside a human-being poster on the wall of a doctor's office. I follow wires, Dave follows directions. Wires going back and forth and people stinking and walking past. One little man in a wheel-chair winks at me as he uses the joystick on the chair to guide himself forward. His wink is friendly. But I yawn at it, like nothing affects me here. And it doesn't. I do not know how people work all day in this. At least at Bob Evans there's the smell of food cooking and people smoking and talking and enjoying what lives they got. I mean it ain't the greatest place in the world. You don't meet the smartest and most interesting people, God knows, but still, compared to the welfare with its honeycomb of cubicles and its bullet-proof glass and exposed wires in the ceiling, at least it's something you don't dread until you have been inside it for a while.

We stand up.

Mrs. Hazelton says, "Well, looks like he'll be eligible. His trailer will have to be sold."

Dave goes, "It's already in my name 'cause the social worker guy told us to do that. I put it over in my name to sell it."

"Yes, that's right," she goes. She looks down at the paper on her desk and goes, "Yeah. He'll be eligible. So when's he gonna move in?"

She smiles at me.

Dave has gotten serious and more awake being with Mrs. Hazelton, like she's some long-lost schoolteacher he once had, and he is trying to impress her.

"Well, we don't know even which place he's going to yet. The social worker at the hospital in Indianapolis is finding one near us."

"Yeah, that can be difficult, finding an open bed," Mrs. Hazelton says, walking us out.

At the door she pulls out her credit-card-looking electronic key and the door buzzes open once she runs it through. We stand there.

"I hope everything goes well," Mrs. Hazelton says.

Right then someone is yelling inside a cubicle, someone we can't see, this husky-voiced hillbilly yelling, "Yeah, but I paid into it!"

Mrs. Hazelton just smiles, whispering, "We get that all the time."

When the Escort doesn't start, Dave starts crying.

I am standing in front of it, waiting to get into the Grand Prix. It's almost five-thirty, and I promised Tammy, my girl-friend, that me and her would go to the mall tonight. I was gonna take Brit. The three of us were going to go out to eat and then to the mall to find some outfits Brit could wear for fall. Plus Tammy needed to buy a fall coat. We were gonna meet at six-thirty. So I feel like I need to leave. But not just that, of course. The anger used to be about making Dave a better per-son, like if I kept on him he would change, but now I realize out in the parking lot it is anger at him for being who he is. His face is a bad joke, crying, and yet I love that crying face. We have been together almost a decade, and yet he does not want to be held. He's stubborn behind the wheel, doors probably locked. It seems like this is the very moment that he needs to be loved the most, with his dad dying and the car not starting. I should be able to break free of my dumb-ass anger at him and go to him, love him the most I can. But in fact I feel the oppo-site. In fact, I feel like saying, "Dave Brewer, why don't you grow up?"

Dave gets out of the car after popping the hood. Maybe he thinks I didn't see him crying. I don't say anything. He just gets out quiet and goes to the engine.

"Dave," I say behind him. "I need to go get Brit at Mom's."

He is in the engine, bending into it. His left leg is up in the air, he is pulling at something.

"Dave," I say.

He turns around then. His face is so pissed I can't catch my breath for a second.

"Go! Go, then!"

I stand in the parking lot for a moment. Humiliated out of my right mind. I wonder if people are looking. He yells so goddam loud. Usually I would have a big old comeback. Something smart-assed, full of right-back-at-you.

Not today. Just this sudden silence, like what an insect might hear inside a jar.

I am tired of it. I am tired of it Dave.

I run to the Grand Prix. When I get Brit, I don't tell Mom nothing.

I go on home, and I put Brit in a comfy outfit. I get into something comfortable myself. My mind is loose and reeling itself in at the same time. Tammy's waiting at her parents' place. She got divorced last year, and she moved back in with her folks. She didn't have kids. Her husband had a low sperm count, and even though Tammy says that wasn't what caused the split, you wonder. I wonder as I pull into the big house out by the water treatment plant, I wonder looking at Brit in the rearview, wonder if Dave fixed the car or what he is gonna do and I feel regret.

Tammy is not fat, but she isn't skinny either. I am so happy to see her I don't know, but I cry. Right then I see her running toward the car in her tank top and long shorts, flip-flops, out from her mom and dad's door, her hair in a ponytail, her face without makeup. If she would have had makeup on, I might not have cried. But she didn't, and I loved her not having makeup on. She gets in and looks at me, putting her purse between us.

"Oh, honey," she says.

I can't talk.

"Is it Dave?"

I nod.

"Dave's dad?"

I nod.

Tammy goes, "Well, we're gonna go shopping and eat and we are not gonna cry all night, now are we?"

Tammy is down-to-earth. You have to respect that. I cry some more, maybe sixty seconds more, and Tammy goes, "Come on, let it out. Get it all out, get it all out, come on."

She makes me laugh, doing that.

I say, "Tammy, shut up." My nose full of crying snot, my eyes stopping finally.

"Here," she says, giving me a pink Kleenex from her rawhide purse.

She turns around and looks at Brit and says, "Your poor mommy."

Brit lets out a holler, and I can see her kick her legs.

I think what if Dave had a low sperm count? Good God I would miss Brit. Miss her like I would miss an amputated arm or leg. I'd feel her even though she wasn't there.

I don't go through anything detailed with Tammy. What would that accomplish? We just go on and eat and shop. He'll find his way home. I know this sounds like I'm treating him bad, but there was simply no choice.

Tammy ends up buying this real pretty lavender windbreaker at Sears. Sears, of all places. I get Brit these two little sweaters that will fit her next year too. Then we walk around the mall, you know, just talking about bull, about the soaps we both tape and watch, about this new perfume Tammy is trying that her mom has, about how her dad said he saw a UFO the other night.

"Crazy fool. He made me and Mom, you know Mom with the arthritis, made her and me get under the dining room table, because he saw it out in the backyard. When he figured out it was nothing he apologized, but still . . ."

With Tammy you never know if she's joking or what. But I just laugh. Push Brit in her stroller. Enjoying life. Today out in the welfare parking lot seems like another lifetime.

We get candy at this fancy candy store. Gooey caramels. Me and Tammy eat it with our packages beside us in the mall, sitting by this fountain that doesn't have water in it.

"Lord," Tammy goes, "I am gonna get so fat, Tara. So fat that I am not gonna be able to fit into nothing."

"Oh, you are not. Me and you will go on Slimfast 'round September like we always do."

"Little Miss Jenny Craig," Tammy says, putting her toe on Brit's stroller. Pushing on it a little, back and forth.

I have caught my breath, yes.

Tammy lets a thin ribbon of caramel droop down from her mouth to her fingers. She laughs at the mess she is making, then twirls the caramel around the pinkie of her other hand. Brit is playing with big plastic multicolored keys on a yellow key ring that Tammy bought her. Shaking the keys, but then with her tiny hand she finds one key and it's like that is the key she is going to use to get home with. The key that starts her car, I think.

The key to everything, the whole damn world.

DAVE

I had to call a cab, but that was okay, I guess. I deserved it. Tara got sick of my attitude. Funny thing, though: I did not care. I mean I did, but the whole part of me staring into that Escort's innards out there in the parking lot of the welfare, the whole part just told me to forget about everybody else. It was my turn. *My turn,* the whole part said. I was sick of thinking of others. I was sick of being Mr. Working Man and Mr. Husband and Mr. Daddy and Mr. Son and Mr. This and Mr. That. Then Tara starts getting pissy.

Honey, I love you but you just better leave me alone, I wanted to say, but it came out in a yell.

The Escort will never start again. I fantasize going out to that welfare parking lot and just setting the thing on fire. Maybe somebody will try to steal it out there. They will bust the window, try to hot-wire the thing, and tah-dah: nothing.

Joke's on them.

I witnessed to Nathan, and then I tried to romance him out by that house, and this romance has taken over. Finally it has taken all the way over, that romance fueled by me not doing anything. This romance will not end. I think I scared him. I think I wanted to scare him. I wanted him to know my love through fear, my love so deep within his tiny soul that there would be no escape, no way to get away from me, and he knows that now because of the fear. He knows my love. As I feel he knows it within me like I know sometimes, at least I think I know, how birds fly. When you let your brain go. When you half-close your eyes and go off into flights of fancy, flights of pure silliness.

This kid named Nathan has become my only reason to live. There you go. Let's just lay it on the table.

Even when I pick up Brittany and smell her. The ribbon has been cut loose. I don't care, or at least I kept on telling myself this.

When I get back home in the taxicab, I see that the two of them are in bed already. I am so glad. Them sleeping is exactly what I wanted to see. I sit down in the dark, remembering witnessing to Nathan in that room off the baptismal pool. How his whole hand could fit into my mouth. How I wanted my mouth to take the rest of him in.

I mean I just sat through welfare for my dying dad, and yet all I could think about was Nathan being born again.

Earlier today I called Nathan's mother to tell her that he was now saved. From a phone booth at a gas station I called, and I told Mrs. Marcum about her beautiful son being born again.

"Did he tell you he got saved?" I laughed.

"Yes, he did," she says, bright-voiced. "He's sitting right here in front of me, Mr. Brewer, eating tater-tots. He told me as soon as he come in, and I congratulated him big-time. Kids need to get saved."

"Dave," I say. "Call me Dave."

She laughs and she says, "Nathan just told me he wants to go next Sunday too."

"Well," I say, scared for him. What must be rushing

through his head. How he must love me too, and that love has screwed him up till he can't eat his tater-tots anymore, just pushing them around in a pool of old ketchup, his mom on the phone with me, the man he loves. How he is confused from being scared and from me being the daddy he's got outside the real world, the one who loves him so much with money and motel rooms and bus rides through the country, loves him in haunted houses and in dreams when he is awake.

"How's your dad?" his mom asks me.

A semi roars past. I pretend like I don't hear.

"I said how's your dad?" she goes.

"Better," I say.

"Thank the Lord," she says.

"Yes," I say. "How's about letting me talk to Nathan?"

"Sure." She gives him the phone.

"Hey, Bud."

"Hi," he says, the tiniest voice.

"You eating?"

"Yeah."

"You eating tater-tots?"

"Yeah."

"I love me some tater-tots. With ketchup?"

"Yeah. Um. I wanna go next week."

"You do, huh? Well I'm glad, yes I am, Bud. I love you, Bud, but I don't want you to tell me you love me on the phone because your mom ain't gonna understand. I don't want you telling her nothing, okay? Something bad would happen, okay? If you told her. Okay?"

"Yeah."

"So I'll come get you Sunday, 'kay?"

"Yeah."

I hang up.

. . .

Now, tonight, Brit and Tara asleep, I did not know anything outside of the fact that all's I wanted was to have Nathan on my lap in my house and have Tara and Brittany on a long vacation away from me and away from him. I sit down in my living room, my sanctuary, but it ain't that now. I have to get up and walk around. Then I wind up down the hallway of my own house, feeling like a trespasser.

Brittany was sleeping. Brittany sleeps on her back. Her mouth so open. Her mouth is small. I think of the smallest things. Of the mouths of fetuses and of amoebas and of seeds still in the ground. Under dirt, expanding out. Her lungs take in air, hungry.

I should have been a preacher, Tara tells me sometimes. I sure have enough BS for it. She says I should stand up in front of people who love the Gospel and trust me and tell them about the Lord. The Lord is our Shepherd. For God so loved the world He gave His only begotten son. Etc. etc. etc.

And Brittany's eyelashes are the pencil strokes of a math problem I ain't ever gonna figure out in this lifetime. The mystery of a man and a woman coming together as one. The mystery of our lives together.

I am my dad and mom's mystery, am I not?

I feel my daughter's legs as she sleeps. They are smooth, and smooth is all that matters.

I am so sorry for forgetting about you, I think to her.

I am so sorry for the growing part of it.

For the forest fire where my heart used to exist. He grows and grows. Nathan starts with the sun shining off of windows and turns into a propane torch that becomes an incinerator and then the incinerator expands until you don't have a vantage point, until all you are is what is inside you, your outside and your inside get confused, Brit honey, and after all this remember me in that part of your brain when one night after I pronounced the Escort DOA, I came into your room and softly touched on your legs.

Please remember me not crying, and not crying here is very important because I am not sad and I ain't feeling sorry for myself, but remember me slowly touching your smooth and tiny legs, and then remember me standing there in your room, standing until my legs start to hurt, until the sun sprouts into the house like roots underground.

Remember how your crazy daddy stood there watching you slowly get lit by the sun in your crib, like a painting in different stages, the way God must have envisioned you to look right before He took the time to make you.

18
DAVE

Tuesday, Tara and me go over to Dad's trailer and go through his stuff so we can sell it. We have to sell it, since it is in my name now, sell it or rent it. Either way, we have to get his stuff out. We silently pack up his clothing, and he doesn't have that many belongings, surprisingly for a man of fifty-seven: work clothes mostly, old shoes, old country records and cassette tapes, lots of uneaten snack cakes and old Zane Grey books.

Dad has dirty magazines inside the coffee-table cabinet. The dirty magazines make me and Tara laugh, from nerves. The man used to sit in here dreaming of Ponderosa Steakhouse and having no troubles with his stomach, used to sit in this very tiny cramped living room with the dogs playing poker in his painting, with the ducks-and-geese-in-the-woods print fabric of his sofa and chair, with the TV going on *Jeopardy,* and this man in his La-Z-Boy would suddenly get the notion to go down on the floor there and pull out a *Playboy* or *Penthouse* or whatever and there those women would be, loving him back with photographed eyes.

Standing near the TV, Tara says, "You ain't keeping them, Dave."

We are still laughing. She was just trying to make jokes. She was just trying to get over the way I was treating her.

Funny what you find in a man's privacy, right? So I laughed too.

Joke's on you, Tara, I could have said. I do not want them! I do not want these filthy magazines!

But we box everything up that is his. Tara sits on the floor in front of Dad's music collection, going through tapes. She looks like a little girl with a toy box.

"You ever heard of some of these? Freddy Fender?" she says, showing me the cover.

"Nope," I say, wanting to leave.

"I mean I know George Jones and Eddie Arnold and Brenda Lee. But Freddy Fender?"

"No, Tara, I do not know Freddy Fender!" I yell. I think I kick something across the floor, a magazine or something.

Tara's face gets red. "I'm making Paul a tape of his favorite music," she says, proud. She gets up in a huff and puts tapes in a shoe box. She stands up slow after doing that. Confronts me.

"Dave, you are . . ." But she does not finish her sentence, standing there with her box of tapes.

"What?"

I mean I'm just standing there, you know, kind of sad, in my dying dad's trailer. Give me a break.

"What?" I say again.

Her eyes are filled with tears suddenly. "You're not right," she whispers.

"What is your problem?" I say, laughing but terrified. I have goosebumps from her saying that, the way she did. Not accusing, but just like she knows now. It is the true fear of being caught, like she has read my mind, like she knows it all. But also the gushing relief of it scares me, like a dam that's busted. I get a hint of what it would be like to truly be found out, and that double-scares me, the relief like dying, the fear like the fear of death.

"You're just not all there anymore," she whispers. "I know it's your dad, but . . ." She doesn't finish that either. She smiles, and it is a strange smile to see, as it kind of shakes on her lips, then disappears. She walks out. There is nothing left to say.

Except I do say something to her back.

I yell, in a kidding voice, trying to save face or whatever, I don't know, trying to maintain: "Thank you, Dr. Tara! Thank you very much!"

I go and see my dad in the hospital one more time before he moves to the nursing home, Thursday. The social worker found a place in Muncie. He asked me if I wanted to go see it first, and I said I trusted him. Dad is watching *The Price Is Right,* half-sitting up in his bed.

"Looky here," he says. His voice is so soft it makes me want to turn around. This is all he is, that soft little dry voice and *The Price Is Right.*

"How's it going?"

He doesn't answer. His head drops back. Spit comes down his bottom lip from where he is having swallowing troubles. His eyes are still open and spit comes down. I go over to where I can see the show on TV. Amazing how Bob Barker has not aged, just his hair going silver. The same sets and games, the same excitement on the contestants' faces. I remember watching this show when I was a kid. It's nostalgic in a good way. I watch it. Some fat lady wins a bedroom set.

Dad says, "Ain't you got work?"

I laugh. "I just thought I'd come and see you."

"Yeah," he says, and more spit comes out.

I watch TV with him. I used to love him in a hateful way, imagined him chained standing up to a wall, in his underwear, and I think I was twelve when I imagined this, I would come by with a whip or a switch dressed in a uniform like a boy scout or a policeman, and we would both be silent and I would switch his belly, whip it. He would wince but not scream.

Now Dad goes back to sleep during the Showcase Show-

down. I stay and finish the show and leave him as soon as Bob
Barker tells me to have my pets spayed and neutered.

I leave my dad. A sleeping dying man.

He does not need to see me anymore, I realize. Nobody
does. Except you know who.

Dad moves into the nursing home that next evening. I don't
show up there when he moves because I am sick and tired of his
goddam tragedy. I mean here I am, this basket case going to
work. Tara has backed off. She doesn't talk about nothing,
always going over to her mom's, or seeing her friend Tammy.

This is where divorce starts, that's what she is thinking.

I fooled you, didn't I, honey?

Thursday me and Tara meet after I get off work, and she is
on her way out. I am doing something illegal, according to
the laws of Indiana Gas. I am taking the gas company truck
home with me. The guys in the shop let me, understanding
my plight, but if any of the Neckties find out, watch out.
So there's Brit already in her car seat in the Grand Prix in the
driveway. It is one of them muggy after-work evenings. Thursday, like I said, the day Dad is sposed to be transferred to a
nursing home, the one the social worker found in Muncie. No
one had open beds in Anderson. I see open beds in my head,
like beds are doors to other worlds. Which they are in a way.

Tara says, "So he is still going tonight?"

"Yeah. All systems go. That's what that social worker called
and said. They paged me and I called. It's in Muncie still, the
nursing home."

Tara in her Bob Evans outfit on our little porch, carrying
Brit's diaper bag. Hair all done up. She loves her work too
much, I think. That was our problem, right? It's like I don't
really know her, you know? Nathan lets me in on all kinds of
secrets, even though he don't know that. The biggest secret is

that I don't know anyone other than him. I see Tara and I picture myself taking off my shirt on the church bus in front of Nathan, and again my stomach goes off like a bomb I've hid.

"You going to go see him?" she asks. She looks impatient.

"I guess."

"Okay." Again that strange smile, shaky and then gone.

I nod my head.

I turn around and Brittany in her car seat is just sitting there, looking out at the maple tree in the yard. On the road a white cat traipses through. Two kids on bikes. The grass is all yellow from the heat. I think of watering it. Just that. The beauty of a hose watering grass. Simple and quiet and dumb: me.

I see Tara walk off after she kisses me. She gets into the Grand Prix. She ain't asking me about the damn Escort. I took the license plate off. I am going to let it stay there. They can't trace it, can they? Took all the papers from the glove box. It would cost money to have it towed to the graveyard, I mean junkyard.

Bye-bye Tara. Bye-bye Brit.

Then I drive over to Nathan's apartment complex. I sit by a dumpster in the gas company truck. I think of Danny and how I got him to the gas company shed that one time by offering ice cream. He wasn't like Nathan. Danny was muscular in a way. My opposite. Me and Nathan, though, we have a lot in common. We have the same brain, I think, except his started later. They cloned a sheep, but we are the same in the spirit. For instance, we are now both born again. I could tell when I had his fingers in my mouth. They did not wiggle. His face relaxed. It was like his hand wanted to be there. I mean we were in church, and I was doing that. But that was the way I could get now.

Because I knew. I knew it was all over.

When I wake up from this nightmare, I tell myself, watching his town house, I will be fifty pounds lighter and have gray hair, but I will love my regular life even more.

The lights in the living room go off at ten-thirty. I get out of my truck and when I go behind the town house, I look up and try to locate his room, but all I get is closed curtains, dead bugs in the sill, gray screen. I am behind here, and to my back is a long line of storage garages with orange doors and a fence with weeds. I don't stay long enough for nothing. Nobody sees me.

Dad! I forgot about him. But I don't go. I go home, take off all my clothes in the bedroom. Tara ain't off till eleven-thirty. Brit is guess where? I am so alone it hurts. Not really. Naked in the bedroom, I pinch myself, and then I jack off repeatedly, but never come.

I get elastic inside as I do it, like I am a wind-up toy. I go on the bed and do it and I go on the floor and do it and I stand on the damn ceiling, I think, doing it. Finally I go into the closet. I actually try to climb into the top shelf and fall. I sprain my ankle practically. I walk around, my thing still hard, trying to work out the kink in the ankle.

Tomorrow, Dad.

Tomorrow I will go. Even if he doesn't want to see me.

Right now I stop the jacking off and I fall to the sheets back in my underwear and T-shirt. I do not hear Tara and Brit come in.

19

TROY

When do you stop living in the past? I guess when it stops coming at you. I guess when it stops, when the past doesn't exist anymore.

There's proof of its existence all the time, however. Too much proof. Hey, people, I am fucking drowning in proof!

When he arrived in an ambulance that Thursday evening, Doris and I were in the wing where his room was located. I don't have anything to do with new admissions at Sunnyhaven, just a grunt. People often come and go without my knowledge. I just show up for my shift. So I didn't have any warning. Doris and myself are at the nurses' station, and I am doing some care notes while she packs meds into her cart. There's some other nurses up there, all female besides me. I am writing the care notes, and then suddenly I see some old man on a gurney. Nothing special. The glass doors at the end of the wing are black with night, and the white and red ambulance is glowing from where this old man just came.

"New patient," Doris says.

"Yep," I say.

She goes over to where the admissions charts are.

"Did Teresa leave his admission stuff here? Was it faxed

from the hospital?" Doris says, all serious. Teresa was the social worker we all hated because she went on and on about her three-year-old daughter.

"I don't know," Missy, the youngest LPN we have, goes.

"I'm looking," she says, going through the admissions files. Finally she finds what she is looking for.

Now remember, I am just doing my notes on all the folks, when I bathed, fed, and changed them throughout the day, about an hour from end of shift, but probably I would get pulled into a double, as people were calling off right and left. It's summer, after all.

Doris, with her roots showing, her Rudolph the Red-Nosed Reindeer pendant on, her fat jutting out like a colostomy bag all over, she says, "Yeah, here it is. Paul Brewer."

I stop right in the middle of the sentence I was writing. I look down the hall, and there is the old man. He has no hair, scrawny as hell. My mouth doesn't drop open, as I don't want to have to explain my surprise to anybody about who he is. I just stand there, pen cap in my mouth.

Doris reads from his admission papers, "Poor guy. Had his stomach taken out and cancer is everywhere, even into his bones. Um. Morphine drip, some of that new pain stuff to go along with it, and he may have chemo. We have that chemo trailer that comes by, don't we?"

Rhonda, the oldest RN we have, says yes.

"It's sad. Only fifty-seven," Doris says, probably thinking about her own age.

I finish my notes, but every muscle, every bone in my body is directed toward that man's room. Rhonda and Doris go back and get him settled in, as I'm just a grunt and don't do anything for him until he needs to be bathed and changed. Maybe I'll do his G-tube feeding if we are understaffed. If the state found out I did that, we'd get cited, but I do it quite often.

I continue writing my notes. Then I stop. I look up. His

door is closed. I feel as if I am someone else, looking on, that I don't work here, now that Paul Brewer has showed up. The heat in my head spreads down into my fingers, but it is more like cold water that feels somehow hot.

Shock? Hell yes. Also this weird nostalgia, as though I have seen my whole life just come in, in one human person, my whole life: School Street, the garage, the haircuts, the pop bottles in the pop machine, all of 1972. All of that innocence, all of that beauty.

All of that crap.

I can't breathe, but I do anyway. That's the one rule you have to follow where living is concerned: you have to breathe.

I talk to Missy about other things, but my head is in only one place. I keep thinking of the way Paul would pay for my hair to be cut, but then give me dirty looks. He did not like that I was trying to be his son.

I think about David and Paul and myself going to get milk at the supermarket. Me up front, David in the backseat, and that feeling that it was just us, and I wondered, like I always did, what if he were to know? But David is love, that's all: a beautiful thing to be held and worshiped. Paul would understand that, I thought in my fucked-up innocence. I thought how Paul was what David would become and I respected that in a way, he made David, along with Irene, and he made me, in a way.

I went back after 1972 only one time. It was 1976, the Bicentennial. I went back to find David, knowing he would be ten years old and myself twenty. I think at that time I was working somewhere, I don't remember: wait, a taco restaurant. I drove my mom's car back to Anderson, the Taboo City, and as I drove I felt as if I were disintegrating, which, surprisingly, was a pretty good feeling.

Close to what I am feeling right now, walking toward Paul Brewer's door at Sunnyhaven as it is twelve midnight almost, and I pulled a double, just like I said I would have to. Now I am doing my rounds.

I drove to Anderson, Indiana, to School Street, on July 19, 1976. A quiet Tuesday night. I drove to the bypass. I drove to the used-car place, and I saw all that chain-link fencing. I saw our old house, the garage back there, still with painted-on windows. Louie's gas station had been turned into an arcade, now decorated patriotically for the Fourth of July. I imagined how Anderson had a parade for the Bicentennial. There was Bicentennial fever everywhere.

I wanted to break into the garage and sleep there. I thought in my car, parked in the arcade lot, how simple it was to come here, how I should have come back sooner, but the thirty-six miles back seemed always like thirty-six thousand in my head, as though Anderson was the South Pole and Muncie the North.

I stopped in the parking lot of the arcade, still not able to see David's house, and I pictured David coming out of the arcade and seeing me and jumping for joy.

"Troy!" he would scream. A ten-year-old is more filled out, more aware of the universe, and that would only make my feelings increase for him.

But I went ahead and started my car.

I went down School Street proper, in my own little parade. The house was gone.

I got out of my car, afraid, shocked, crazy. The slab foundation seemed very small, as if storybook midgets had lived here. I stood where I thought David's mom and dad's bedroom had been. Right where the closet was. Then a little girl riding a bike stopped on the road.

I looked at her, and she looked back, but did not say anything. Her bike was tiny and so was she. She had on a pink jumper, her face pale with freckles. No shoes. Short boy-type hair.

"It blew up," she said. "Last year."

I nodded.

"Anybody hurt?"

"No," she said.

"Nobody was living here?"

"No."

"Do you—"

Maybe she got scared or maybe just sick of questions, but she rode away then, disappearing down below the used-car place. I remembered cutting my wrists then with Mom's shaver that night she found David and me in the bathroom. I remembered wanting not to cut my wrists, but just simply going down to this house, where this house used to exist, going and claiming him and telling everyone in the town the truth: that you can love a child like you can love an adult, you can actually be in love with a child and that child can love you back!

It is not wrong, I wanted to say.

Not wrong, I wanted to say, but instead I did the slit-wrist thing. I was weak. I was stupid. I was me.

Now I guide myself to Paul Brewer's Sunnyhaven door. I open it slowly. His roommate is in a coma. There are no TVs in here. I go over to Paul, his heart monitor bleeping solemnly, and I know he is sleeping the sleep of a dying man. It is a hard drunk sleep, as if he has been beaten into unconsciousness. He does not look at all like the Paul Brewer from 1972, of course. He is the Paul Brewer of now, the dying one, but then again there are subtle things I can see. His eyebrows, thick like David's. His hands, long slender fingers, like David's. His feet with the high knobbed bone near the toe. Like David's.

Why did your house blow up, Paul? I want to ask.

Where's David?

But it would be David as a thirty-one-year-old, right? David who I ruined. When you are fucking someone up like I did, you only think of them as the age in which you fucked them up: that is the eternity of your longing.

The eternal garage feeling. He is six and innocent forever,

waiting for you in the painted-window garage in heaven. His
dad is at a union meeting getting drunk. His mom is answering
the phone at a motel. Your mom is getting drunk in her bedroom with her dog Shar. Shar who got run over in 1974 by a
semi.

No.

Paul is here. The present tense. Paul. Is. Here. Paul is waiting to die.

Would you do this?

Would you go up and kiss this Paul Brewer? Kiss each eye-
brow, feeling the eyebrows with your lips, like mustaches. Not
disturbing him—he is so dead asleep.

I do. I have to.

The next day he is awake. He doesn't recognize me. Morphine, other drugs, just the exhaustion of dying. It takes a lot of
work. His eyes are open, and he looks right at yours truly.

He says, "Where is this place?" His mouth can hardly open.

"Sunnyhaven, Muncie, Indiana," I say. My voice is shaky,
almost gone.

"Oh," he says, and he closes his eyes.

I am to bathe him. I usually use a shower chair, and take the
patient into the shower room, but Paul's getting a sponge one
for now, as I'm afraid to move him with all the equipment. I
have my plastic dish of Phisoderm and water, my sponge and
towels on a cart. The comatose roommate has the whitest hair,
like a classical music composer. I give him a sponging off too,
but now it is Paul Brewer's turn.

I lift up each arm. The skin is hot. The soap and water
stream down onto the sheet, but I am careful to wipe it up. I'll
do his linens later. Right now I am bathing him. Slow. Slower.
Elbows and wrists, each finger, each space between each finger. The soap smells good on his skin. I sponge off the stitches
where they did his ectomy. The stitches are smooth, not tight,
since they have been in two weeks, and they have healed over
and will be taken out soon. Not stitches really, though: staples.

I sponge Paul's neck and I sponge off his cheeks, and he wakes up.

"What?" he says.

I do the clichéd response: *"Shhhhhhhhhhhhh,"* prolonging it.

This is my religion, like I said before, only now it is more religious than religion. What if the preacher got directly to God in the flesh? What if your prayers were actually kisses right on the mouth? What if God had a dying body, what if God gave birth to the son you loved so much, and he stayed six years old forever?

He fathered my child, I'm thinking, or something like that. Something really sick, and yet I am bathing the man who fathered David. I am knowing this now, this strange pleasure, if that is what it is, the soapy water almost like warm blood. I rub it around and on that body, the one that's dying, and then I think of David's young skin, pale, almost translucent in a candlelit garage, his tiny elastic arms wrapped around my neck, his small lips being licked by my tongue. And I think of the times David and I had, all those wonderful yet evil things I did to him because I wanted to, and these being the only times I can think of as "good" in my life, the only times I felt I actually existed—well, then I am damned, right?

Damned to this cleaning up of the dying father. Then again, this is my blessing and my curse both. I always feel this when I get this intimate, this close to a dying body. I feel this need to prolong the little pleasures in life for that person. Make sure the person is comfortable. Make sure the dying person is clean.

Each eyelid, slowly. The scalp is done.

I roll him over carefully, and he grunts.

I wash shoulder blades, spine, butt, and groin. I look at his purplish dick. It's small, retracting into him, as if he is going to change into a woman at the end. His balls are up there too. I wash where they are. Wash out his asshole.

After this, he is so clean. He is clean and he is clean.

"Paul, do you know who I am?"

He isn't listening.

After work, I go home and go straight to bed, in my clothes.

He didn't even recognize me. Paul did not recognize the past, now that he is dying.

Maybe this is why we die, I think, under blankets and sheets. Maybe this is why we die, so we don't have to remember the past anymore. Maybe this is why we die, I think, drifting off to dream about a grown-up David who is really the six-year-old one. A dream of David swimming in the ocean as a thirty-one-year-old. But the body of a six-year-old. And me in a little boat, saving him. Pulling him into my boat. It is Paul, though, I have saved, I see. A dead Paul. A dead Paul brought up from the bottom of the ocean.

I push him back in.

20

PAUL

He ain't David. He ain't my dad. He ain't the preacher. He ain't the doctor. He ain't no buddy of mine. He ain't nobody I worked with in my life. He ain't my brother. He ain't the guy down in the next trailer who smokes pot. He ain't the guy I roomed with when I was working cutting timber when I was sixteen. He ain't the lawyer for the divorce. He ain't her new husband. He ain't the gas station attendant I caught crying one time. He ain't Frank 'cause Frank's black. He ain't Arthur the mechanic. He ain't Lloyd the mailman. He ain't Red the barber.

He is Troy.

He is Troy Wetzel.

Why Troy Wetzel!

He is washing my elbow and he is washing me good.

I see them sheets on the line, and Troy is hanging them up.

Troy is washing each eyelid. The soap is warm. He doesn't say nothing. I can't move my mouth.

I fall down the mountain. Me and Dave fall down the mountain. I hold on to my son to protect his skin and bones. We fall and the tree trunks hit, hit our faces and our bones. We keep falling like it won't ever end.

Why, Troy Wetzel, after all these years!

In the end I will see all the people I know and used to. In the end when I just don't think no more, other thoughts can come. In the end I will be falling down a mountain with my son in my arms and then not. More like I will fall off of the bed and break into a thousand pieces, each piece growing up into people I used to know.

Why Troy.

What ever happened to your mother? Fine lady.

Why Troy.

What ever happened to that little yapper of a dog? Goddam thing.

Why Troy.

You still go to church?

21

DAVE

Friday at noon, I make the trip to Muncie. To this place called Sunnyhaven. I thought the lady I called said Sunny Heaven. I told her that. She did not laugh.

Muncie is a little bigger than Anderson, farther north. I am smoking cigarette after cigarette on the interstate. When I came in today at the shop, Biggun, the main mechanic, told me I better be careful about driving that truck around on non-company business. Biggun's got burn scars all over his face, poor guy, always looks scared and freaky from the pink scars. A car blew up in his face one time while he was working on it.

"I won't take it over the weekend," I said.

"Okay, good," he said. "We don't want you losing your job."

You reach this point after a lot of waiting around, a lot of thinking you aren't actually doing anything. You reach the point of staring at closed curtains behind an apartment building around this time 'cause you have lied so much to yourself and those around you, and then it clicks: you know there is no God and there is no Jesus coming back in the clouds. It hurts to know this, that all this time you've been this big atheist, pretending to love God, but you don't really, come on. Not really.

You only love the feeling that the boy gives you. That jolt, that flash in your blood. That's all you love, pervert. Just now the devil is telling you all this and you believe it, but even then you question the devil's existence because if there is no Jesus, there is no devil either, and if neither of them exist, what the heck are you?

Biggun says, "Kent's been asking around about you."

I laugh.

"Oh he has, has he?"

I laugh so loud people stop working. They look up from their working and give me one great big dirty look.

I apologize and leave.

Sunnyhaven is this big, long, three-story colonial, almost like an old hotel but shabbier. Near the road, surrounded by pulled-up trees where they are starting a housing development nearby. I park in back. It is a sunny, not-that-too-bad hot day, and there are green trees and flowers landscaped around the building, which is sweet. Takes your mind off things.

I go into the reception area, after walking around. It kind of stinks here like pee. The carpet is purple and there is furniture to sit on and paneled walls and paintings. Old people in wheelchairs, but some are walking and getting their mail and bothering nurses. At the back is a long hall that leads to the separate wings. I go up to the main desk and there's a big fat dyed-blond lady there with a Frosty the Snowman on next to her name tag that reads DORIS, LPN EXTRAORDINAIRE.

"Hi," I say. "I'm David Brewer. My dad, I think, came here last night."

Doris smiles.

"Yes. Yesterday evening. You want to see him?"

"If you don't mind," I say, smiling back.

She picks up the phone and on the intercom she says, "Troy, could you come up to the front desk, honey?"

She puts the phone back. An old lady with a corsage on and a beautiful blue dress is sitting on the couch next to the out-of-order candy machine. Why is she wearing a corsage at noon on a Friday in a nursing home? For that matter, why does Doris have Frosty the Snowman on her uniform? It doesn't matter. The old lady's face hangs off her skull like dough. But she used to be quite a looker, I bet.

Doris says, almost in a whisper, "People get lost in this place. I'd tell you how to get there, to your dad's room, but we're remodeling some parts, and it's just easier if one of us takes you through. I'm waiting on a call, so Troy can take you."

Of course, Troy is a name I don't want to contemplate, but it ain't that Troy, I am sure. He is dead or he is in Africa walking around in a desert or he is under the water having become a fish.

But then I see at the back of the hall as if in slow motion I see a man who is balding and kind of awkwardly tall, who has the complexion of the underside of all things, white as a white-covered Bible. I think of a Bible without words in it. And as he comes closer I can see his face disintegrate backwards, like a movie of a bomb in reverse. His eyes are big and shiny. He has a plain face, but it is a face I know, like a latex mask of a real-life public figure, Richard M. Nixon or possibly Ronald Reagan or even Bob Hope, and that mask, that mask is Troy Wetzel. That face is Troy Wetzel. I stand by the front desk.

As he approaches, hair raises up on the back of my neck.

Think of two dogs looking at each other who have never seen another dog in their lives. These two dogs have been pampered separately by their owners to think they only are the only dogs in the world. Now they have been trained by their owners to be dead-eyed and dumb and full of hate. Yes. Think of these two dogs seeing each other for the first time.

Think of what the Bible says about the way God created the earth out of nothing, and then look into Troy Wetzel's shiny eyes.

I am angry in a way I have never been angry. Not at Troy
Wetzel, but at the way things have fallen into me. Angry at this
fucking nursing home for hiring such a person as Troy. Troy,
who is dead to me! Dead! Only a memory of Troy should be in
the world, not even written down.

The anger makes me stand still.

Troy walks up to me. He has stooped shoulders.

"I thought you might be coming," he says. His voice
reminds me of a vapor in the shower when you get it too hot,
but you go ahead and get in.

Doris is looking at him. "You know him?" she says.

I am shaking.

My God, the dog who had never known other dogs existed:
it's him. It's another him. It's me.

Troy has the voice he had, only it's cooked down to a small
amount of voice. His voice has been left on the stove too long.
It almost caused a grease fire. I see curtains catching. I see curtains of fire when I see Troy, tall, in white pants and white
smock, Troy is balding, but he fixes his hair to make it look like
he is not.

"David?" Troy says.

He walks to me. He walks to me, the boy who the first day
he saw me must have fallen deep into love 'cause he first saw
me without my shirt on as my dad made me go shirtless that
day they moved in, him and his dad and his mom in that house
next to the used-car place. "Get you some sun, Dave," Dad
said, and then I had my shirt off and the sun ate into my white
skin, and he, my dad, turned on the hose and he sprayed me
with cold water, and then Troy saw me, in an instant, and I am
Troy seeing me see me, and I see me in the water, white and
cold and small being burnt by the sun and I love me with all
my heart, like someone has given me a very strong drug with a
needle.

Troy says, "David? Your dad is . . ."

Troy is up close. I smell him.

I reach out to him in slow motion. I take his hand in my hand and I shake it. I shake it like a politician, like a preacher at the end of church. I smile with tears of joy in my eyes.

"How have you been?" I say in a robot's voice.

Troy doesn't know what to say.

Doris laughs. "So you two know each other?"

Troy looks at Doris. "Would you mind, honey?"

Doris says, "Sure."

She looks suspecting.

I still shake his hand. Squeeze it.

"Your dad's condition is, um—"

I stop shaking. "So how have you been?" I say again.

Troy backs up against the desk. He looks to me like he wants to run. So do I. But he takes me back to see my father. Back and back into the back part of the nursing home, where they keep the dying. Back into the smelly hallways, the smells of shit and food and pee and body sweat and dying. The halls lose their shine. The walls lose their pictures. They are remodeling some parts, and walls have been busted down. We go past busted walls and chunks of plaster. Troy does not talk.

In his room, Dad isn't on as many tubes and things as in the hospital. He is not awake. He won't wake up very much from now on. Troy goes over and pushes at a pillow to comfort him.

"I can't believe this," says Troy. Bending up from pushing in my dad's pillow. That little gesture infuriates me.

I go, looking at my dad, I go and I don't know where this has come from, except from Troy pushing on my dad's pillow, I go, "Remember how we used to get our haircuts together?"

"Me and you," Troy says. His smile seems to realize that I forgive him automatically. Even though I still want him dead.

"Yeah," I say.

"I always think about that. Jesus Christ, I can't believe this," he says, in a whisper. He smiles. He is vulnerable. He is full of memory.

I go closer to my dad. I know that he loved me, and I know

that I will always love him, but there is a point where love and whatever don't matter, out past yourself, in outer space where I seem to be. And maybe I never did love him. I see him whipping me good outside at sundown. I feel the switch burning my legs and my chin against the bark of a tree. I lick bark, screaming. Later he gives me ice cream with a gigantic spoon.

Troy looks at me like I am a little off.

"So," he says.

This is when I yell.

"Get the fuck out of here!"

This comes from deep inside my heart. Like I have wanted to scream so long it is louder than real.

"You leave him alone!" I yell.

Troy nods his head. He ain't even near Dad.

Dad one time had me climb up on the roof of the house 'cause I threw the Frisbee up there and Dad pulled the ladder away and he was laughing. I got scared 'cause I did not think I would ever get down.

"You get the fuck out of here!" I yell.

I watch Troy walk out while people gather at the door to see. The back of him is the back of him when he would turn around and padlock that garage door. Me sitting on the cot, his back, me seeing him do the lock, me sitting there waiting for his love. I look up one time 'cause the thing would not lock. Up in the rafters, the bird's nest like a wad of hair in the sink. I imagine birds stirring up there in it. Baby ones. Baby black birds small as baby mice breaking out of their eggs while the mother is away getting food for them. There is a horror to birth. There is terror to it.

Eggs crack open. Wet small faces creep out with beaks.

People at the door look in.

"You okay, buddy?" someone asks.

I don't say nothing.

Dad must have heard. His eyes are open to me.

"Do you know what he did to me?" I whisper to Dad.

He has a look on his face which I cannot say what it is. Helplessness. And I like that. Or maybe it's just that he doesn't know who I am. Or he doesn't want to know anymore.

I go to his face, and I kiss his mouth.

I say good-bye and rush out the back doors somewheres. Hills, trees, cars, asphalt. Where is Troy? Hiding from me. We hid together, remember? Hid in the closet in the house on School Street. I climbed up, hoping to disappear from him. I did not want that dirty boy touching me! All he wanted all the time was me, me, me. All he thought and all he dreamed of. His blank dead wanting face. I did not want him loving me, his face all serious as an animal's about to eat you. No! But I climbed up there and he found me, and then when he found me, after he counted slowly to twenty, when he found me it was like *Good he found me this is over now I know what is going to happen now.*

And I think I must have loved him too.

22

TROY

"What is that guy's problem?" Alice says, some RN I have never liked.

I have traveled to another part of Sunnyhaven to hide, but hiding is not the point. I now understand you can never hide really. That's good to know.

"He acted like you were the Antichrist," she says.

She actually says that. This is when I laugh.

I laugh and I settle down onto an empty hospital bed, shaking from the experience. I saw him, David Brewer, and I saw him with Paul Brewer. I escorted him to see his dying dad.

"He acted—"

I look up at Alice, who has a fat baby face like she doesn't know what the world does to people. She just administers meds and goes home to the fucking suburbs where her lookalike husband waits for her on his riding lawnmower.

"Listen, I just want to be left alone."

Alice nods, obviously miffed at me.

I lay on this broken bed. This broken bed, in a small storage room off of the main wing. This room with a broken bed and a broken pop machine and three crutches leaning against the scaly walls. Those crutches seem to stare at me, aluminum with white rubber handles. There is a window letting in sunlight. I look out in my prone position and I can see him out there, I see David get into his truck, and I see David drive away. I stay right where I am, as if I might become (if I'm lucky) another stashed-away piece of equipment, put here to be forgotten.

Is there a moment I need to return to? Some perfect moment as I lose my mind? Is it the first time I showed him who I was, who I really was, in the garage? The *first* first time when he got completely scared and tried to run, but I, the fifteen-year-old evil genius, had padlocked the goddam door. Naked and hard, I stayed there, as he went to the door to undo the padlock. I can still hear the sound of his little hand trying to undo a padlock, so pathetic, the lock hitting the door, the wall.

"You can't leave until you kiss me," I tell him. Naked, white, and skinny as a skeleton. I am so naked then in my mind I *am* a skeleton. A Bible-believing skeleton with a hard-on.

He sees this horror but must get over it, for a boy of five has to survive to become a boy of six, and the boy of six must live to seven.

And so on, so forth.

But back then I was the bastard who trained him. For this, my life is ruined, but still the rest of the memory must unfurl. How he did come back to me. How the padlock did not unlock, and he turned around, crying, whimpering, and yours truly still rock-hard, standing by the cot. He comes back pissed off, defeated, and crying. He comes back and tries to hit me. I knock him down onto the hard floor.

"You don't hit!" I say.

He is on the floor crying, but then he stops and stands up.

"If you want to leave, you got to kiss me. Here. Kiss me here," I say, pointing to the end of my dick.

And he does. He does so, crying again. But then after that, I lift him up to my face, and I kiss his face. I kiss him and tell him it will be okay.

"You love me," I say. "You just proved it. You just proved that you love me, David. Thank you. Thank you."

I take him to the cot. By this time he is a tired animal. For I have fucked up his brain quite well. Still, there is the pleasure of tucking him into the cot. When he asks, exhausted, if I will ever unlock the door, I tell him, "No. Not now. Only when I want to."

Only when I feel like it, I think is actually what I say, and then I crawl into the cot beside him, sharing with him the old army blanket.

No one will ever know, will they? But me and him. And now I am here.

Here at Sunnyhaven Nursing Home Incorporated. I know what it feels like, to sleep next to him when he is five, and I know what it is to be hated by him when he is thirty-one, but there is no reality to any of it. I sit up from the bed and I go out into the hallway. I am not human anymore, but realizing this only makes me that much more human.

Doris finds me in the break room. I bum a cigarette.

"What happened in there with that Brewer guy? Did you know him before or something?" she asks, serious. Her black roots make me smile, like old friends, her mascara, pancake makeup, her caring about me.

Maybe someday I will tell her what I did, tell Doris. Confess to Doris, who sits here in front of me, lighting my Vaginal Slime. I can imagine her as wanting to know, her face full of compassion, leaning into me. Her pendant today is Frosty the Snowman. At the end of *Frosty the Snowman,* Frosty went into the greenhouse and melted, did he not? Melted into a puddle of warm water.

I smoke.

Doris says, "What did you do? Was he just like really crazy about his dad or something?" Doris laughs. "You are spooking me, kiddo," she says.

"Don't worry," I whisper. I smile. My face isn't tear-streaked. My heart is not broken. I'm getting it all back together.

Doris lights up her cigarette then.

I can't talk anymore. Don't want to. Don't need to. Just want to smoke. Smoke here in the break room with Doris. That's all I really want to do.

When I go back and see Paul Brewer Sunday night, all I think about is his son. I have worked a long-assed double (again). Since Friday, Paul's son has not come back to see me, and I am grateful to God. David's wife and her mother have come back several times. I try to hide from them, of course. I worry that Dave has told them, or told the police, whoever you are supposed to tell. But, no, they just come and talk to Paul the way relatives here do, as if he is a three-year-old in traction.

Paul says nothing, for he is in his own morphine fairy tale now.

I bump into David's wife and her mother. This is how I find out who they are, actually.

"Are you his nurse?" Tara asks. Her face is raccooned by crying with mascara on. She's skinny and energetic, her mom slow and tired.

"No. Just an aide. I help bathe him and stuff. Troy," I say, automatically wondering if she will go home and tell David about me. This nice aide named Troy she bumped into.

"This is my mom, Martha. She and Paul had a pretty good relationship."

Martha smiles at me.

"He's dying, I mean for real now, isn't he?" Martha whispers.

"I don't know," I say.

We stand there.

"He likes old country music a lot," Tara says. She wipes her eyes. "Old old country music. I brought him a tape. Do you all have a player?" She takes a cassette tape out, a black one with writing on it, shakes it at me.

"I think I can find one," I say.

"Thank you."

She gives me the tape. This stranger in a nursing home— she gives me that sacred tape.

They leave, Tara and her mom. I see them walk out to their car.

I hope David is happy.

Now, Sunday night, I walk into Paul's room, with the tape and an old tape player I have brought from home. I have already given him a bath. I stand beside his bed. I notice Paul still wears a gold wedding band on his finger and has on a brand-new wristwatch, but really all I can think about is what I did out of love, in a secret place in 1972, to his only begotten son.

I put the tape player on the tray-table at his side, plug it in. Once it starts, it startles me. Eddie Arnold's "Make the World Go Away." If you are not familiar with this song, it's slow and sad, can give you the creeps with its slowness, with Eddie Arnold's voice like the voice from a lullaby, his masculine voice singing sorrowfully above the ghostly violins, the twangy steel guitar. Makes you feel drunk. I think of Paul, I think of David. They merge into me somehow. I am no one just then.

Some people, other freaks and molesters, would tell me to give up guilt, to go on with my bad self, to do it again and again and again, so that I may forget what it actually does to the boy. Find some other boys, some others to do it with, so that all this guilt I feel might be of use somehow, pushing me on. Forget about David, and go on. But he was the only one I could ever love. Don't ask me why. I think I've already said enough about it. Of course, I could be lying to you, but I swear to God I'm not.

Here comes a great big cliché. True love never dies.

Dogs die. Plants die. Cars die. People die. Dads die. Moms die.

But true love, my friend, does not.

The music goes on. Patsy Cline, Loretta Lynn, Tammy Wynette, Brenda Lee, Merle Haggard, Freddy Fender, Willie Nelson, George Jones.

Funny how Sunday night often is the night a lot of people give it up. It is the most popular night. Everyone who works at Sunnyhaven knows that.

Paul Brewer's eyes are open when he dies. When Paul dies, he is looking at me and hearing George Jones. *For the treasure of love, the treasure of love makes me a king . . .*

The last air comes out in the sound of a childhood whistle, like *Come over here I have something to show you.*

His eyes are open, and his face has the peace of the quietest days.

He is a no-code, it says it right there on his chart. I stay with him an hour after he dies. I stay with Paul and think of other days, when I sat next to my mother and watched her go off. Her hair was not auburn anymore, her face was not her face anymore. Death took her off. I wanted her to go, so that she could see someone else besides me.

And then, right then, with Paul, I think of when I die.

I think: Who will be staying with me? What music will be playing? What will I lose?

23
DAVE

The days before the final time I saw Nathan, the days after I saw Troy, I did not work, but rode around and drank more. In the truck, often I fell drunk-asleep inside sleepy, beautiful neighborhoods, hiding from Neckties and coworkers, waking up just in time to go in, fake my paperwork, and go on home.

I told Tara I was not going back to that goddam nursing home, no matter what she said.

"He is your dad," Tara says. She is in jeans and plaid shirt with a frilly collar and high heels and earrings. She has made Dad that tape of his favorite music.

"I am not going," I say, sitting in the chair.

"You have to."

"Listen," I say. I look at her with a dumb look, like I am too tired to say anything else about it. She looks so hurt I want to hurt myself back.

"Listen, Tara, I don't think I can handle it right now," I say.

Tara sees me in my Indiana Gas Company clothes, still a little lit up from screwdrivers all day, and this is when maybe she starts to understand completely that I have started to turn into a ghost. I am a dead being in the house we once shared.

She says, "Do what you want."

Yeah, I will.

Then I have Brittany on my lap, clapping her hands, and me even clapping along a little. This is on Saturday night after her bath. This is on Saturday night after I have spent all day hiding in our house from outdoors. Me holding Brit and clapping.

That same night, Tara and me hold each other in bed. She is wanting something from me more than sex, not even in her red nightie this time, and me not even able to provide the sex part. Of course, I never really have, let alone the lovingness. Still she holds on to me, and I hold on to her. I wish that I could tell her that stuff. About Troy. About how Troy and me did that stuff. About all of it, but it is too late. You know that. I know that. Even she does, I think. This is why she is holding me like this. Because she knows, and she does not want to.

The next morning, Tara's mom comes and gets Brittany to take her to church as I drive the church bus. Tara has to work breakfast. She is gone, and Brittany is gone.

I am sliding on my necktie. I look at myself in the mirror. *Lord,* I don't pray it as much as just talk. *Lord, look at me. Look what I am doing.*

I shave with a necktie on, getting shaving cream on my collar. As I shave, I smile at myself because I have to do that to pull my skin tight so that the shaving works right. My smile is the smile of a desperate little man.

My smile is tight-lipped and surrounded by white foam.

Nathan gets on my bus, Nathan who I scared last week on this very bus, who I scared and kissed last week on this very bus, Nathan who has come back for some more of me.

You do not know the feeling of him coming back to me after me doing that to him. I want to cry. It's a victory. He has come back to me after I revealed to him my true self, and in the moments he walks up the steps to the front seat he doesn't look at me. I think of Troy Wetzel, and I think of me, me and Troy, Troy through me looking at Nathan who could be me. There is a finality to this emotion. An ending which I am grateful for. Oh God, it is finally over.

Nathan sits in his seat, and I pick up all the others, and we go through the motions.

That day Pastor Lewis preaches about the Rapture yet again. He just loves that Rapture.

"The end of the century, it is written in Revelation, read it, people. The end of the twentieth century is a watershed for the coming of Christ. Now I am not saying Jesus is coming on New Year's Day, the year 2000. No, but what I am saying is it is a great event to watch for, as Jesus is watching for it."

Smiling. Like Christ will take him up first.

Pastor Lewis after his sermon says to me in the foyer, "So your dad. I'm gonna get out to see him I think Tuesday."

Tuesday seems like so far off, so far away, like a pendulum has swung so slow it became a planet and I am on that planet where time has no time. Me and Nathan and a dog named Blue on a faraway planet time has forgot.

"Yes," I say. "He's doing pretty good."

"He's in Muncie, right?" Smiling again. Pastor Lewis, you don't know anything.

"Yeah, Sunnyhaven Nursing Home, on Route 9."

I smile.

"Well, yes," Pastor Lewis says, shaking my hand.

I shook Troy's hand. I shook it till it came off like a malfunctioning robot's. I shook and shook. I look at Pastor Lewis's face then. Its fat is the surface of clouds. He has no eyes suddenly. His eyes have been removed by God. His eyes have gone to the other side of his big fat head. To watch for what is back there behind him.

"Good-bye," I tell him.

The boy and me drop all the others off. We drop off people like they are parachuting to hell once they get off our bus, which is the Golden Chariot that took Enoch back to heaven. Enoch is the only man in the Old Testament to be able to go to heaven without dying.

Do we even stop the bus for them to get off, or do we just push them out the door?

I am on my way to the abandoned house. I look at him in the rearview.

This is the image I want to keep: Nathan looking back at me. Me looking back at him. A mirror we are sharing. Troy is somewhere in the back, hiding behind a seat. Or maybe Troy is the mirror.

Troy is hiding, so he can watch, and I feel the bus stop. Nathan does not look scared yet. He must want this. I feel the heat right then because the wind has stopped. We are secluded here, the house right before us. I stand up and take my shirt off. I am burning up.

"Come on," I say.

Like he knows.

He gets up and runs to the back of the bus. He is whimpering.

"Come on."

I can't stand it anymore. He knew what he was doing, getting on the bus this morning. He better stop his running. I am tired of his running. I run to him, and he starts to scream and kick.

"You come here today for this, Bud," I say. I act like I'm shocked. "Listen, if you don't settle down, I'm gonna do stuff!"

I swat his head. He stops his kicking. He goes limp, lets me carry him without my shirt on. I hold him close to my chest, and his face is in my face. I kiss him. Kiss him on the cheek. His body next to my naked chest makes me feel like I am going to fly away. I am so excited I am busting out of the skin I have on.

I unfurl like a holy flag. Nobody has felt this before. Not even Enoch.

I carry Nathan into the shell of a burned house. I carry him into a burned room that has a burned floor and burned walls. All the glass is broken on the windows. There are remnants of cabinets. A kitchen. I put him down, and I take off my pants then. I throw off my shoes and pants to the side, and then I take off my underwear.

I stand before him who was once me. No, who *is* me.

I picture Troy looking at us through the windows. Picture Troy that time at Indiana Beach in the Port-O-Let. He is touching me there. There! Wanting into me!

The boy is crying. He sees who I am.

"No," he says slow, in a whisper, shaking his head.

I am so naked it is making him cry. I am the nakedest thing he has ever seen.

"Oh, honey," I say in a crackpot voice.

"No!" he howls now.

I go to him crawling on my knees, get into his face, smell his breath, kiss him with my tongue and I lick his eyes, face, and nose, bite into his skin a little, laughing from pure bursting joy.

"No!" he screams.

But I don't stop. I push him onto the floor and taste every part I can and I feel like I am finally the thing I have always pretended to be afraid of. I am all black inside, but bleaching out from finally just doing this, just letting myself do this. Bleaching out white as a beautiful cloud.

Nathan squirms, bites, does more than I could have anticipated to break away from me, and as we struggle and wrestle I feel my disappointment already start. He kicks me in the belly and I understand that I may need to hurt him, hurt him worse to shut him up, to get what I want. I pull away for a sec. See his face as he lies there on the floor, his face suddenly froze, like he is reading my mind, his tiny dark eyes clawing into me.

Then I see that I am trying to strangle him.

This must be when I stop, my hands turning limp. When I stop, he breaks away from me. He runs away. I can't think he has actually done this to me. Run away. It does not compute. There is an instant of whiteness. There is an instant of being alone not just in Indiana, but in the universe. One instant that stretches out into a lifetime of traveling through time and space. Not remembering no more. Just reexperiencing a lifetime of being here in this one exact spot, naked in a burned-out house. Sorry for everything, but then again not. I look and see Troy. Troy the boy I loved back then like I was sposed too, but I did not could not love you the way you wanted and this love has stayed inside me spoiling like milk spoiling and turning back into itself.

I wake up. Not wake up. Just realize.

I realize Nathan has escaped.

I go outside into the hot sun, naked.

"Nathan!"

Out of my mind.

"Nathan!" I call. Naked. I hate him, I know now. This hate is part of my being naked. I hate him for being him and I hate him for running, but still I love him for being Nathan, for being alive.

And I run, looking for him through the tall scorched weeds, the dirt and rocks hurting my feet. The blades of grass all over my skin, cutting slightly, itching into me. Poison ivy? I look up at the sky. White-hot like a spaceship has exploded. Is that where Nathan is? Is that where my Nathan is?

I look up in a sycamore tree. I look up into several trees.

"Nathan!"

I run. I call his name into a cornfield. I call and I call.

"Nathan!"

Naked and running and chasing.

When it is over, and it already is, there is no life left.

When it is over, there is no life left at all.

No life left to lead, to fall into, or under. I am this way the rest of my time on earth. No matter where they put me or who they tell me to talk to. Who I bare my soul to ain't a problem anymore. I can talk and talk and talk, and they have medication and they have prison and they have this and they have that. I have a suicide watch and a plastic plate of sausage and eggs and a little bit of knowledge.

Love is knowing who you are, love is knowing who you want to be, and I realized that out in that hot field that day, chasing after Nathan. *My* Nathan, who had run all the way to the interstate, screaming his head off, who was picked up by a nice gentleman and his wife in a nice car and they took him to the police.

Like I said, I realized who I was out there in the hot field that day, left there in that field, calling Nathan's name at the top of my lungs. You see, I was pursuing Nathan without any alternatives on that day. I had to find him for my own survival, and this was who or what I was meant to be.

You see?

Pursuing and chasing him in a world lit as bright as a concussion, bright and brighter and brightest, me naked as the day I was born

A NOTE ON THE TYPE

This book was set in Adobe Garamond. Designed for the Adobe Corporation by Robert Slimbach, the fonts are based on types first cut by Claude Garamond (c. 1480–1561). Garamond was a pupil of Geoffroy Tory and is believed to have followed the Venetian models, although he introduced a number of important differences, and it is to him that we owe the letter we now know as "old style." He gave to his letters a certain elegance and feeling of movement that won their creator an immediate reputation and the patronage of Francis I of France.

Composed by NK Graphics, Keene, New Hampshire
Printed and bound by Quebecor Printing,
Fairfield, Pennsylvania
Designed by Virginia Tan